Ana Seymour

IRISH  EYES

Rose in the Mist

"Her writing style
draws you in from the first page."
—*Rendezvous*

JOVE

$5.99 U.S.
$8.99 CAN

ISBN 0-515-13254-3

9 780515 132540

5 0 5 9 9 >

S > EAN

Praise for Ana Seymour . . .

"Ana Seymour takes her legion of loyal readers into a fascinating new realm of medieval lore."—*Times Record News*

"Seymour's plot is a heady brew—she stirs in a generous measure of conflict, spices it with tension, then serves her readers an unforgettable tale."
—*Rendezvous*

"Ms. Seymour has captured the historical era and given us a romance filled with wonderful characters and several unique subplots. *Lord of Lyonsbridge* is a highly enjoyable read."
—*Romantic Times*

"Exciting . . . The story line is loaded with authenticity. . . . The characters are intelligent and warm. . . . Fans of this sub-genre already know that they see more of the era when Ana Seymour is the author, and this tale enhances her deserved reputation."
—Harriet Klausner

"[Seymour is] again filling pages with her mastery of plotting and the sweet joys found in family, friends, and the simple pleasure life affords. . . . It is always a joy to read a novel of this caliber."
—*Under the Covers*

"*A Family for Carter Jones* shows why Ms. Seymour is noted for her outstanding writing skills. She always keeps her readers entertained at the highest possible level."
—*Rendezvous*

"Readers will be enthralled as they follow spunky Jennie's struggles to keep her family together with a never-give-up determination. Superb."
—*Bell, Book & Candle*

Rose in the Mist

Ana Seymour

JOVE BOOKS, NEW YORK

If you purchased this book without a cover, you should be aware that this book is stolen property. It was reported as "unsold and destroyed" to the publisher, and neither the author nor the publisher has received any payment for this "stripped book."

This is a work of fiction. Names, characters, places, and incidents either are the product of the author's imagination or are used fictitiously, and any resemblance to actual persons, living or dead, business establishments, events, or locales is entirely coincidental.

ROSE IN THE MIST

A Jove Book / published by arrangement with
the author

PRINTING HISTORY
Jove edition / February 2002

All rights reserved.
Copyright © 2002 by Mary Bracho.
Cover art by Bruce Emmett.
This book, or parts thereof, may not be reproduced
in any form without permission.
For information address: The Berkley Publishing Group,
a division of Penguin Putnam Inc.,
375 Hudson Street, New York, New York 10014.

Visit our website at
www.penguinputnam.com

ISBN: 0-515-13254-3

A JOVE BOOK®
Jove Books are published by The Berkley Publishing Group,
a division of Penguin Putnam Inc.,
375 Hudson Street, New York, New York 10014.
JOVE and the "J" design
are trademarks belonging to Penguin Putnam Inc.

PRINTED IN THE UNITED STATES OF AMERICA

10 9 8 7 6 5 4 3 2 1

For my mother,
who is my securest anchor.

For my dad,
who is my sunshine.

Prologue

*Angels fold their wings and rest
In that Eden of the west.*

"*Ye're a shameless* tease, Cat O'Malley, and I've done with bein' the victim for yer wicked games." The gangly boy punctuated his words by stomping his right foot, then spinning around to turn his back on his companion.

Catriona's green eyes glinted with mischief. "Ye've been sayin' the same since we were scarce out of birthin' clothes, Bobby Brosnihan. Shall I be believin' it this time?"

Bobby's shoulders sagged as he slowly turned back to face her. "Nay," he said with a sigh.

" 'Tis as I thought." She was about to add an additional smug remark, but something in the boy's expression made her pause. It was true, she'd teased Bobby unmercifully since the two were youngsters, but in recent weeks there had been a change in the way he'd been treating her. Today when they'd ridden up into the hills through a thick morning mist, he'd seemed much more serious than normal.

She looked up at her red-haired friend. When had

Bobby become so tall? she wondered suddenly. She'd never thought much about it, but she and Bobby had always seemed about the same level. Suddenly he towered above her. His shoulders had grown broader and the fuzz on his face had darkened.

"I'd not thought to make ye angry," she said more soberly.

He shrugged. "Ye know well that I'd not stay angry with ye for long."

They'd left their horses tied and had been scrambling along the slippery rocks of the stream that tumbled down the hill to the valley where the O'Malleys had lived for generations. An autumn chill was in the air, and they could see the remnants of the morning fog settling over the valley floor below them. Though they'd spent similar days dozens of times before, this afternoon seemed different.

More than once Bobby had taken her arm to help her over one of the larger boulders, though he of all people knew that she was as surefooted as a goat. She'd amused herself taking advantage of his sudden gallantry by leaning on him more and more. Finally, when he'd had to half-lift her over a big rock, she'd jumped nimbly away out of his arms with a taunting giggle. That was when he had had his short-lived outburst.

"I should think not," she said. "'Twould be a sorry thing to be angry with your best friend."

He stiffened his shoulders. "Mayhap I don't want to be yer best friend, Cat."

She cocked her head in puzzlement. "Whyever not?"

"Ye've grown up, sweetling. Did ye ever consider that it might be more than friendship I'm wantin'?"

Catriona could not have been more shocked if he had thrown her into the icy stream at their feet. At thirteen, she was old enough to know something about the ways of men and women, but she'd never associated any of that with her friendship with Bobby.

"I—faith, Bobby Brosnihan," she stuttered after a moment, "now who's the one doin' the teasin'?"

He took a firm hold on her arms and bent his head to give her a quick, dry kiss on the lips. It was over before Catriona even knew what he'd done. Her mouth dropped open.

" 'Tis no tease, Cat," he said. "I want ye."

"Don't be a dolt, Bobby!" she exploded, pulling herself backward out of his grasp, then felt instant remorse as she saw the hurt in his eyes. " 'Tis like a brother ye are to me, Bobby," she continued more gently. "Like the brother I never had."

"But I'm not a brother, Cat, nor any relation a'tall. If yer father were not head of the richest barony in Kerry, I'd have made it clear long before this. I know he'll never accept me as a husband for ye, but I can't stop the wantin'."

Catriona had begun to feel sick. It was as if an ominous cloud was threatening to shroud the memories of her carefree childhood. Bobby was her dearest friend, but she understood nothing about this "wantin'" he spoke of. She shivered as a breeze lifted suddenly from the valley below.

"Can we not just stay the friends we've always been?" she asked, turning away from the new, hungry look in his eyes. "I've no desire for more, truly. Why, 'twill be years on before I must wed."

"Ye're almost fourteen, Cat. Your father will soon be getting offers for your hand, if he hasn't already."

She looked up at him, her mouth set. "Aye, and he'll be turnin' them down as fast as he receives them, for I'll wed no man until I'm ready—which mayhap will be *never*."

Bobby shook his head sadly. "Ye're the last o' the O'Malleys, Cat. The Valley of Mor will belong to you one day." He flung out his arm to indicate the vast green basin below them. "Ye'll be needin' a man to help ye keep it."

Her gaze followed the sweep of his hand, then she shuddered and crossed herself. "My father is head of the

O'Malleys and master of the Valley of Mor. God willing, 'twill be so for many more years."

The laughter of the morning was forgotten as they stood side by side for several minutes looking down at the O'Malley estate, lost in their own thoughts.

Suddenly Bobby grabbed her arm. "Cat, look! Riders!"

Catriona became rigid. For weeks her father had been worrying over the possibility that the English troops who'd been sent to achieve dominion over the unruly Irish subjects of the English Crown would find their peaceful valley. "Are they soldiers?" she asked.

"Aye." He squinted to make out the tiny figures that were fast closing in on the O'Malley manor house below them. "Well armed and wearing breastplates."

"The English?"

"Aye."

She whirled around and began running back up the stream to where they had left the horses. "Come on!" she yelled back to him. "We must get down there."

Bobby ran to catch up to her and pulled at her arm. "Are ye daft? Yer father has only a few men. If the English are set on taking over the O'Malley lands, he'll have little hope of standing against them. He'd want ye away from here."

Catriona shook off his restraining hand. "I need to be with him, Bobby."

The boy caught her again. "Nay, Cat. I won't let ye go down there. Lord O'Malley would never forgive me."

This time his grasp was firm and her struggles to free herself were having no effect. "Don't make me fight ye, Bobby," she pleaded. "Not now."

As they argued, the troops below had reached the main house. The low-lying mist made it difficult to see, but they could hear shouts and the sound of clanging steel, oddly distorted by the distance. She pushed forward with all her might, forcing Bobby to clamp both arms around her middle to keep her from running.

"I'll not let ye go, Cat. And the days are far gone when ye could best me in a wrestling match."

She knew that he was right. For some time now she'd had to acknowledge that her friend was superior in a contest of sheer physical strength. She stopped struggling and stood with his arms around her as she turned her attention back to the scene unfolding in the valley below.

The English soldiers had dismounted, leaving their horses scattered around the yard to trample the neat O'Malley gardens. Women and children and animals poured from the big house and the outbuildings, running for their lives into the hills. Here and there men came together in clashes as O'Malley retainers tried to defend their liege's home and land.

"Don't look, Cat," Bobby said after several minutes.

She ignored his plea. "Do ye see Father?"

"Nay."

"Bobby, we have to do something." Tears of rage stung her eyes.

"I'd be down there fightin', Cat, but 'tis more important for me to keep ye safe. Yer father would tell me so himself."

"Oh, no, Bobby, look!" A sob reached her throat as flames suddenly burst from the north side of the house. The stream of people evacuating the manor slowed to a trickle, then stopped. The fire raced along the dry timbers of the big house, and within moments the entire structure was ablaze.

"Do ye see Father?" Catriona asked again, her voice low and urgent.

Bobby tightened his arms around her. "Nay," he said grimly. "Cat, I fear he didn't come out."

She wriggled around until she was facing him. "Take me down there, Bobby. I need to find out what's happened."

"Cat, if we go there, we'll be killed or captured, too.

God knows what they'd do to you, especially if they find out that you are Lord O'Malley's daughter."

Below them the roof of the big house crashed inward, sending columns of sparks high into the sky. Catriona's tears dried on her cheeks as they watched. When she finally spoke, her voice was hollow. "I don't care what they do to me. I have to find Father or . . . or I have to know. You can ride with me or no, Bobby, but I'm going down."

Bobby looked down at her for a long moment. Finally he said, "May God forgive me, Cat, for I could never say ye nay." He dropped his arms from around her, then took her hand as they made their way back toward the horses.

One

Niall Riordan rocked back on his heels and gave a low whistle as he surveyed the long gilded hall. Lavishly dressed courtiers bustled back and forth in an endless stream interrupted only by an occasional lady gliding through like a silken water lily. "God's teeth, John, I've never seen the like!"

His companion laughed. "There is no like, my friend. You're at the center of the world now, the court of the great Queen Elizabeth."

"Everyone's in such a hurry."

John Black's smile died. "Aye, 'tis the way of things here at court. Never let anyone get ahead of you or 'tis like to cost you dear. You'd do best to keep your wits about you at all times."

Niall grinned. "I thought that was to be your charge, Doctor. I'm here because of the Riordan family name, but you're the one who knows these games. I'm depending on you to be the wits of the team while I enjoy myself."

John Black did not return his smile. "You're young,

Niall, and no doubt will find amusement here. God knows, there's much amusement to be had. But never forget that we are on a deadly business. There are many here"—the Irishman waved his hand to encompass the length of the hall—"who have no desire to see Ireland and England at peace."

Niall nodded and grew serious. "Aye. I'm not likely to forget the lads who died with the O'Neill to keep our liberty. We must be sure they didn't die for nought."

John Black nodded, then turned as one of the courtiers steered toward them, his face pinched into a fixed smile. Niall's eyes widened as he took in the man's scalloped-edged shoes and bright yellow hose.

"Gentlemen," the newcomer addressed them with an indifferent roll of his hand that was apparently meant to replace a bow. "Alger Pimsley, at your service. Lord Wolverton is ready to see you." His tone held no hint of apology, though after arriving at the palace, Niall and John had been ignored in a small antechamber for nearly four hours before they'd been ushered into the hall.

"I'd understood that we would be presenting our credentials to the queen," John said.

"My good fellow," Pimsley said with a slight sneer, "Her Majesty has more important things to do than deal with petty squabbles in the outlands." He turned his back and started walking quickly down the hall. "Come this way," he told them, motioning for John and Niall to follow.

Niall couldn't take his eyes away from the man's plump, yellow-clad legs. The courtier's short doublet rode up as he picked up his pace, revealing puffy breeches of bright purple silk. As they lengthened their strides to keep up with the man, Niall leaned close to John and whispered, "The popinjay wouldn't last ten minutes back in County Meath."

"Nay, but we're not in Ireland anymore, and we'd do best to keep our opinions of their fashion to ourselves, lest they think that all of us from the 'outlands' are ignorant bumpkins."

"I'd sooner be a bumpkin than encase my backside in silk and show it off to the world," Niall muttered.

John chuckled. " 'Tis a rare sight, I'll admit," he agreed, nodding at the man, who was now several yards ahead of them. "But you're missing the real view."

Niall turned his head to see that his friend was looking toward the end of the hall at two young women.

"Elizabeth's court is known across the continent for its beauties," John continued.

"They'd not last long among the lads of County Meath, either," Niall said with a grin.

The women appeared to be engaged in a lively conversation. The smaller one, a curvy blond, was laughing, but Niall's gaze fixed on the taller woman. Her face was not as merry as her friend's, but the features were striking. As he and John approached the end of the hall, he could see that her eyes were a true green. Beneath a small Dutch cap, her chestnut hair was coiled into thick rolls that, if unbound, would surely reach her waist.

"I'll let you have first pick, lad, since you're new to the hunt," John said hurriedly as they drew within a few yards of the ladies.

"The blonde's all yours," Niall whispered back.

John laughed. "Ah, Niall, you always were one to go for the most skittish colt on the lot. The green-eyed wench has the look of trouble, whereas the other's a little sweetheart, ready to warm a man's heart and his bed."

"I'll trust my own judgment in horseflesh," Niall replied quickly as the two men stopped directly in front of the ladies and bowed. Without looking back, the courtier, Pimsley, disappeared through the door at the end of the hall.

The ladies appeared surprised at the interruption in their conversation.

"Forgive the intrusion, m'ladies, but perhaps you may

be able to help me with a problem," John Black said, his expression serious.

The blonde gave them a tentative, questioning smile, but the green-eyed beauty's expression was wary and slightly hostile.

Niall looked through the door after the courtier, who had disappeared among the moving throng.

"I had promised my friend here that when we arrived at court, he would be seeing the most beautiful women in the world," John continued smoothly. "Yet all morning we've seen nothing but grumpy politicians, though, I grant you, some of them were dressed with more ribbons than any of our girls back home."

The little blonde giggled. "You gentlemen are new to court, then?" she asked. " 'Tis why you're not perhaps aware that 'tis proper to be presented to a lady before addressing her."

John cocked his head. "Let it never be said that John Black is less than proper, milady, but tell me this. How is a stranger to present himself without addressing the lady first?"

Niall's gaze was on the taller woman, who was listening to John without expression. Suddenly she shifted her startling eyes to look at Niall. Her voice was cool. "If you are strangers to court, you have yet to learn that Her Majesty guards the virtue of her ladies closely. 'Tis a lesson you'd do well to learn quickly."

Niall spoke for the first time. "Surely even your queen would not consider a simple inquiry to be a threat to a lady's virtue."

"My queen?" The dark-haired beauty's arched brow rose with sudden interest. "Is she not your queen, as well?"

John and Niall exchanged glances. " 'Tis a matter of some debate, milady," John said after a moment. "We are Irish."

Niall thought he saw a sudden flare in the green eyes,

but in an instant it was gone, replaced with the cool hostility he'd first seen.

"Irish!" said the blonde. "Why then, you are strangers, indeed. Perhaps we need to make an exception to the usual propriety, Cat." She looked hopefully at her companion, who responded by taking her arm and turning her away from the two men.

"Nay, Bella," her companion said. "If they are foreigners, 'tis all the more reason to be wary." Without another word she began to walk away, pulling the blonde she'd called Bella along with her. Bella looked back at them with an apologetic smile, but let herself be led back up the hall.

As they left, Pimsley puffed toward them from the opposite direction, his face turning a mottled purple that nearly matched his breeches.

"Are you gentlemen mad?" he asked, sputtering. "It's not bad enough that you're keeping Lord Wolverton waiting, but you tarry in the hall to insult his ward."

John started to speak, but Niall interrupted him. He'd had enough of English manners. "If Lord Wolverton has the right to be angry over a few minutes' delay, then how are we to feel after being kept waiting all morning? And furthermore, where we come from, 'tis worth a man's life to accuse him of insulting a lady when such a thing never occurred."

John put a restraining hand on Niall's shoulder and addressed Pimsley. "Forgive us, my good man. We were merely introducing ourselves to the ladies, since we know no one at court. Which one is Wolverton's ward?"

Niall's anger seemed to deflate some of Pimsley's pompous manner. He was almost civil as he answered John's question. "The tall one. She's Mistress Catriona Sherwood, ward to Lord Wolverton these past seven years. His Lordship would not take kindly to anyone showing her disrespect."

"None intended and none shown, Pimsley," John said

briskly. "Now let's not keep His Lordship waiting any longer."

As he followed along behind Pimsley and John, Niall's thoughts lingered on the woman they'd just met. He would have liked to ask the courtier more about her. How had she come to be the nobleman's ward? Had she no family of her own? But John and the Englishman had moved on to a discussion of how the negotiations were to proceed, and Niall decided to quell his curiosity. In spite of his earlier banter with John, they'd come to Elizabeth's court to cement the peace, not for personal entertainment. The green-eyed beauty was intriguing, but she hadn't seemed the least receptive to their attempt at acquaintance. He'd be better served to keep his mind on his mission.

"'Twould have done no harm simply to talk with the gentlemen, Cat," Lady Arabella Houghton told her friend as they reached the private solar that was reserved for Elizabeth's ladies-in-waiting.

Catriona sniffed. "You've plenty of gallants to choose from here at court, Bella. There's no need to entangle yourself with a couple of strangers."

Bella frowned. "As they said, they have no acquaintances here. 'Tis not like you to be so uncharitable." She giggled. "And they were bonny, in case you failed to notice."

Catriona shrugged. "I simply see no need to associate with men we know nothing about. We have enough trouble dealing with the ones already established here."

"Aye, well, *you* do, at least. There's not a man at court who'd not like to get under your skirts, Cat, though you'll have none of them."

"Men don't interest me."

Bella giggled again. " 'Tis only because you've not met the right one yet. Once you do, you'll not be so quick to dismiss them."

She and Bella had had the same discussion countless times in the two years since Catriona had come to court, but Catriona remained unconvinced. The only truly good man she knew was Bobby, and, while she did love him in her own way, she had long ago confirmed that they would never be more than friends.

She sighed, feeling inside the dull ache she always did when she thought of her childhood companion. She hadn't seen him for several months, but she knew he would show up one of these days, and they would both be keenly aware once again of just how much he had given up for her sake.

He'd refused to tell her the details of his days of captivity by the English while she was being raised in the gilded prison of Lord Wolverton's home, but the scars on his body bore witness to what he had had to endure. If she ever did pick a man for herself, it would undoubtedly be Bobby after all he had suffered.

She walked over and knelt on the stone hearth to build up the fire with sticks from the wood basket. "Mayhap I have found the right one, Bella, and 'tis why none of the others interests me."

Her friend's eyes grew round. "Why, Catriona Sherwood, don't tell me you've had a lover all this time and never told me!"

Catriona bit her lip in reproach for her loose tongue. She'd been foolish to give Bella grist for the court gossip mill. "Nay, Bella, I've no lover, nor ever hope to have. I was but teasing you."

The glint in Bella's eyes faded as she joined her friend at the fireplace. "Nay, how could you have a lover? We're together day and night. 'Twould have to be a ghost," she added with a giggle.

Catriona nodded, relieved at Bella's easy acceptance of her denial. Bobby was not her lover, but in some ways he did come in and out of her life like a ghost, a ghost from a past that would haunt her every day and every hour for as long as she lived. They could give her an English name and English speech and an English bearing, but she would never forget who she was and where she had come from.

"I reckon a ghost would be less nuisance than a flesh-and-blood man," she answered lightly, tossing a final stick on the flaring blaze.

Bella shook her head. "Ah, Cat, 'tis as I said. You've not found the right one. When you do, you'll see that flesh and blood is a definite advantage."

Cat busied herself dusting the soot off her hands and made no reply. After a moment Bella said, "The tall one appeared to be interested in you."

Cat looked up in confusion. "What tall one?"

"The Irishman. The tall one had that look in his eye, the look a man gets."

Cat stood. "You're ever seeing things that aren't there, Bella."

"Nay, 'tis true. His gaze was fixed on you. He never glanced my way once."

Catriona sniffed. "Do you intend to keep chattering or did you want me to help you with that Latin text?"

Since Elizabeth herself was such a scholar, she approved of all her ladies' attempts to educate themselves, and employed a number of tutors for the purpose. Catriona had found her own abilities in French and Latin and Greek were superior to those of the teachers employed at court, but she often helped the other ladies with their studies.

"Could we not leave it until tomorrow?" Bella asked wistfully. " 'Tis much more enjoyable to talk about the new men at court. Yours was by far the brawniest of the pair—you couldn't have failed to notice that chest and those shoulders, Cat. He was standing right in front of you."

"I noticed nothing about the man, Bella. I'd have forgotten the encounter entirely if you didn't keep bringing it up."

"Oh, very well," Bella said grumpily, rising and going over to the big oak table where the manuscript they'd been studying lay open. "But 'twill be interesting to see if he continues to watch you so at supper. You could at least give the man a smile."

"Bella, if you studied your Latin one-tenth as much as you study the court gallants, you'd be the most renowned scholar in England."

Bella laughed and laid her hand on the open book. "Mayhap, but I can't picture the day when one of these dusty tomes will give me the satisfaction I get from the twinkle in a man's eye."

They pulled up two stools and Bella began laboriously spelling out her translation, but Catriona's mind was only half on her friend's labors. She hadn't entirely told the truth. She *had* noticed the Irishman's shoulders and his handsome features, as well. She tried to tell herself that this unusual interest was because he was Irish, but the truth was that the interest had begun before she'd known the man's origin.

"Cat, have you fallen asleep? 'Tis the third time I've asked. *Vita brevis*—life is short. Correct?"

Cat sat up straight on the stool. "Forgive me, Bella. Aye, you have it right." *Vita brevis*. She'd learned that lesson seven years ago in the Valley of Mor, and she wasn't about to forget it. Life was short. Too short for silly daydreaming about broad-chested strangers with dark eyes. She had much more important things to do with her life. If Bobby didn't show up soon with instructions, Cat intended to take matters into her own hands.

"I'm not sure Wolverton has any intention of helping us with the queen," Niall said, slapping the leather sheath of his dagger against his hip in frustration.

"I told you to leave the weapons in our quarters, Niall," John said, his humor not much better than his friend's.

"I've no intention of going unarmed into a room full of

Englishmen," Niall answered. "And I'm beginning to think that this whole venture was a mistake. We'd be better off fighting the English with O'Neill in the forest than here among mincing politicians who smile politely and do absolutely nothing."

Their afternoon meeting had not gone as expected. In spite of Alger Pimsley's assurances, Lord Wolverton, the nobleman who had been Elizabeth's special choice to oversee the Irish question, had never appeared. He'd sent a messenger with a proposed settlement that met none of the goals John and Niall had come to achieve. It gave no guarantees that the usurpation of Irish lands by the English conquerors would end, nor did it grant amnesty for the rebels who had fought against the English in the most recent conflict.

The two friends were walking toward the great dining hall where, according to the manservant who had helped them find lodging in the sprawling palace, they would be served supper.

" 'Tis but the first day, Niall," John said finally. "We need to give it a chance. This is a fight that's been waged for years. 'Twill not be settled in hours."

"Nor in centuries with men like Wolverton in charge," Niall grumbled. "I've a mind to search the palace until I find the man and demand a meeting."

"We'll try again on the morrow. In the meantime, there's nothing stopping us from enjoying ourselves for the evening. I, for one, could eat an entire boar, head and all."

"Aye, I'm hungry, too, but I see little prospect of enjoyment."

They'd reached the door of the dining hall, which was already teeming with people. Niall calculated that there were close to a hundred diners interspersed with an almost equal number of servants busily carrying full platters among the rows of tables.

"Mayhap you'll see that green-eyed wench you fancied," John said in an undertone as they paused in the doorway.

"I'd rather see a fat leg of mutton and a measure of ale," Niall replied.

John laughed and clapped his hand on his friend's shoulder. "Aye, 'tis the proper order. Food and drink first, then ladies."

No one seemed to pay them any attention as they made their way into the room, so they took two empty seats at the end of a bench. Almost instantly, a trencher appeared between them, heaped with meat and roasted leeks slathered in a berry sauce. They'd not eaten since dawn, so they wasted little time in digging into the platter.

After several moments of silence, John leaned back with a sigh. " 'Tis like wakin' from the dead."

"Aye," Niall agreed. "We were nigh starving." He looked around the room. Now that the pangs of hunger were addressed, he had to admit to some degree of curiosity. This was the court, after all, and the servant had said they might see the queen here. But the carved chair in the center of the raised table at the end of the dining hall was empty.

"There she is!" John said.

Niall followed the direction of John's pointing hand, looking for the distinctive red head that would indicate the presence of the most powerful woman in Christendom, but John had not been referring to the queen. Entering the dining hall from a side door was the lady they had met that morning, Catriona Sherwood.

Her companion had called her Cat, Niall remembered, and as he watched her cool gaze from across the room, he decided that the name was apt. She moved with the grace of a feline, and her green eyes were just as compelling . . . and just as indifferent.

"That must be Wolverton escorting her," John added. "Pimsley said she was his ward, remember?"

Niall had not even noticed the girl's companion. She held the arm of a man who was certainly old enough to be her powerful guardian, Lord Wolverton. Wolverton—the man who had kept them waiting all morning and then had failed to show at the audience.

Niall pushed back the bench and stood. "I believe we're about to keep our appointment with His Lordship."

John got to his feet, cautioning, " 'Tis not proper etiquette to discuss matters of state at supper, Niall. We should wait until the morrow and try again."

"So that we can waste another day being kept waiting in an antechamber? Why, when the man is finally here in the same room?"

He started to weave his way between the tables and the diners to cross over to the side of the room where Wolverton and his ward still stood, surveying the crowd. John followed reluctantly. "We'll just introduce ourselves, then," he said. "The rest can wait."

Though Catriona Sherwood was a tall woman, her guardian towered over her. Wolverton was wearing a gold velvet coat that bloused at the shoulders, making his already large frame look huge. He had silk hose and the same kind of fancy shoes Pimsley had been wearing, but on him, the ensemble did not look at all ridiculous. Even in County Meath, Niall admitted, this was a man who would be given a wide path.

There was no flicker of recognition in Catriona's eyes as the two Irishmen approached.

John stepped in front of Niall, evidently deciding that if the confrontation was inevitable, he was not about to let Niall's temper turn it into a disaster. He stopped before Wolverton and gave a flourish of a bow.

Niall's eyes widened. He'd known John Black as both a fierce fighter and a skilled physician, but it was the first time he'd seen his friend adopting courtly manners.

"Lord Wolverton, forgive the informality of our approach," John was saying. "Since you were unable to see us this afternoon, Master Riordan and I would like to introduce ourselves."

Niall's gaze was on Catriona. Her expression had not changed. She looked slightly bored . . . and exasperatingly beautiful.

Wolverton sniffed and took a step backward, pulling Catriona with him. "Who are you?" he asked. "And what devil's maggot would make you think I would care to meet you enough to interrupt my supper?"

Niall stiffened. If his horse were within reach at that moment, he'd consider mounting up and riding straight back to tell the O'Neill to start up the fighting once again. John, as usual, stayed calm.

"I am Dr. John Black, at your service, and this is Niall Riordan, third son of the Riordans of the Midlands. More important, we represent Shane O'Neill and your queen's best hope to end the fighting that has cost many English lives, as well as Irish."

Once again, Niall thought he saw an odd flicker in Catriona's eyes, but it was gone in an instant.

"I don't discuss politics at supper," Wolverton drawled.

"Nay, nor would I ask you to. I'd not keep you and your fair lady from the table," John agreed smoothly, acknowledging Catriona with a smile and a nod. "I merely wanted to get past the introductions and perhaps set up a time for a more productive meeting tomorrow."

"I believe you gentlemen have already received our terms. I see no need for a meeting."

From the tightening of John's jaw, Niall could see that his friend was also losing patience, but his tone remained steady as he said, "The papers we were given today contained none of the promises that were made to the O'Neill himself by your queen's own emissary. Perhaps after all, 'tis the queen we should be seeking."

Wolverton's lips turned up in a sneer. "Her Majesty has no time for impoverished petitioners from the godforsaken end of her realm."

The nobleman had scarcely finished the last word when a commanding voice rang out from behind him. "Perhaps you should let Her Majesty decide whom she has time to meet, my lord Wolverton."

Niall stepped to one side in order to see around Wolverton's big frame. Walking quickly toward them was a small woman with flaming red hair.

Wolverton backed up a step and doubled over in a deep flourish. "Your Majesty," he said in a tone entirely different from the one he had used with the Irishmen.

Niall glanced briefly at John, and then, for the first time in his life, bent at the waist and bowed.

TWO

Niall had never seen so many jewels adorning one body—pearls, diamonds, emeralds, rubies. They were stuck on gold pins in her hair, attached to a thick leather strip around her neck, encrusted on the bodice and sleeves of her dress, and studded on big rings on every finger of her hands.

Yet, oddly enough, after taking in the queen's incredible display of wealth, Niall found all of it fading into the background as his attention riveted on the voice and features of the woman herself. She was not beautiful, as some had claimed, especially not when she was standing next to Catriona, whose features were as near to perfection as Niall had ever seen.

Niall searched his mind for the word. *Powerful.* It was a term he would never have thought to apply to a woman, but in this case, it fit. In a way, Elizabeth reminded him of the rebel leader Shane O'Neill himself. She had the bearing of a leader who was ruthless with enemies, yet possessed of a deep humanity.

The queen spoke again to Wolverton, her voice rich with authority. "You may present these gentlemen to me," she said.

Wolverton gave another bow. "Your Majesty, I have scarcely made their acquaintance myself. They're from the ragtag band of outlaws who've been bedeviling our troops these two years past."

"Aye, 'twas the O'Neill these two years past and before that his brother and before that another and another before him," the queen snapped. "And if we never figure out a way to put a stop to it, I reckon they'll keep up the bedeviling until you and I are cold in our graves."

"That's precisely why we've come, Your Majesty," Niall interrupted. "To find the way to stop it." Out of the side of his eyes he caught a glimpse of John wincing. Wolverton's expression grew dark and even Catriona looked surprised at his breach of protocol, but the queen turned to him with no sign of annoyance.

She studied him without hurry, appearing to take in every detail of his appearance, from his thigh-high leather boots to his decidedly plain linen tunic. The Riordans were the richest family in the Midlands, but they had never felt the need to use their wealth for fancy garments.

Finally she spoke. "If 'tis so, young man, you are welcome at our court." She shifted her gaze to John and gave him the same thorough head-to-toe survey. Then she added, "Gather your papers and your promises and bring them to me tomorrow."

"You have our gratitude, Your Majesty," John said. Niall could see that his usually unflappable friend was disconcerted by the queen's sudden attention, but John continued gamely, "We will look forward to it."

Wolverton's expression remained stormy. " 'Tis not necessary for Your Majesty to be bothered by such affairs. Your ministers can deal with these men."

The queen dismissed his suggestion with a wave of her hand. "Lately my ministers seem to have trouble lacing their own breeches, much less solving affairs of state. We will see these men on the morrow, Wolverton. Arrange it."

Catriona had been listening to the exchange in ladylike

silence, but at the queen's comment about her ministers and their breeches, her lips turned up in a slight smile. The simple gesture made a remarkable change in her expression, transforming her from an icy beauty to a mischievous girl. Niall found himself smiling at her in return.

Elizabeth's sharp eyes caught the exchange. She did not sound entirely pleased as she addressed her lady-in-waiting. "They are handsome creatures, these Irishmen, are they not, Catriona? Mayhap you would enjoy helping them feel welcome during their stay here at court."

"As Your Majesty wishes," Catriona murmured with a little curtsy. But when her gaze lifted to meet Niall's once again, all sign of the smile was gone.

Elizabeth appeared suddenly impatient. She reached up to tap Wolverton none too gently on the cheek with her jeweled fan. "Bring them to me tomorrow," she said again. Then she turned around with a sweep of brocaded skirt and stalked into the dining room. The several retainers who had been waiting a respectful distance away scurried to catch up with her.

John and Niall waited as Wolverton watched her go. His tone was resentful as he turned to them and said, "My man Pimsley will call on you in the morning." Then he turned to his ward and held up an arm for her to take. "My dear," he prompted.

Catriona shook her head. "Go on ahead, Uncle," she said. "I'll be along shortly. The queen bade me welcome these gentlemen to court, remember?"

Wolverton looked at Niall and John as if they were beetles that had suddenly appeared in the middle of the queen's dinner platter, but after a moment he nodded and followed the queen into the dining hall.

When he was out of hearing, John turned to Catriona and said, "You are something of a surprise, milady." His words echoed Niall's thoughts. In both their encounters, the girl had been nearly as hostile as her guardian. It was hard to believe that she was suddenly making an overture of friendship.

Catriona looked up at John and said, "Ladies are supposed to be surprising, Dr. Black. 'Tis part of our power." Then she smiled again, slowly, and Niall felt his limbs go weak.

Catriona watched the Irishmen's confusion with secret amusement. The queen's orders had, in fact, pleased her. They gave her the opportunity to satisfy her own curiosity about the two newcomers. Though, of course, she wouldn't have refused to obey even if the task had not been to her liking. Elizabeth was not easily crossed.

Catriona's feelings about the sovereign she had come to court to serve were mixed. In her deepest core she would always hate England and everything about it, but she couldn't help admiring a woman who, on ascending to the throne at the age of twenty-five, had used her keen wits and strong spirit to earn authority over so many powerful men.

Now at the height of her powers, that authority was rarely tested, but Catriona still enjoyed watching how easily Elizabeth controlled her ministers, including the man who had taken Catriona into his household after the death of her father.

Catriona had never known exactly how she came to be taken into the home of Lord Wolverton. She and Bobby had ridden directly into the chaos of the fighting that horrible day seven years before. She'd seen Bobby beaten by the invaders and dragged away. Then she, herself, had run into the burning house, only to be confronted with the sight of her father's charred body just inside what was left of the massive front door. After succumbing to smoke and shock, the next thing she remembered was finding herself on a boat to England.

It had been some weeks before she could summon the will to care what would become of her. She'd let Wolverton's staff begin the process of turning her into an English lady. Wolverton had insisted that she take on one of his own family names, Sherwood, to replace her Irish surname, and he'd offered to give her a modest dowry as he would one of his own distant relations. But she had never been comfortable in his home, and she had never been able to feel warmth toward Wolverton himself.

Though she'd never been the recipient of his wrath, she'd seen him act cruelly toward servant and peer alike. The only one he couldn't bully was the queen, which was one more reason Catriona regarded her with respect.

But it had not been respect for the queen that had made her decide to acknowledge her two countrymen. She'd thought about them much of the afternoon and had already decided that if they had indeed come to bring about a peace between Ireland and England, she needed to know more about their mission. As Bobby had always told her, the way things stood, the only possible peace for her homeland was surrender to English rule. And surrender was something that neither she nor Bobby were willing to accept.

She would make an effort to learn more about these men. She turned once again to the shorter Irishman, John Black. It was easier talking to him. The tall one's gaze was a little too unsettling. In addition, as Bella had said, he was extraordinarily handsome, too much so for her to keep her wits about her. "Are you not often surprised by the ladies in your own country, Doctor?"

"Aye," John admitted with a grin. "I'm regularly surprised by almost everything about them."

Catriona had quickly learned this kind of flirtatious banter after arriving at court, though she indulged in it much less frequently than Elizabeth's other ladies. Most of the time she found it tedious, but tonight she felt a kind of exhilaration. " 'Tis one of our ancient secrets," she teased. "Men are best kept off-guard."

John laughed. "Then my friend here and I must be at our very best, milady, for we've understood little of what's going on since we arrived at court."

Catriona looked at Niall. "Is that true, Master Riordan? Are our court manners so mysterious?"

The taller Irishman appeared to be more serious than his companion. For a moment, she thought he might not even reply to her question, but after a pause he smiled and said, "So far, I've found court manners to be more rude than mysterious, milady, but I'm beginning to think that I could change that opinion any moment now."

The man was not only handsome, Catriona thought, he was honest. A rare quality at court. "We shall endeavor to make you change it," she said. "Let it not be said that visitors to Her Majesty's court were received with discourtesy."

Ever the diplomat, John clarified, "I'm certain that no one has meant any offense. As you heard, the queen herself has promised to hear our petition tomorrow."

With a start, Catriona realized that she'd been so focused on Niall Riordan's intense black eyes that she'd forgotten that she was against everything that these men were trying to accomplish.

Careful not to reveal too much interest, she asked casually, "Do you gentlemen think that an audience with Her Majesty is likely to solve the problems that have been simmering for decades?"

Niall answered her. " 'Tis worth the effort to try, milady. We've already lost too many good men over this struggle."

"Are there not some in your country who feel that Ireland should be free from England entirely?" Catriona let her long lashes sweep languidly over her eyes in a fashion that she knew distracted the thinking of most men. She wanted to learn the Irishmen's position, but she did not want them to suspect that she had any involvement in the matter.

Her strategy appeared to be working as Niall Riordan stumbled over his words in answering. "Not everyone was in agreement about suing for peace, but the leader of the uprising, Shane O'Neill, has agreed that it is time to reach a compromise."

Catriona had a sudden memory of Bobby Brosnihan's last secret visit. He'd been bitterly disappointed by the O'Neill and had called him a coward for appearing ready to give in to English demands.

"Ah, but 'tis a heavy topic for a colleen as beautiful as yourself," John interjected. "And 'tis ungentlemanly of us to keep you standing here when you've not yet supped."

Catriona hesitated for a moment. She'd like to know more about exactly what the men were going to be telling the queen the following day, but perhaps she'd asked enough questions for now. "Aye, I should go join my uncle."

Niall looked into the dining hall for the imposing form of Lord Wolverton. He was not difficult to spot seated up at the raised table only a few seats down from the queen. "Is Wolverton truly your uncle?" he asked.

Catriona nodded vaguely. She was used to skirting questions about her past and her family. As far as most people at court knew, she was an English orphan who was some kind of distant relative to the powerful lord.

She looked at the two men facing her. They both had the look of Ireland about them. It would be comforting to be able to tell them the truth about her family, to spend an evening with them talking about home. But she didn't dare reveal her true origins, especially not considering the task that had brought them here.

"I should take my leave," she said again. "No doubt I'll see you both again, since the queen has instructed me to make you welcome."

"We'll count on it, milady," John said with a practiced bow.

Niall nodded his head but remained silent. He watched her make her way up to the dais to join her uncle at the table, then turned on John. "What ails you, John? I'd thought to take courting lessons from you, but the way I see it, the lady was happy talking with us until you practically suggested that she leave."

John looked thoughtful. "I suspect there may be more to Mistress Sherwood than we are aware."

"What do you mean?"

"Her questions about Ireland were a little too casual."

Niall snorted in disgust. "You've been living in the woods with O'Neill too long, John. You see conspiracies everywhere. You're just confused because the girl's a beauty but appears to have a brain in her head as well."

"She's also Wolverton's niece," John added.

Niall looked up to the dais where Lord Wolverton and Catriona had their heads together in earnest discussion about something. He watched them for a long moment, but finally shook his head and said, "She was merely showing polite interest as the queen herself commanded. And since she's one of the few people who has spoken civilly to us today, you'd do well to be grateful rather than suspicious."

John sighed. "You're probably right. In any event, I'm done thinking for this night. Shall we go find the closet they've given us as sleeping quarters?"

"Aye," Niall agreed firmly. "After this day, I'd sleep in a dustbin if necessary."

John nodded and they turned together to start down the corridor.

They'd been at Whitehall for a solid week, and though Queen Elizabeth had received them and briefly listened to their proposal, her ministers had not followed through with any results. Alger Pimsley continued to bring them sheaves of documents each day, but they had still not received the kind of agreement they had hoped to take back to Shane O'Neill and the other rebel leaders.

"The next time he shows up with a proposal that says nothing, I'm likely to plant a boot in the center of his puffy silk breeches," Niall told John as they reentered London after a long ride. They'd spent the afternoon away from the city, in search of air that smelled of trees and grass rather than the greasy cooksmoke and heavy perfumes of the palace.

John gave a long sigh. "I warned you before we left home that this would be a long prospect. You claimed to be eager for the chance to learn a new place."

Niall scowled. "Aye, but I hadn't realized 'twould be a place where people are too busy to give you a simple 'good day' and where they consider anyone Irish to be one step less civilized than a pirate."

"You're exaggerating, lad. If the court ladies think you a pirate, it has only heightened their interest. They swarm around you like bees at a honeycomb. Ah, to be young again," John added with a grin.

Niall snorted. "You're not exactly in your dotage, John. From what I've been able to see, you've had plenty of them buzzing about yourself." The streets had become narrower and more crowded as they neared the palace. They slowed their horses to a sedate walk. "But you're right—the ladies, at least, are not unfriendly. 'Tis the men. Every time we catch a glimpse of Wolverton, he turns his back and walks the other way."

"Aye. Mayhap we were not the right ones for this job. Neither one of us is a politician."

"Cormac or Eamon should have come instead," Niall agreed gloomily. The two older Riordans had always had more patience and more diplomacy than their younger brother.

They had reached St. James Park, and their horses, spurred by the sudden expanse of green, began to trot. "But the O'Neill appointed us, and we're not going to let him down," John countered. "If we keep badgering them, eventually they'll have to give us what we want." His tone brightened. "And in the meantime, we've all those fair ladies to charm."

Niall shook his head. "I'm finding the chase less interesting than I'd thought."

John grinned. " 'Tis your own fault, lad. I told you not

to set your sites on that green-eyed feline. You have a whole garden of sweet roses ripe for the plucking, yet you insist on seeking out the one who offers nothing but thorns."

"She sometimes seeks us out as well," Niall argued.

"Aye, she seeks us out to get information, no doubt to pass along to her guardian."

John had voiced this warning before, and Niall himself had suspected the same thing. The lovely Catriona did seem to confine her conversation to questions about the progress of their negotiations. Yet every time Niall was in her company, he grew more fascinated.

The two friends remained silent as they arrived at the outer yard of Whitehall and allowed their horses to be taken by a stable boy. Walking toward the palace, Niall said, "If she's truly a spy for her uncle, mayhap two can play the same game. While she's trying to get information from us, we could get it from her."

John looked at his friend with an expression of amused pity. "Justify it however you like, Niall. The truth is, you're smitten with the lass, and, thorn or no, you're likely to keep after her until she's pricked you enough for you to come to your senses."

"I've had wounds before."

"Aye, but in battle. You're likely to find that wounds to the heart are an entirely different thing and much more painful."

Niall was about to make a mocking reply, but when he looked over at his friend, he saw an expression in his gentle gray eyes that he'd never seen before. "I don't intend to receive any wounds while at the English court, John, not of the heart or any other kind."

"If I were you, I'd stay away from her," John advised soberly.

Niall looked up at the imposing façade of Whitehall. Elizabeth's ladies, including Catriona Sherwood, were mostly housed in the upper floor of the new north wing.

"I'm not sure I want to do that, John," he said softly. Then he gave a nod to the footman who held the big iron door to the palace and walked inside.

John was right, Niall admitted silently as he headed toward the Queen's Garden where Elizabeth's ladies-in-waiting customarily strolled each afternoon after the midday meal. He could tell himself that he was seeking Catriona out to gather information for his cause, but the truth was, he simply wanted to see her again. Each time he turned a corner in the palace corridors or entered a new room, he found himself looking for her.

Today she was among the roses. Niall smiled, remembering John's warning about thorns. A basket with several cut flowers swung from her arm. She was wearing a brown skirt with a tightly cinched overdress of soft leather, dyed as red as the roses that surrounded her. The gown emphasized her narrow waist and the gentle flare of her hips.

"Good day, milady," he called to her.

She looked over at him, startled.

"Have you taken up gardening duties?" he asked.

She lifted her right hand to reveal shears. "Flowers for the queen," she explained. "She likes them to be fresh."

He moved toward her. "Aye, and pretty, as well. You can tell that from the way she chooses her ladies." He hoped his tribute would draw a response, but Catriona remained unsmiling and silent. " 'Tis a fair day," he continued, less certainly.

"Aye, 'tis," she replied.

By the rood, Niall thought with frustration, the woman made him feel like a milk-faced stripling. "Where is your companion, the Lady Arabella? She seems to be your perpetual shadow."

"I doubt Bella would appreciate that description, Master Riordan. She's no one's shadow."

"I just meant—"

"For that matter, you seem to be missing your own companion," she continued.

Niall grinned. "John's meeting with another representative of your uncle. We drew lots to see who would have to sit through yet another useless session."

"Useless?"

"Aye. English politicians are not the same breed we are used to back in Ireland. They prefer talk to action."

Catriona appeared to be only half listening to his words as her gaze shifted behind him.

He turned briefly. "Are you looking for someone?" he asked.

She looked vaguely uneasy as she answered, "Nay, 'tis just that I should be getting on with my cuttings."

He had hoped to walk with her for a spell, or perhaps persuade her to sit with him on one of the shady benches deeper into the garden, but her tone held obvious dismissal. Niall gave an inward sigh. John had been right. The beautiful Catriona Sherwood had her thorns.

"Shall I see you at supper tonight in the dining hall?" he asked.

"I rarely eat in the stables," Catriona replied dryly.

"Of course, I meant—"

"It was nice talking with you, Master Riordan," she said coolly. "Now you must excuse me."

Niall frowned as she turned away from him and walked down the rose-lined path. He'd never had this kind of problem back in Meath. If he'd seen a girl he wanted, she'd been available. It was as simple as that. Of course, he'd never seen any girl in Meath who was remotely like Catriona Sherwood.

Slowly he turned back toward the palace, trying to remember how Cormac had acted when he had first discovered he was in love with Claire.

Back in Meath the Riordans had a reputation as fierce fighters and generous lovers, but it was well known among the provincial girls that to lose one's heart to a Riordan was a fool's game. With the death of all three of their mothers, the brothers had grown up in an all-male household that no woman had been able to penetrate, at least not until his older brother Cormac had finally fallen under the spell of Claire O'Donnell.

He wished Cormac were here now. He could use some advice from his big brother on what to do about the first woman he'd ever met who seemed to be able to set his heart pounding with a simple glance.

Catriona let out a long sigh of relief. How could she have had the bad luck to run into Niall Riordan, of all people? He hadn't appeared to be following her or to be suspicious, but she watched out of the sides of her eyes to be sure that he was heading back to the palace.

She wiped the sweaty palm of her hand along the side of her dress. Master Riordan's appearance had made her nervous, and if she were honest with herself, she'd have to admit that it was only partly due to worry about her mission. Her palms had grown equally moist the previous evening when he had approached her in the dining hall, and she'd had to force herself to be cool and distant.

The roses ended as the path led into the dense shrubbery of the arbor. Catriona reminded herself that she had more important things to think about than Niall Riordan's sparkling black eyes. She squinted her eyes to see in the sudden shadows. Perhaps he wouldn't come today after all, she thought, though the signal had been unmistakable.

Inside the arbor it was suddenly cool. She closed her eyes and took a deep breath of air that smelled of moist greenery. Suddenly from behind an arm snaked around her waist.

She smiled and opened her eyes. Without turning to see her assailant, she said, using her former manner of speech, "Bobby Brosnihan, 'tis a wicked lad ye are fer stayin' away from me so long."

Three

Bobby's laugh was as hearty as in the old days—before the troubles—and Catriona felt as if her heart had suddenly lightened. It had taken him many years to regain that laugh.

"I'd not stay away from ye a minute, if ye'd only come back to Ireland where ye belong, scamp," he said in her ear.

She turned around and beamed at him. Once they had finally come to terms with the nature of their relationship, Bobby had ceased trying to use loverlike endearments and had reverted to the name he had used for her when they were growing up together in the Valley of Mor. His affectionate teasing always lifted her spirits. But she knew that the plea behind his words was serious.

"The day will come when I can go home, Bobby," she answered him. "But you know I can do more for the cause by staying."

Bobby looked doubtful. "I mislike the thought of ye with this scurvy lot," he said, nodding in the direction of the palace. "Especially that so-called guardian of yours. I ask myself why he's kept ye all these years, and I keep coming up with the same answer."

Catriona gave a dismissive wave of her hand. "I've told you before, if Lord Wolverton had evil designs on me, he'd have shown it long before this. Most of the time he scarcely appears to notice me."

Bobby's smile had faded. "I find it hard to believe that any man could fail to notice ye, Cat, especially when you're living as part of his household."

"Forget about Wolverton, Bobby. I want to hear what's going on with the Clearys." The Cleary family of the southwest had taken up the cause that the O'Neill had seemed to abandon with his decision to negotiate a peace settlement. The Clearys had sworn never to give up the fight until all the English were out of Ireland. Bobby and some of the others from the former O'Malley estate had joined with them.

Catriona looked around the little clearing. The greenery was thick, but the Queen's Garden was a popular place for afternoon strolls. "Come on," she said, grabbing his hand. "I'll take you to a place I've found where we can find some privacy."

Bobby grinned and gave an exaggerated sigh. "Ah, Cat, many were the days when I would have sold me soul to hear ye say that very thing."

Cat dropped his hand and gave him a little push on the shoulder. "Enough teasin', ye silly lad. I've much to tell you. O'Neill has sent men here to sue for peace."

Bobby's expression turned sober again. "I know. Dr. John Black and one of the Riordan brothers. Those are two men I'd never have thought to see selling out their country. Yet here they are, pretty as you please, supping with the English queen, the bloody traitors."

His characterization bothered Catriona, but she wasn't sure why. Hadn't she been saying much the same thing about the two erstwhile rebels? Inexplicably she found herself defending them. "They say that too many men have already died. 'Tis time to reach a compromise."

Bobby looked at her as if she'd turned into a ghost. "Ye've talked with them, then?"

"Aye."

He bent his head to scrutinize her face. "Surely they've not convinced ye, Cat?"

She shook her head, but it appeared that her murmured "Nay" was not as convincing as Bobby would have liked.

He tipped her chin up with his fingers so that she was forced to meet his eyes. "I've heard the Riordans are a devilish lot with the ladies. Mayhap the blackguard's put a spell on ye. Or mayhap 'tis the rebel doctor who's making that blush creep up yer neck."

"John Black's old enough to be my father," she answered sharply.

"So 'tis the Riordan, after all," Bobby said, dropping his hold on her chin. He sounded suddenly tired.

Catriona felt the heat fade from her cheeks. " 'Tis not either one of them, Bobby. I'm just telling you what the two men are saying. It doesn't mean that I've gone over to their way of thinking."

Bobby didn't look particularly convinced, but he nodded and said, "Very well then, show me this secret place of yours, Cat, and we'll see what kind of plan we can figure out to send Master Riordan and Dr. Black running with their cowardly tails between their legs all the way back to Tara Hill."

"You have the right of it, John," Niall said, giving his mouth a twist.

John's expression was amused. "I usually do, lad, but precisely what right are we referring to at the moment?"

"About the ladies. And thorns."

"Ah. About a certain lady in particular, you mean. I warned you from the beginning to seek out sweeter fare."

"Like your Bella."

"Nay, my friend, not *my* Bella. The lady Arabella is a

pure love to flirt with, but she's far too young for an old rake like me."

They were in one of the palace's endless antechambers, once again waiting for Alger Pimsley. The previous day, after John had threatened to leave and return to Ireland without any settlement, the man had agreed to try to convince Lord Wolverton to bring the matter before the queen's privy council.

"God's teeth, if you're old, John, then I'm a dancing bear. Why, there's scarce an eligible lady at court who's not set her cap for you."

John gave a rueful grin. "Which is precisely why I'm feeling that it's time for us to leave."

Niall laughed. "You'll hear no argument from me. I've given up on my quarry. But, seriously, John, aren't you the least bit interested in Arabella? She does appear to be interested. If there's to be peace at home now, you could settle down with a nice little wife to warm your feet at night when the cold creeps in from the bogs."

John leaned over and slapped his friend's shoulder. "I reckon 'tis my lot in life to live alone, Niall, but I'm grateful that you're concerned about my comfort in these waning years."

Niall snorted and once again insisted, "I don't picture you with a foot in the grave quite yet, John. Have you never wanted to marry?"

The doctor shifted his gaze away from his friend. "Mayhap. But 'twas long ago."

Niall waited for him to continue the story, but John remained silent, staring into space as though he were looking back through the years to another time and place.

After a moment Niall said, "Ah, well, mayhap we'll be happy bachelors together."

John turned back to him, straightening his shoulders, and said lightly, "So you really have abandoned all hope for snaring the attention of the lovely Catriona?"

Niall nodded. " 'Tis as you said from the very beginning. She's not interested."

Both men looked up as a young page approached them and gave a small bow of his head. He held an envelope in one hand. "Dr. Black?" he asked.

When John nodded, the boy handed him the envelope, then gave another nod, pivoted, and left.

John opened the envelope and withdrew a paper.

"What's Pimsley's excuse today?" Niall asked with a grimace of disgust.

"The message is not from Pimsley," John answered.

"What is it, then?"

His companion smiled. "It seems that we've been invited to a ball at Wolverton House."

Niall looked puzzled. "Lord Wolverton has invited us to his home?"

John held up the paper and waved it in front of Niall's face. "The invitation is signed by his ward. Lady Catriona Sherwood."

Catriona never knew how Bobby made his way in and out of London. He seemed to be able to come and go without anyone being aware of his presence. She'd felt safer about meeting him when she was still living at Wolverton House. No one had paid any attention to her there. She could probably have met with the O'Neill himself without anyone taking notice. But the movements of Elizabeth's ladies-in-waiting were more closely watched. She and Bobby had devised a signal—a small piece of yarn tied around the last of the queen's prized rosebushes—to let her know when she should expect him and make arrangements to get by herself.

The yarn was there again. She was due to leave for Wolverton House in less than an hour to begin preparations for the ball, which was to be in two days. She hoped Bobby had no last-minute changes, since she was nervous enough about the plan they'd made.

Looking around to see that she wasn't observed, she bent to remove the thread, then hurried off to the secluded spot she'd shown him the other day. It was a little walled garden that had apparently been abandoned since it was at some distance from the regular palace lots. It had once been an herb garden. Pungent odors still drifted up here and there from beneath the overgrown weeds.

Bobby was sitting on a rock, waiting for her.

"Is everything all right?" she asked at once.

His smile was reassuring. " 'Tis the very same question I was about to put to ye, scamp. I wanted to be sure that ye're no goin' soft on me again."

She stuck her tongue out in an old childhood gesture. "I'm as tough as you are, Bobby Brosnihan. Never think otherwise."

Bobby jumped to his feet as she picked her way toward him through the weeds. He took her hand briefly and gave her a kiss on the cheek. "Aye, lass, ye're as tough as they come. 'Tis proud I am to know ye, Cat O'Malley."

Tears stung her eyes. In fact, she wasn't feeling tough at all. The plan she and Bobby had devised could do more than end the peace negotiations. It could mean a sentence of death for the two men who had come to bring them about. Bobby had scoffed at her qualms.

"But I wish there were another way to do this," she said again.

Bobby's eyes narrowed. " 'Tis Riordan who's put that quivery tone in yer voice, isn't it? If he means so much to ye, I reckon ye could seduce the bounder and convince him of the error of his ways," he added bitterly.

"What a hateful thing to say, Bobby!" Her voice was stiff with hurt.

Bobby's shoulders sagged. "Aye. I beg pardon, Cat. 'Tis just that I can't stand seein' ye take on the cause of a couple of bloody turncoats."

"I'm not taking on their cause, Bobby. Haven't I made all the arrangements for the ball just to make this happen?"

Bobby looked sullen. " 'Tis much on your shoulders. Mayhap it would be better after all if I just did away with the two of them." He pulled a hunting knife from his belt. "Quick and easy."

Catriona shuddered. The thought of Niall's dark eyes growing still with death gave her a chill. "I'd not see them killed."

Bobby looked concerned. "Cat, ye do realize that when they are caught with yer uncle's jewel, they may be executed?"

The lump that had seemed to take up residence in her throat over the past three days grew larger. She nodded. "Aye, but I'm thinking that I can convince the queen to grant leniency. All she needs to do is send them back to Ireland. That would solve the problem for the nonce."

Bobby stepped back and motioned for her to sit on the rock he had abandoned. "Are ye certain ye can do it all yerself, Cat? Ye'll be alone with Riordan. What if he catches ye planting the jewel on him?"

Catriona felt the heat rise on her neck. "I can deal with Niall Riordan, Bobby. You have the hard part—opening my guardian's strongbox and taking the emerald. How will you be able to get into his study without anyone seeing you?"

Bobby grinned. " 'Twill be like plucking feathers off a dead chicken. Wolverton House is an easy mark. I've already been in and out twice."

"Inside Wolverton House?"

"Aye, I always scout before I steal, Cat."

The words were said in jest, but there was a hard edge to his tone. Bobby had never wanted to talk about what he had had to do to survive after he had escaped from the English, and Catriona had never pressed him for details.

She reached up to take his hand. "If there's a chance that you'll be caught, Bobby, then I think we should make other plans. Halting the peace negotiations is not worth you ending up in English hands again."

"Halting the peace talks is worth anything, Cat," Bobby answered firmly. "But I'll not be caught. I'll retrieve the Wolverton emerald from your guardian's strongbox, and I'll hide it where we discussed in the orangery. The rest will be up to you."

She looked up at him from her perch on the rock. "Aye." The word came out a half-whisper.

Bobby frowned. "I'm countin' on ye, Cat. Can ye do it, lass?"

"Aye," she said more firmly. "I can."

He nodded approval, then bent to plant a kiss on her forehead. "That's me girl," he said.

The groom at Wolverton House who took their horses looked impressed as he eyed their mounts, both of which had come from the famous Riordan stables, Niall's particular love. The lad appeared less impressed with the horses' riders. The two Irishmen were as plainly dressed as they had been at Whitehall.

"We look like two wrens in a yard full of peacocks," John said wryly as they nodded at the liveried doorman and walked into the entrance hall of the huge manor.

Niall laughed. "I offered to send for a tailor to do you up some yellow stockings, but you refused."

"There wasn't time. These English appear to be a spontaneous lot. In Ireland we'd be planning a gala like this weeks ahead."

Niall shrugged. There had been no lady in the Riordan household since his mother had died giving birth to him, so social gatherings had always been haphazard affairs at best. "I reckon if one has enough servants, anything is possible."

"Aye," John agreed, looking around. Half the hall seemed to be filled with maids and lackeys performing one kind of task or another.

Niall scanned the hall as well, but he was not focusing on the servants. "Do you see our hosts?" he asked John.

His friend grinned. "Patience, lad. You have an entire evening to woo her."

Niall flushed. "I meant Wolverton. You were questioning whether he had some special motive for inviting us here tonight after ignoring us for days."

John cocked his head. "Ah, my friend, 'tis because I'm old and jaded. I see conspiracy everywhere I go. You, on the other hand, are still young and eager. Forget politics for tonight and go after your fair lady."

"She's fair enough, John, but she's certainly not mine."

John shook his head. "I'd always thought 'twas a Riordan pledge never to admit defeat." They had made their way to the far end of the hall, where double doors led into a grand salon that was filling up with guests.

Niall grimaced. "Aye, if my brothers were here, they'd roast me for cowardice."

John gave him a gentle shove on the back to push him into the crowded room. "Then onward, lad. The evening is young and so are you."

"I can't believe your uncle simply let you hold a ball with a week's notice, Cat," Arabella said with a little giggle of excitement. "And I'm so glad the queen decided not to come. We can be as naughty as we please."

Catriona smiled at her friend's eager face. "Everyone says that Uncle Henry is a harsh man, but he's always given me everything I wanted. I can't fault him for lack of generosity. As for acting naughty, Bella, I have no doubt that our behavior here will be duly reported back to the palace."

"Unless we're very careful," Arabella said in a laughing whisper.

"Aye," Catriona agreed. "Unless we're very careful."

She would have to be more than careful this night, Catriona told herself. She'd have to be clever and quick and devious. Most of all, she'd have to be cold. It simply wouldn't do to think about Niall Riordan's crooked smile or those eyes. It wouldn't do to remember that he was trying to serve their common country in the way he thought best, just as Bobby was.

It especially wouldn't do to think about what could happen to the two Irishmen if this night's work had the outcome she and Bobby intended. She'd seen Elizabeth sign death warrants for less, but she also knew that the queen had a soft side, especially for charming men with handsome faces. Elizabeth had been taken with the two Irishmen. Catriona didn't think she would want to see them hanged.

"What ails you, Cat?" Bella asked impatiently. "You haven't heard a word I'm saying."

Catriona forced her thoughts back to the present. "I beg pardon, Bella. I'm trying to remember if everything is taken care of for the evening's festivities."

Bella linked her arm through her friend's and pulled her toward the grand salon. "Anything that's not ready by now will have to stay undone, my fretful friend. The dancing has started."

Catriona's palms grew moist. It was time. She and Bobby had gone over the details again and again. He undoubtedly was already at the far end of the house retrieving the famous emerald from her guardian's study. There was no help for it. She had to keep her mind on the brave rebels who were ready to die to rid their country of English oppression. She couldn't fail them.

Arabella tugged at her arm. "Stop dallying, Cat. I think I see those two brawny Irishmen across the room. Isn't that doctor simply the most distinguished older man you ever saw? I didn't know you'd invited them."

"It seemed the polite thing to do," Catriona said, her voice hollow. "They have no friends at court."

"They have me." Arabella giggled. "Come on. Let's go claim a dance."

• • •

"You may have an easier time than you thought, Niall," John said in an undertone. "There's your thorny rose with her shadow, Lady Arabella, coming across the room to us now. It seems that the quarry is coming straight to the hunter."

Niall didn't need John's advisory. He'd seen Catriona the moment she and her friend had appeared in the doorway. As usual, the two were the most striking pair in the room—Catriona in a rich purple silk gown that made the green in her eyes glow like a candle. Arabella wore a pale pink that was nowhere near as dramatic, but that showed off her blond prettiness to perfection.

He gave a low bow as the two women approached. It was, at least, one thing he had learned from his stay at court. He hated to think of the teasing he'd get from his brothers if he tried the gesture back home.

"Mistress Catriona and Lady Arabella," John said as he lifted his head from his own bow. "May I say that you are nothing short of stunning tonight? I vow, the candles dimmed when you entered the room."

Niall shot his companion a sardonic glance, then turned back to the women. "Aye," he agreed simply. " 'Tis no exaggeration about the beauties at Elizabeth's court."

"Nor 'tis an exaggeration about the gallantry of Irish gentlemen," Bella replied with a small curtsy. Her eyes twinkled and her curls bobbed. "Are their dancing skills equally fine?"

John glanced at Niall, whose gaze had not left Catriona's face. With a smile he extended his hand to Arabella. "Shall we put it to a test, milady?" he asked.

Arabella gave Catriona a wink and let the Irishman lead her away toward the lines of dancers.

"You have our thanks for the invitation," Niall said after a moment. Catriona seemed less self-assured than usual. Perhaps she was nervous about her hostessing duties. " 'Tis a fine assembly," he added, looking around the salon.

She gave a slightly brittle smile. "Wolverton House is a beautiful setting for festivities."

"Has this always been your home?" Niall asked.

A shadow seemed to cross her face. "Nay," she answered briefly.

Niall bit his lip. If Wolverton was her guardian, she was evidently an orphan. He of all people should know how painful childhood memories could be when one lacked a parent's love. He searched for another topic. "I've not seen Lord Wolverton."

She smiled. "He's not likely to leave the gaming room the entire evening. 'Tis the only reason he's willing to suffer these galas."

"He likes gambling, then?"

"Aye. I've heard that Uncle Henry can be a ruthless man, but the only evidence of it I've seen is at the tables. He refuses to be beaten."

Across the room Niall could see John smiling at Arabella as the two lined up to begin an almain. Niall had not the slightest idea how to do the popular French dance, but John seemed to know exactly what to do. Niall shook his head in amusement as the music started and his friend gave a deep bow. Except for the plainer clothes, he looked much like all the other gentlemen courtiers, but that wasn't surprising. John Black was the kind of man who could fit into any circumstances. He was equally at ease sitting around a campfire with a band of woodcutters as he was dancing as gracefully as any courtier.

He turned back to his companion. "Gambling is a sport that brings out the competitive side of a man. Much like politics. 'Tis why I've decided that I like neither activity."

"Yet you participate in both," Catriona observed.

"Nay, I'm not a gambler. And as for politics, I intend for these negotiations to be my first and last venture into the realm."

She looked surprised. "You have the look of a man who relishes a fight."

He laughed. "Because my hose are not pink? The only fights I relish are wrestling matches with my brothers. There's something clean and true about a contest of strength between men. You match your mettle honestly and aboveboard. Best man wins. In politics, as in cards, nothing is as it seems. The game goes to the one who can be the most devious." He made a grimace of disgust.

Catriona shifted her glance to the dance floor. "Sometimes the game may be worth the price," she said softly.

As usual, her words were not what he had expected. It was one of the intriguing things about Catriona Sherwood. Just when he thought he was beginning to read her, she would take a different turn. When she'd been so cold to him in the garden the other day, he'd been sure that she was not interested in his company. Then they'd received the invitation for this night's gathering.

Which was it to be tonight? he wondered. The icy beauty who could freeze with a look . . . or the flesh-and-blood woman whose smile had turned his blood to liquid heat?

As if reading his question, she turned her face back to look at him. Her eyelashes swept upward and her voice was inviting as she said, "I should go now and greet our other guests, but perhaps later in the evening, you would care to have me show you my guardian's orangery."

There was an unmistakable implication to her invitation. Niall's body responded instantly to the thought of spending some time with her alone, even as his mind sounded a bell of warning. Was it simply her nature to be cold one moment and hot the next? Or was John right that there may be something more sinister behind Mistress Sherwood's interest? Either way, at that moment he could no more turn down her invitation than chop off his right arm.

"I would love to see . . . er . . . your orangery," he answered with a smile.

Once again the long lashes swept. "At midnight?" she asked.

Niall's answer came out hoarse. "Aye," he said. "At midnight."

Four

Catriona glanced for the hundredth time at the big golden clock that hung on the wall behind the food tables at the end of the hall. She had not touched the heaping platters of roasted duck and quail and grouse. Her stomach was too jumpy to think of eating. Every time the clock had chimed the hour all night long, she'd felt her heart give a little skip. The evening had seemed endless.

Keeping busy with her hostess duties, she'd gone from the dancing to the game room to the East Wing salon, where some of the ladies were talking while their husbands gambled. She'd avoided the long hall that led back to the orangery. Part of her didn't want to know if Bobby had been successful. If the jewel wasn't there, the plan would have to be abandoned.

She'd also avoided the Irish visitors, though she'd seen them both dancing. It was obvious that John Black had more experience than Niall, but the younger Irishman managed well enough. He had a natural strength and agility that made the unfamiliar steps seem easy.

Some of the older guests had already departed, but Catriona knew that there would be plenty of younger courtiers to serve as witnesses for the scene she and Bobby had planned as the finale to the night's festivities.

Over the tinny sound of the music, the deep bong of the clock began its twelve strokes. Catriona's throat went dry. She glanced across the room to see that Niall was looking at her, his expression questioning.

She forced a smile and nodded at him. He bowed quickly to the group around him and started toward her across the salon. As he approached, she took a deep breath, willing herself to stay strong and calm. Bobby would expect nothing less.

"I trust we still have our engagement, mistress," he said, "for 'tis all I've thought of this whole evening long."

"Aye," she said. "The Wolverton orangery is known throughout England. You'd not want to miss it."

Niall laughed and leaned close to her ear. "You could be taking me to the rubbish heap, Mistress Catriona, and I'd not care. I find it hard to notice anything beyond a certain pair of green eyes."

Her neck grew hot—the cursed blush that always seemed to betray her no matter how hard she tried to appear strong. Ignoring his implication, she said, "Shall we go, then? There are some varieties of trees that my guardian has had brought from the New World. I think you'll find them quite exotic."

Niall took her arm and let her lead the way out of the hall. "Lord Wolverton is interested in more than gaming and politics, then?" he asked.

Catriona nodded. "He's an expert on plants. They say his collection is one of the best in England."

Niall found it hard to reconcile his image of the callous English politician with the man who had taken in a young orphan, held dances at his home, and collected exotic plants.

"I appreciate your offer to show it to me," he said, suddenly impatient to be alone with her. Though he'd done his best to keep up with the tangled steps of the fancy English dances, his mind had been on Catriona and their midnight meeting. A dozen times he'd asked himself why she'd agreed to meet him. A dozen times he'd tried to convince himself that the answer was nothing more than the age-old spark between a man and a maid.

" 'Tis at the rear of the manor," she said, guiding him down a darkened hall. "Designed to get full exposure to the morning sun."

He nodded. Back at Riordan Hall he'd always taken an interest in the gardens. Though the racing of his heart had nothing to do with plants, he would find her uncle's collection interesting.

The musky scent of the plants greeted them even before they entered the room. Glass windows that extended nearly floor to ceiling undoubtedly provided daytime brilliance, but this night the room was dimly lit with scattered wall sconces. A tiled walkway provided a path through the beds of plants and trees. Niall had never seen a room quite like it.

" 'Tis quite remarkable," he said.

She turned back to smile at him, and all at once the plants and the unique nature of the room were forgotten. "I've always liked the room," she admitted. "There are benches at the rear where I used to sit and read when I wanted to be away from everyone. You feel completely hidden from the rest of the world."

He studied her face to see if the words held invitation, but her expression appeared to be nothing more than that of the polite hostess giving a tour to a guest.

He followed her along the walkway, pausing now and then to question the origin of an unfamiliar plant. She knew the names of some and not others. The collection was entirely ornamental—no new varieties of fruits or sturdier vegetable stock.

" 'Tis true your uncle's tastes run more to adornment than practicality," he observed when they'd made their way halfway down the room.

"Aye. He says it appeals to him to be able to own something beautiful. Something that has no purpose other than to be beautiful just for him."

"It would appear that your uncle has never experienced hunger, then. For most of the world, food comes first, then beauty."

"I know," she said briefly.

Once again, Niall wondered about her background. Had she once known hunger? Up to now, she'd shied away from his questions. "My surmise is that you've had little experience with hunger yourself, milady, in these surroundings."

Her tone was sharp as she replied, " 'Tis true I've led a privileged life, Master Riordan, but that doesn't mean I know nothing about—" She hesitated and seemed to be reconsidering her words. Finally she ended, "About how the poor of this world must live."

Niall had the feeling that she'd been about to say something entirely different, but he wasn't inclined to press the point. She'd been cordial to him all evening. The last thing he wanted was to turn her back into the ice princess. "Forgive me if I said aught to annoy you, mistress."

The candlelight from a nearby sconce caught a troubled glint in her eyes, but she said hurriedly, "Nay, you've said nothing amiss. And"—he could see a hard swallow travel the length of her slender throat—"and mayhap ye'd like to call me by my name, since we're alone."

Her invitation surprised him, but he wasn't about to wait for further explanation before taking advantage of her offer of more familiarity. Leaning toward her, he whispered, "Then I'll call you my beautiful Cat. As alluring and provocative as the name."

She looked up at him with a smile that on any other woman he would have called seductive. But there was just a hint of nervousness to her manner that disturbed him. Perhaps she was new to this game, he thought. He'd have to progress slowly, though his body had been racing since she'd come toward him across the dance floor.

"Would you care to find one of my private benches to sit for a spell?" she asked.

Niall looked around the overgrown orangery. From down the hall behind them, the noise from the dancing was a distant din. None of the other guests appeared to have found the secluded place. Catriona might have been new to trysting, but she had chosen the place well. "Aye," he agreed with a smile.

She led him to the far end of the long greenhouse, and around the twisting path to a shrouded nook where a bench was nestled among thick rhododendron bushes. He took her hand to help her to a seat. The circular alcove was hidden from the rest of the room. "Are you sure 'twas reading that brought you to this place?" Niall teased. "Were there no young swains you invited here?"

"Nay, you're the first." Her face was so close that he could see the almost imperceptible quiver of her lower lip. She *was* nervous. The thought helped temper his rising hunger.

"I'm glad," he whispered. Then he slowly put one hand behind her neck and bent to kiss her.

Catriona closed her eyes, willing herself not to feel. But his lips were every bit as tender as she had imagined, and her body melted at his first touch. She leaned back on the bench in mute surrender, letting him deepen the kiss, letting the magic spread through her shoulders and her limbs and her hands. She made a small moan of surrender at the back of her throat.

"Tell me this is why you brought me back here, my sweet Cat," Niall murmured. "Tell me that you've wanted this as I have." Without waiting for an answer, he kissed her again, less softly, this time using his tongue to tease her lips and gently explore her mouth.

He held her head with both his hands as his thumbs gently stroked along her neck. An unfamiliar wave coursed the length of her body. He moved his hands down her back and drew her closer, all the while continuing his kisses. She felt her breasts harden against the pressure of his chest, and of their own accord, her arms went around him.

For several moments she gave herself up to the sensations. This was it, she was thinking in wonder. This was what the minstrels sang, what the bards penned. Then she stiffened, suddenly remembering what it was she had come here to do. When she'd made her plan with Bobby, she'd not imagined that it would be like this. She'd thought she could bring Niall to this private place, give him a quick kiss or two, then plant the emerald in his coat and that would be that. She hadn't expected the instant heat or how it could melt her into surrender.

She turned her face away from his kiss and pushed against his chest. It was time to regain control.

He released her instantly. "Forgive me. I'd intended a more measured approach, but"—his voice was hoarse and slightly desperate—"surely you must feel it as well."

His face was inches away. She could see the rough whiskers along the square line of his jaw. Her lips still tingled from his kisses. She drew in a ragged breath, but instead of clearing her spinning head, it seemed as if she was still inhaling his masculine essence.

He smiled and in a swift movement lifted her to his lap. "I'll not rush you, sweetheart, I promise," he murmured. "We'll take our time learning each other's delights." He was punctuating his words with brief soft kisses that made her go weak again in his arms. *Jesu,* what was happening to her?

From her new position, her gaze caught a flash of green in the dirt at the base of the rhododendrons nearest to the bench. It was the Wolverton emerald. Bobby had left it there for her, just as they had planned. A sudden chill raised bumps on her skin. Misinterpreting their nature, Niall chuckled and kissed the base of her neck. "Are you cold, sweetheart?" he asked. "Myself, I'm feeling the heat has become intense."

Catriona closed her eyes and willed herself back to the Valley of Mor. She forced herself to remember the sight of her beloved home in smoking ruins, the charred bodies of her father and Terrence, the old manservant who had not left his side in life or in death. The man who was now holding her in his arms had come to London to make peace with the people who had done that.

The chill subsided, along with the heat from Niall Riordan's kisses. She slipped off his lap and forced herself to smile at him as she cautioned, "'Twould be best if you keep that promise not to rush me, sirrah. I vow 'twould be quite a scandal for the lady of the house to be seen entangled with one of the guests."

He let her go without resistance. "Aye, especially when that guest is a foreigner who is little trusted at court," he added ruefully.

His voice was still raspy and his breathing rough. She steeled herself. She had a mission to accomplish, and she had best do it quickly.

On the pretense of straightening her voluminous satin skirts, she reached over the edge of the bench and collected the small brooch that contained the prize emerald that her guardian had recently added to his collection of precious gems. The piece was an unadorned circlet of gold surrounding an emerald that rivaled the most perfect of the crown jewels. Lord Wolverton had shown it to her a number of times, though he'd never suggested that she or anyone else wear it. Like his exotic flowers, it was beautiful and it was his. That was enough.

Her head was finally beginning to clear. Once again she was becoming Cat O'Malley, determined to do what she could to give Bobby and his fellow rebels the time they needed to drive the English out of their country. The memory of those moments in Niall's arms was already becoming unreal.

Niall put a hand against her cheek. "What we need, sweetheart, is a place that is truly private. Will you ride with me tomorrow?"

"I'd like that," she replied with a smile, though she knew full well that if her plan succeeded, Niall would not be riding anywhere for a long time.

"Shall I come for you here, or will you be at the palace?"

"I return to the palace in the morning," she answered. This was the riskiest moment. She knew that Niall had a purse at his belt, but, unlike Bobby, she had never had the chance to learn the skills of the cutpurses and sneak thieves of the London underworld.

"Though not early, I trow, after this night's work," he said. "Shall we meet at midafternoon?"

There was no help for it. She would have to distract him again. She tried to make her smile suggestive. "Would you like to seal the arrangement with a kiss?" she asked.

He grinned. "Since I've already given up the idea of being able to sleep this long night . . ." He leaned toward her and she offered her lips.

This time, with the hard jewel pressing into the tender flesh of her palm, she had no trouble keeping her mind on her task. While he kissed her, she ran her hands down his side. Feeling her way with her fingertips, she found the top of the small leather bag that slung loosely over his belt and slipped the brooch inside. Then she pulled away and looked into his eyes. He was still smiling at her and appeared to notice nothing amiss. She took in a deep breath of relief.

"Until tomorrow, then," she said brightly, standing.

"Aye," he said, coming to his feet more slowly. "Until tomorrow. Only a mere eternity for me to wait."

She smiled at him and let him lead her back along the tiled path.

•   •   •

"Are you going to tell me where you disappeared to for so long with our lovely hostess?" John asked with mock disapproval.

"Nay," Niall answered with a grin.

"Since you have the look of a boy who's eaten the entire pantry full of pastries, I warrant I don't need to ask."

"Gentlemen don't reveal the details of their assignations, John."

The most diehard guests were finally collecting their cloaks and taking their leave. Niall paid little attention to the assembly. His mind was on the past hour he had spent with Catriona in the orangery. His heartbeat had still not returned to normal.

"So it *was* an assignation, then?" John asked. His tone was teasing, but Niall could see a trace of worry in his expression.

"Are you still suggesting that she's a spy for her uncle? Because I assure you—"

John cut him off with a raised hand. "Nay, I'm not suggesting anything, lad. It's just that we can never forget who we are or what we're doing here. Not for an instant."

Niall grew sober. "I know that, John. But what passed between Catriona and myself tonight had nothing to do with politics. I'd stake my life on it."

John smiled. "I'm glad to hear it. You're young and bonny, the both of you, and I've not become so jaded that I'd stand in the way of young love."

They began moving toward the door amid the crush of guests. "We're going riding tomorrow," Niall confided.

"Just remember to be careful. You may be sure of your charming companion, but there's more to consider. I've heard the queen does not always take well to the romancing of her ladies."

"We'll be careful," Niall assured him. "After waiting this long, I'd not do anything to jeopardize the negotiations."

The predawn air coming from the open door of the

manor felt good after the stuffy heat of the salon. Niall drew in a deep breath and prepared to step outside. Suddenly someone put a hand on his shoulder and spun him around, none too gently.

He began a startled protest that died in his throat as he saw Catriona standing before him with Lord Wolverton. Her expression was set in the haughty mask he had seen on their first meeting.

Two liveried servants held him by each arm as John asked sharply, "What is this about, milord?"

Wolverton looked down at his ward.

"Aye, Uncle," she said, pointing at Niall. "He is the one I saw entering your study."

Niall felt the blood drain from his face.

"Search him," Wolverton said.

Rough hands pushed at his legs and sides. One of the servants ripped the purse from his belt. "This is it!" the man said, opening the leather bag to produce a brooch with a glittery stone. He reached to hand the jewel to Wolverton, who snatched it from the man with a smile of triumph.

"I have no idea how that got in my bag," Niall said, but even as he said the words, a horrible certainty was growing. He looked at Catriona, but she refused to meet his gaze, and his worst suspicions were confirmed. "It was the girl," he said to John.

His friend gave a dismayed nod of understanding.

"Seize them both and convey them to the authorities at the Tower to await the queen's pleasure," Wolverton said, signaling to several other retainers who had gathered around the group.

Catriona remained silent.

"They'll see what we do with traitors who come on the guise of peace only to plunder our nation's treasures," Wolverton continued, his voice booming out to the entire assembly of remaining guests who stood watching the incident in eager silence.

Niall looked at Catriona. "Is this what you wanted?" he asked her. When she continued her silence, he persisted. "Was it your plan or Wolverton's?"

Her eyes were as glittery and hard as the emerald Wolverton held in his hand. "I don't know what you're talking about," she said.

"Don't even speak to them, my dear," Wolverton said, putting an arm around her shoulder. "I'm sorry I ever agreed to have them in my home."

John, whose arms were now also pinned by two men, spoke to Wolverton. "Milord, I know not who is behind this plot, but if you are not involved, I'd ask you to consider the sense of it. Master Riordan's family back in Ireland is wealthy. He's here on a political mission. Why would he risk it to take a bauble, especially in the midst of a gathering of witnesses?"

Wolverton appeared as unmoved as his ward. "Who knows why any of you ruffians do anything," he said. "The emerald is extremely valuable, valuable enough to purchase many weapons to use against Her Majesty's government."

"We're done with weapons. We're here seeking peace," John argued.

"So you say." He held out his hand to show off the brooch. "But the evidence is unmistakable."

Niall felt a rushing behind his ears. All the while she'd been kissing him, soft and yearning in his arms, she'd been plotting his downfall. And to think he'd thought her an innocent. It would appear that the innocent one was he himself. And the fool.

"You'll win no argument here, John," he told his friend. "We'd best wait and plead our case to the queen. I believe that she, at least, is an honorable woman." He looked directly at Catriona as he said the words, but her expression didn't change.

John nodded in agreement.

"Take them away," Wolverton said.

The crowd of onlookers cleared. Niall turned his head to keep his eyes on Catriona as the Wolverton men led them out of the house. She watched them leave without so much as a flinch.

Five

The Tower of London was slowly being transformed from a home for kings to a home for the prisoners of kings. Elizabeth herself had spent time there, and it was there that her mother's head had been struck from her small body by a swordsman especially brought from France.

John and Niall's quarters were, at least, not among the most grim in the maze of Tower buildings. They were being held together in the Wakefield Tower in a roomy chamber with two beds, a long window, and a sitting area that included a carved table and benches for dining.

In spite of the comfortable quarters, Niall was finding the confinement nearly unbearable. Up to now they'd been unable to see the queen. They'd been refused the help of a barrister. The only representative of the palace who had visited them had been Alger Pimsley. The fussy little man made regular visits to stutter and stammer and wring his hands as he tried to explain the progress of their case.

It had been over a fortnight since the ball at Wolverton House, and Niall still felt his insides churn every time he thought about Catriona's treachery. He had actually begun to think that he had met a woman he could love with the kind of passion he'd seen between Cormac and Claire, but he should have known better. Such love was rarer than a bluebell in winter.

He had to admit that part of his bitterness stemmed from sheer embarrassment. John had carefully avoided the subject, but he suspected that his friend must think him an utter fool for letting Catriona put them both in such peril. He'd risked their lives and destroyed the peace negotiations—all because he was too infatuated to see through the clever scheming of a beautiful woman.

"What do you see staring out that window so incessantly, John?" he asked his friend. It was the morning of their sixteenth day of incarceration.

"The river. Come look at how it sparkles in the sunlight. If you let the mind drift, you could think 'twere the River Boyne."

Niall joined his companion at the window. "Aye, if you ignore the black, smoky air hanging over the city yonder. 'Tis not exactly the blue sky and green hills of home."

John smiled. " 'Tis a game of the mind, lad. When you're as old as I, you become an expert."

"You never seem to be disturbed by anything, John. Don't you ever feel anger or sadness or . . . I don't know . . . *despair*?"

John's expression was gentle. "I'll leave the raging to the young."

"And the happiness, as well?" Niall asked.

His friend made no reply.

A thump on the door made them both turn. "Dinner's come early," John said. After they had arrived at the Tower, they'd given the warden the coins they'd been carrying to ensure that they would receive twice daily meals consisting of more than rat-infested gruel.

But when the thick wooden door swung open, it was not the usual bailiff who brought their food.

"Eamon!" Niall shouted, bounding across the room to engulf his older brother in a rib-crushing embrace.

Eamon extricated himself with a laugh and responded

with an affectionate cuff to his brother's head. "God's teeth, baby brother, 'tis a nice way to lure me to London—landing yourself in the Tower."

"How did you get here?" Niall asked, elated.

Eamon shrugged. "The O'Neill sent me. I warrant he had his own special ways of keeping accounts on the progress of his peace brokers."

Niall didn't question further. Shane O'Neill was a true leader, one who had a vast web of informants to keep him abreast of any developments that would affect his command. "I'm glad," he said. "The bloody English wouldn't let us see anyone or send any messages."

"We've already seen to that," Eamon told him.

"We? Is Cormac with you?"

"Nay. Claire's with child again. He won't leave her side." For generations so many young Riordan brides had died in childbirth that the Black Swan emblem of the clan had turned into a symbol of what was called the Riordan Curse. The oldest Riordan brother had fully believed in the curse's power until the healthy birth of his first child the previous year.

"Again?" Niall grinned. "After resisting the idea for so long, it appears our brother has turned into a prize breeding stud."

"I'll challenge you to say that to his face when we get back home." Eamon grinned. "He'll have your hide."

"Or at least attempt to have it," Niall agreed.

John had been waiting over by the window while the brothers had their reunion, but he stepped forward now to offer the newcomer his hand. " 'Tis a glad sight you are, Eamon," he told him. "Mayhap we can get this straightened out now. I trust Shane sent others with you to help us?"

John Black was the only man Niall knew who called the powerful O'Neill by his first name.

"He sent no one," Eamon told them, but before they

could protest, he continued, "But he authorized me to hire Truly Fitzpatrick."

Niall and John both smiled. Truly Fitzpatrick was an Irishman whose talents both in business dealings and at the bar of justice had become so legendary that he was now sought by the wealthiest and most powerful men in all of Europe. He'd been living in London for the past several years.

"If this is in Truly's hands, I'll stop fretting," Niall said.

"He's talking with some people at court this morning, but he'll come here this afternoon. In the meantime, he asked me to get your account of how all this happened. Where do we start?"

Niall motioned for his brother to take a seat at their table. "You'd best start with the lady," John said wryly, taking a seat at Eamon's side.

Niall frowned and sat across from them without speaking.

"The lady?" Eamon prompted.

Niall leaned forward, elbows on the table, and gave a hefty sigh. "Aye, a lady. Turns out that here in London they can be as treacherous as they are alluring."

Eamon seemed surprised and glanced at John, who nodded a quick confirmation. Then he turned back to his brother with a new look of sympathy. His voice was gentle as he said, "I warrant 'tis not only in London, nor is it the first time a man's been ensnared."

Niall gave his brother a brittle smile of appreciation for his understanding, then settled himself to tell his brother the whole story. "Her name is Catriona Sherwood," he began, "but they call her Cat. I should have been warned from the beginning. Everyone knows that felines are the craftiest beasts on the face of the earth."

"What if they kill them, Bobby?" Catriona asked, her voice catching.

"What if they do?" he answered with a shrug.

They were in the little hidden garden, sitting on the ground in the midst of the weeds, their backs against the brick wall, and Bobby had come to say goodbye. Once again, he was returning to Ireland, leaving her here surrounded by English people with English clothes eating English food in English houses. Everything she hated. She was so tired of it all. She wanted to go home, but there was no home for her in Ireland. The O'Malley lands were in the hands of some English lord. Bobby lived the wandering life of an outlaw. Where would she go?

She'd thought often of her family estates back in Killarney in the Valley of Mor. With her father dead, she should have been the rightful heir, but Lord Wolverton had explained that her estates had been forfeited and awarded to one of the English lords, who had fought for the queen in the recent conflict. Catriona had never asked to know the usurper's name. She doubted she could be civil to him if he ever showed up in court.

The truth was, she had no home—not in England or in Ireland.

"You might be a little more understanding of how it makes me feel," she snapped.

He sat up straight, surprised at her tone. "What's wrong, scamp?" he asked her.

She shook her head, not even sure herself what was wrong. For two weeks she'd been unable to get the picture of Niall Riordan's accusing eyes out of her head. She'd tried to banish all memory of those moments in the orangery when his kisses had sent wild rushes through her body, but she'd been unsuccessful. Somehow Bobby's glee at the success of their scheme made everything seem worse.

Nor had it helped that her guardian had been openly jubilant that the peace talks were at an end. Wolverton had refused to listen to any of her suggestions that the two Irishmen be sent back to Ireland without further punishment.

" 'Tis not a matter for you to concern yourself with, my dear," he'd told her with a pat on her head. "They'll hang, just as they deserve."

She leaned back against the wall and closed her eyes before answering Bobby. "Is it so difficult to understand that I don't want to be the cause of these men's deaths? They are not evil. They were merely working for a cause they believe in, just as we are."

Bobby knelt beside her and took her face in his hands. "Look at me, Cat," he said sternly. "Since the raid on the Valley of Mor, ye've led a sheltered life." As she began to protest, he continued, "I know it has not been an easy one, and ye've not been happy, but ye've not had to face death day in and day out as have I and the other rebels struggling for our land."

She pulled out of his grasp. "I've not pretended to endure what you have, Bobby, but—"

He shook his head and interrupted her again. " 'Tis no fault against ye. I'd not have had ye living in the wild and seeing what I've seen. But ye have to understand that great causes require great sacrifice. Black and Riordan mean nothing. If the queen decides to execute them, it's of no matter to us, just two fewer people we have to fight."

Catriona choked back the rising tears. " 'Twould be the same as if I had murdered them," she said.

Still on his knees in front of her, Bobby nodded grimly. "Aye. And it's no more than I would expect of a true patriot and the daughter of Lorcan O'Malley. Remember, ye're doing it to rid yer lands of the usurpers."

Catriona shook her head. "Nay, this has nothing to do with the O'Malley lands. I'm doing it for Ireland." Her voice had regained some of its strength.

"For Ireland, then," Bobby agreed. "That's me girl."

"I hope it will be over soon," she said. "There was talk at court today of a trial. It seems someone has come from Ireland and hired an important lawyer to defend them."

Bobby rocked back to sit on his heels, a frown on his

face. "Someone else from Ireland? I thought it would be weeks or months before they would send someone. Is this newcomer going to continue the peace talks?"

"I heard nothing of peace talks. They are only saying that they are going to help the two accused in the theft of the Wolverton emerald."

He was silent for a long moment, lost in thought. "Maybe I'd best not leave for Ireland just yet. If this man has come to resume the talks, we may have to find another way to thwart the proceedings."

Catriona groaned. She couldn't imagine going through this all again. At least this time, she'd take care not to let her heart get entangled with this new Irish arrival. Even as the thought came to her, she realized that it was the first time she was admitting to herself that she had become more interested in Niall Riordan than she had ever thought possible.

" 'Tis glad I am that ye're staying, Bobby," she said softly, lapsing into the old brogue.

He jumped to his feet and reached for her hand. "Aye, ye're right, Cat. I should not leave ye to yer frettin' conscience. Until this matter is settled, I'll stay around, near enough to remind ye of why we're fightin'."

She took his offered hand and let him pull her to her feet. "Just be sure that you're careful, Bobby," she cautioned.

He grinned. "Ye may be the cat, but over these past few years, I've learned to become as sneaky and silent as a little mouse. I've been in and out of Whitehall dozens of times with Her Majesty's guards none the wiser. Don't worry about me." He dropped a kiss on her cheek, then winked, and before she could so much as blink, he'd disappeared through the crack in the wall, much like the darting mouse he claimed to be.

Truly Fitzpatrick was a man of style. Instead of the plainer tweeds and linens of his homeland, he'd assumed the fashion of his adopted city—silks and a high ruffed collar that would rival any dandy at court. Niall found it strange that although Truly was one of the shrewdest men he had ever met, the finery did not look the least out of place.

"I mislike everything about this case," Truly said as the four men met in Niall and John's Tower chambers. "They're painting you as nothing more than petty thieves who don't deserve the attention of the queen's ministers. Some are even saying that the incident proves that they were wrong to think that they could bargain with outlaws in the first place."

"And Wolverton is rabidly pressing the case," Eamon added.

Niall listened in silence. He was as concerned as any about the resolution of their dilemma, but every time Truly or his brother brought up something about court, he found himself waiting to hear *her* name. Finally he brought it up himself.

"What of Mistress Sherwood?" he asked. "Has she steadfastly continued with her story about seeing me leave her uncle's study?"

"Guardian, not uncle," Truly corrected. "She is no relation to Wolverton. But, aye, the girl says she saw you, and the jewel was found in your purse."

"So what do we do?" John asked.

Eamon smiled. "Truly, as usual, has a plan. 'Twill require some cooperation from you two."

John made a wave with his hand to indicate the small chambers. "Since I've already made the acquaintance of every spider and counted every brick in these handsome quarters, I find I'm at leisure for anything you have in mind."

Truly pushed back his bench and stood, rubbing a hand at the small of his back. " 'Tis damned uncomfortable, they are, if you don't mind the observation, gentlemen. The sooner we have you out of here, the better."

"I'll second that," John agreed fervently.

Truly walked across the room to look out the window. "What we're going to do," he said, turning around slowly to face Niall, "is catch your lovely Cat at her own game."

"What do you mean?" Niall asked warily. He'd spent much of the past two weeks considering ways he'd like to avenge himself on his beautiful betrayer, but hearing Truly refer to her so callously brought out an unexpected and unwanted surge of protectiveness.

"You are utterly sure that she's the one who planted the jewel on you. Am I correct?" Truly asked.

"Aye."

"Then this becomes a simple case of her word against yours. We need to prove that she's a liar."

"And that she's working for Wolverton," John added.

Truly shook his head. "We know that she planted the jewel. We don't know that she did it for Wolverton."

"Who else?" Niall asked. "You don't believe that this was a scheme of her own devising?" It was bad enough that he had been so taken in by a woman. It was intolerable to think that his betrayal had been Catriona's own idea.

"Our informants are not totally clear, but it's possible that Mistress Sherwood has been working for the Clearys."

"The rebels who broke with O'Neill?" John asked in surprise.

Truly nodded. "Aye. Parker Cleary and his followers say they'll fight to the death until every Englishman is out of Ireland. They refuse to consider any compromise."

Niall's mind felt foggy. Nothing was making sense to him. He'd give anything for a brisk ride in the countryside, racing his horse along an unknown path into the fresh spring air. John seemed as confused as he was.

"Why would a proper English lady have anything to do with the outlaw Cleary clan?" John asked.

Truly took a moment to adjust his new collar. Then he said carefully, "Because Catriona Sherwood is not a proper English lady. She's as Irish as we are. The O'Neill's agents have discovered that she's the daughter of the former lord of the Valley of Mor, Lorcan O'Malley."

Niall sat back in astonishment, but his reaction was nothing compared to John's. His friend leaped to his feet, shouting, " 'Tis not possible!"

The other three men in the room stared at him. John looked around at their faces, then appeared to regain some control. "She appears English in every way," he said more calmly.

"Aye," Truly agreed. "But she's not. The O'Neill's agents have discovered her true identity. So the question is, when she deceived you, was she following Wolverton's orders . . . or someone else's?"

"Or was she acting on her own?" Eamon added.

Niall looked at his brother. The Riordans were fierce in each other's defense. He was sure that if Eamon had a chance, he would do everything possible to see to the downfall of a woman who had put his brother in such a grave predicament.

John resumed his seat, but his face was still white. His reaction puzzled Niall. It was shocking to learn that Catriona was not what she seemed, but of the two of them, Niall himself should be the more outraged. After all, he was the one she had chosen to trick.

He leaned toward his friend. "Is everything all right, John?" he asked.

John shook his head and remained silent.

Truly Fitzpatrick, still standing, continued speaking. "If the girl is working with Cleary agents, Shane O'Neill would like to see them all uncovered so that he can continue the peace negotiations. Understandably, he feels it's bad enough dealing with the English without having his own people working against him."

"I can't believe that Catriona is part of a hotbed of agents," Niall insisted. "Why, she's one of Elizabeth's ladies-in-waiting. They're guarded day and night."

" 'Tis possible she's just a rogue agent, acting by herself," Truly acknowledged.

The idea seemed equally preposterous to Niall, but the events of the Wolverton ball made anything possible.

"Truly has a plan to expose her," Eamon said. "With luck, she'll soon be inhabiting these quarters herself, and you two will be on your way back home."

"If she is working for the Clearys and we expose her, she may be accused of treason," Niall said slowly.

"Undoubtedly," Truly agreed without emotion. " 'Twill serve the baggage right for tricking you, and it will be one fewer outlaw rebel you all will have to contend with."

"Aye," Eamon agreed.

"The queen does not take kindly to those who betray her. She could send Catriona to the block," Niall said. Catriona had tricked him. She'd pretended to care for him—had let him kiss and caress her—all in order to send him to prison and perhaps to the block himself. He should care nothing about what became of her. But somehow he found that he couldn't bear the thought of being the cause of her downfall. "There must be another way," he concluded.

Truly and Eamon looked at him as if he had lost his mind, but John nodded agreement. "We can't reveal her to the queen. It would be a death sentence."

Niall glanced at John, surprised to find him as an ally.

Truly's expression was implacable. " 'Tis not exactly the time to summon your chivalry, gentlemen. The girl hoodwinked you, and she must pay the price. If she doesn't end up at the executioner's block, you very well may stand there in her place."

For a long moment all four men remained silent. Finally Eamon said to his brother, "You've no choice, Niall."

Cursing himself for a damn fool, Niall stood to face the others. "Aye," he said, "I do. I want to take my chances convincing the queen of my innocence. I'll not have Catriona exposed."

"I'm with Niall," John said quickly. "We'll argue our case before the queen."

Eamon began a loud protest, but Truly held up a hand to stop him. "If that's the way you gentlemen feel . . ." He looked to each for confirmation.

Both John and Niall nodded.

All waited while Truly pulled a tiny snuffbox from his waistcoat, opened it, took a pinch, and sniffed. "Care for some, gentlemen?" he offered, holding the box out. " 'Tis the latest rage, don't you know?"

When he was finished, Truly turned to Eamon. "It appears our business here is concluded, Riordan. We'll take our leave."

Eamon looked at the lawyer in amazement. "This solves nothing, Truly. We can't listen to these two. I believe they've both lost their wits." He stood and went to stand beside his brother. "Don't be a bloody fool, Niall. We have no choice but to expose the girl. Would you rather have me returning to Riordan Hall with your dead body?" he asked.

"Are you coming, Riordan?" Truly asked, his tone even. "I've an appointment back at the palace within the hour."

Niall shook off his brother's hand and said, "Go on with him, Eamon. We've not lost this battle yet."

Truly pounded on the door to alert a guard that they were ready to leave. With a final bewildered glance at his brother, Eamon followed the lawyer out of the room.

When they'd left, Niall turned to John. "Eamon's probably right, you know. We're a couple of bloody fools."

John's smile was wan. He hadn't appeared his usual self since Truly had revealed Catriona's true heritage. " 'Twould not be the first time men made themselves into fools for a woman's sake."

"I warrant," Niall said glumly. Then he walked back to the table and reached for the bottle of wine his brother had brought them.

• • •

"I'll talk to Niall tomorrow," Eamon said as he and Truly mounted their horses for the return trip to Whitehall Palace. "I'd never have believed that Niall would be one to get so muddled over a girl. But I'm sure I can talk some sense into him."

"Perhaps you can, Eamon," Truly said, "but we don't have the luxury of waiting. At any moment the English prosecutors could decide to put your brother and Black on trial, and then it might be too late to do anything about it."

"We can't just give up," Eamon said angrily.

"I have no intention of giving up." Truly pulled a handkerchief out of his sleeve and leaned over to polish the silver amulets that surrounded the upper rim of his saddle.

Eamon frowned. "Then what are we going to do?"

When the silver was shining to his satisfaction, Truly stowed the cloth back inside his sleeve and took hold of the reins. Finally he answered, "The O'Malley girl must be exposed. If your brother is too much the cavalier to do the dirty work, then we'll just have to do it for him. I trust you do not share your brother's scruples about seeing that the little deceiver meets her deserved fate."

Eamon shook his head. "If 'twill save Niall, I'd see the witch hang."

Truly nodded approval, then signaled to his mount to move.

Six

"*Perhaps Truly was* offended," Niall said to John. "He came here to help us and we both were unwilling to listen to what he had to say." It had been two days since Eamon and Truly's visit, and they hadn't heard a word from either of them.

John was lying on his cot, staring at the rough beams of the ceiling. "Nay, Truly is not a man to take offense. They may be busy trying to arrange some kind of settlement."

Niall had spent much of the morning pacing back and forth across their Tower chamber. " 'Tis unlike Eamon not to let us know what's happening."

John sat up and swung his feet to the floor. "Why don't you summon a guard and have a chessboard brought in? I hate the bloody game, but anything 'twould be better than watching you wear the floorboards through."

Niall gave a weak grin. "My apologies. I'm finding it harder and harder to endure this place." He started toward the door to signal a guard, but as he approached, it swung open. In the doorway stood the last person on earth he expected to see. He stared at her in stunned silence.

John pulled himself to his feet, his gaze fixed on the visitor's face.

Catriona looked from one to the other. Then she turned back to the guard who had opened the door and said, "My pass says I'm to see the prisoners alone." He nodded and grasped the window bars to swing the door shut.

By the time she turned back to him, Niall had found his voice. "Why, how kind of you to pay us a visit, Mistress Sherwood," he said.

He was pleased to see that his tone was properly indifferent, since the rest of him was decidedly not. The sight of her had been as staggering as a blow.

She looked uncertain and there was puzzlement in her green eyes.

"What brings you here, child?" John asked.

Niall looked at his friend sharply. John's words held none of Niall's bitterness. His tone was gentle. What possessed him to treat her so charitably? Niall wondered. This woman had betrayed them both.

Catriona frowned. "I was waiting for you to tell *me*," she said.

"For us to tell you what?" Niall asked sharply. "To tell you what it feels like to be locked up in an English prison awaiting a call to the executioner's block?"

She took a step into the room. Niall couldn't take his gaze from her. She was dressed in a red velvet gown with a tightened bodice that pushed her breasts into tantalizing fullness. The color heightened the blush of her cheeks and the rusty highlights of her shining hair. She was as breathtaking as ever, and Niall realized with dismay that if she tried the same tricks of seduction on him she had used at Wolverton House, he would undoubtedly succumb, even now, even knowing her treachery.

Disgust at his own weakness made his voice harsh. "Do come in, mistress. I'm sorry we haven't a proper repast to offer you, but you might enjoy some of the special Tower ale, for which we've paid a king's ransom."

Catriona bit her lip. "I'm in no need of refreshment," she said. "I've come about the—" She glanced back at the little barred window in the door, but there was no one in sight. The guard had evidently left them to talk in private. "I'm here to discuss our plans."

Now Niall was the one frowning in confusion.

"What plans, mistress?" John asked, walking toward her.

Her wide eyes blinked. "The plans to destroy the peace negotiations." She reached into the side of her skirt and pulled out a folded paper.

Niall stepped closer, willing himself not to notice the sweet, lemony scent of her. "I believe you've already effectively accomplished that, my charming traitor," he told her. "Negotiations are difficult when the emissaries have been arrested as jewel thieves."

"I must ask your forgiveness for deceiving you," Catriona said. "We thought you had come to sell us out to the English."

"So you pretended that you had some affection for me, all the while you were actually trying to frame me for robbery." Niall was not paying much attention to the sense of her words. All the anger that he'd been building up since the night of the Wolverton ball was threatening to explode. If he'd been two steps closer to her, he'd be tempted to put his hands on her slender shoulders and shake her.

"I wanted to put a stop to the negotiations without violence," she said. "That's why I thought about my guardian's jewel."

"Without violence? Ah, then you consider hanging as a jewel thief to be a peaceful form of death?"

"I thought I could intervene with Her Majesty. I just wanted you sent back to Ireland."

"Because you're working for the Clearys," Niall spat.

Once again, she looked perplexed. "As are we all," she began slowly, but even as she said the words, her eyes widened with dawning comprehension. " 'Tis true, isn't it? You two are also working for the Clearys to delay the peace?"

John had been listening carefully to their exchange. Suddenly he moved toward Catriona and put his hand across her mouth. "Don't say another word, Catriona," he said in a low, urgent voice.

But his warning was too late. The door behind them swung open.

On the other side were Eamon, Truly Fitzpatrick, Alger Pimsley, and two other English officials Niall recognized from the negotiations. Behind them stood three of the queen's guards.

Truly said in clipped tones, "I trust you gentlemen have heard enough to make your case against Lady O'Malley."

Pimsley and the other two officials nodded. "I'll report directly to my lord Wolverton to see what's to be done with her," Pimsley said.

But the taller of the two officials shook his head. " 'Tis a matter for the queen's justice now." He turned around to the guards and told them, "Hold her here in the Tower until you receive further orders."

Catriona's face had gone pale. Though it was the men at the doorway discussing her fate, her gaze was on Niall. "I congratulate you, Master Riordan. You have managed to trick me at my own game."

"I had nothing to do with this," Niall protested.

But Catriona appeared oblivious to his words. "I only regret that I've spent the past two weeks worrying over your fate. I doubt you'll spend two minutes crying over mine."

Before Niall could say anything more, the three guards surrounded her and ushered her out of the room.

Truly watched them leave with a slight smile of satisfaction. "Nicely done, gentlemen," he said to Niall and John. "It could not have gone better if we had coached you."

Eamon looked at his brother with a shrug of apology. " 'Twas the only way, Niall. I wasn't about to see my little brother hanging from an English rope."

Niall was not totally sure what had just happened. He leaned over and picked up the paper that had fallen from Catriona's hand when the guards had taken her. Scanning it quickly, he could see that it was a note, signed by someone named Bobby. He read the words more carefully. This Bobby was telling her that the two prisoners were actually on their side, and that she should visit them in the Tower to plan the next move.

He looked up at Truly. "You devised this?" he asked.

Truly nodded. "With some help from my agents."

"Who's Bobby?" Niall asked.

"Her lover, I warrant. He's another of the Clearys's agents who's been meeting with your Mistress O'Malley regularly since she first moved into Whitehall Palace."

Her lover. Niall felt a tightening under his jaw as if he were about to be sick. No wonder she'd seemed so unpredictable. She'd been welcoming and pleasant to them when it served her purposes, but all the time she was meeting in secret with another man who was her true sweetheart. Of course, there was no longer any reason for him to care. Catriona Sherwood or O'Malley or whatever her name was would now receive the justice due to someone who had clearly committed treasonous acts. She was no longer his problem. Yet he could taste the bitter bile in his mouth.

Eamon seemed to sense his brother's distress. "Forget about her, Niall. The girl's a liar and a renegade, and evidently a trollop as well. Who knows how many men she's enticed before you, all the while sleeping with her rebel lover?"

Truly had been conferring with the three Englishmen. Now he turned to Niall and John and said, "You're free to return to your quarters at the palace. I suggest we arrange for you two to give your testimony on this matter to the prosecutors and then you can leave immediately to return to Ireland. It would be best if we wait until this matter is settled before we try to open negotiations again."

Eamon nodded agreement. "The sooner we're out of this country the better, I say."

John was looking out the door as if trying to see what had become of Catriona. "What will happen to her?" he asked.

Truly pulled a handkerchief from his sleeve and dabbed at his brow. "Jesu, Black, what is that to us now? We've got the truth out. I warrant that if her erstwhile guardian Wolverton doesn't throttle the wench himself, the queen will have it done officially."

"I'd like to meet with her," John said.

Truly shook his head in exasperation and said to Eamon, "Would you get these two dimwits out of here before I have an entirely new case to untangle?"

Eamon nodded and went to take John and Niall by the arm, none too gently. "Come on. You both need to get out into the open air," he told them. "The confinement has addled your brains."

Without further discussion, the two men let themselves be led out of their prison quarters and down the stairway to freedom.

"It's the perfect solution, Pimsley." Lord Wolverton's tone was uncharacteristically gleeful. "My poor little ward will be hanged as a traitor, leaving the O'Malley estates without any heir to ever question how they came to be in my hands."

His aide nodded agreeably, unsurprised by his master's easy acceptance of a gruesome fate for the young woman he'd had in his care. "I never could understand why you didn't dispatch the chit right there in the Valley of Mor, Your Lordship."

As usual, when any of his actions was called into question, Wolverton frowned. "She was a child, Pimsley. Do you think me a monster?"

Pimsley knew better than to try to answer that question. Wolverton leaned back on the cushions of the oversized couch in his sitting room. "Then, too," he began, his smile returning, "she was such a pretty little thing. I couldn't resist. She does brighten up the place, after all, like one of my prize flowers."

Pimsley shifted from one foot to another. He was rarely invited to sit in Lord Wolverton's presence. "All the same, 'twas a danger taking her into your very household when you knew the raid on her father's estates was illegal." As Wolverton's face darkened once again, he hastened to add, "I just mean—'twas a *bold* move, Your Lordship. Bold. Worthy of your genius."

Wolverton nodded. "Aye. Pity. There was a certain satisfaction in receiving her gratitude for the things I did for her, when all along I was receiving twenty times that amount in rents from her estates."

"Yet no one knows they belong to you."

"Someday they will. Killarney is the most beautiful part of Ireland, Pimsley. I fancy spending some time there when I get old."

After a moment in which his master seemed to have lost himself in contemplation of his far-off Eden, Pimsley cleared his throat. "Will that be all, Your Lordship?"

Wolverton looked up in surprise. "Aye, just see to it. Make sure they convict her."

Pimsley stretched his neck in an attempt to keep his new ruffled collar from chafing. "Er . . . What if the queen should decide not to . . . er . . . hang her?"

Wolverton sat up straight. "The little wretch deceived me, Pimsley. What's more, if she's still in touch with people in Ireland, she's dangerous. One way or another, she must be eliminated. If the queen's too squeamish to do it, we'll find another way."

He lay back on the pillows and closed his eyes. Pimsley waited several more minutes, but when Wolverton's breathing became even, he turned and crept out of the room.

•   •   •

The fresh air had not helped rid Niall of the haunting visions of Catriona. Asleep or awake, he could see her green eyes as they had looked when he had been holding her that night in the orangery. He could swear that her response to his kisses had not been *all* pretense. Yet she had tricked him, had been content to see him arrested, even hanged. And now Truly said that she had a lover, an Irishman she'd been meeting for at least two years. The thought was surprisingly disturbing.

He sat up on his cot and looked around the palace chamber he and John were sharing with Eamon. Their room was smaller than their prison quarters at the Tower, but here, at least, no guards stood outside their door. John was still sleeping, but Eamon's cot was empty.

He rubbed his fists into his eyes to try to rid them of their unwanted visions. Eamon wanted to leave immediately for home, and every shred of reasoning within Niall was telling him that his brother was right. It was the only course that made sense. He would return to Riordan Hall and the hills of Tara, to his horses and the village maids who were generous with their kisses and easy with their demands. Simple maids who neither schemed nor lied.

The door opened and Eamon looked in. " 'Tis past time you slugabeds woke up," he said cheerily. "I've made arrangements for us to leave today. Truly says he can handle any final questions on the case. So up with you! I'm ready to get out of this city." He screwed his face into a grimace of distaste.

John opened one eye. "Is it still night?" he asked, his voice thick with sleep.

Eamon strode across the room and threw an apple at each of the two men lying in bed. Niall caught his, but John's rolled to the floor. "Nay, old man. 'Tis nearly time for dinner. You two have gotten lazy with the soft life they've been giving you. 'Tis past time you got back to home and some real work."

His brother's high spirits didn't help Niall's humor.

Every time he thought about riding away from London and leaving Catriona to face possible execution as a traitor, he felt a wave of nausea.

"Don't the prosecutors need us here?" he asked. "They've scarcely spoken to us."

Eamon picked up the apple from beside John's bed and took a bite. Between chews he explained, "I reckon they're mostly taking Truly's version of the events. 'Tis not a difficult case to prove, since the girl refuses to defend herself." He looked over at John, who still hadn't moved, and took another bite of the apple. "I'll be eating your breakfast, Doctor, if you don't get yourself up."

John was looking at Niall. "We're not in such a hurry that we can't stay to see the outcome of all this, Eamon," he said. "After all, these events may affect the continuation of the peace negotiations. The O'Neill will want a complete report."

Once again, Niall wondered about John's interest in the case and Catriona, but he merely said, "Aye. I'm not comfortable leaving until we've had some resolution."

Eamon frowned. "You mean until you find out what's to become of your Mistress O'Malley." He spat an apple seed on the floor, shaking his head. "I can't fathom it. The traitorous wench has bewitched you both."

The door behind him opened and Truly entered, carrying a sheaf of papers. "It appears she's bewitched more than a few people at court," he said.

He was dressed impeccably in royal blue linen trousers and a silver studded jerkin.

Eamon turned around. "Now what news?" he asked.

Truly smiled. "Her erstwhile guardian, Wolverton, is being curiously quiet about the case. But Lady O'Malley's friend, Arabella Houghton, is leading a campaign for clemency. And it appears that the queen is more than a little inclined to grant it. Turns out she's rather fond of the girl and is experiencing some reluctance at the thought of chopping off her rebel head."

Niall felt a wave of relief. "You mean they'll let her go free?"

Truly waved with the batch of papers. "She's a professed rebel trying to interfere with the queen's business. I don't see how they can set her free. In truth, the queen's own prosecutors are in a bit of an upheaval about this case."

Eamon dropped down on the bed beside his brother. " 'Tis beyond belief. I'd always heard that London was a miracle of modern efficiency. Turns out people know less about what's going on here than almost anywhere I've been."

"What do you think is going to happen?" Niall asked the lawyer.

Truly gave one of his eloquent shrugs. "We may find out shortly," he said. "I've come to fetch you all to an audience with the queen."

Her Tower room had had no windows, and Catriona had wondered if she was ever going to see the sky again. Finding herself back at Whitehall was a welcome surprise, even if she still had no clue about her ultimate fate.

She'd spent the five days since her arrest going over memories of her childhood—of Bobby, her father, and all the others she had loved in the Valley of Mor. If she closed her eyes and ignored the musty odor and the cold coming off the walls of her cell, she could picture herself back at the O'Malley estate sitting on her father's lap while he told her stories about her mother.

Rhea Kelly had been the daughter of a simple farmer, the most beautiful woman in County Kerry, when Lord O'Malley had fallen in love with her and taken her to his big manor to be his bride. Their love had been as intense as it was short. Rhea had died a year after their marriage, giving birth to Catriona. Lord O'Malley had never married again, and Catriona's one consolation following the horrible fire that had taken his life was that her parents were now together again.

Perhaps she would be joining them soon, she thought as she waited in an antechamber outside the queen's throne room. She had been brought to Whitehall that morning, and she could only assume that it was to hear the queen's pronouncement on her fate.

While in prison, she'd been visited by a procession of officials and prosecutors, but she'd refused to talk with any of them, not wanting to implicate herself and especially not wanting to tell them anything about Bobby. The trap that had caught her had been baited with a note using Bobby's name, which meant that the English knew about him. No doubt they knew about his activities for the Irish rebels, as well. She could only hope that he'd been able to get away from London before they could catch him.

On the third day she'd had an unexpected caller—her guardian, Lord Wolverton. She'd expected that he, of all people, would be furious with her. After all, she'd repaid all his kindness to her with treachery. But he'd merely asked about her welfare and promised her that he would speak to the queen on her behalf.

Perhaps he had done so, and that was why she had been brought to the palace, she thought with a moment of hope. But the hope was fleeting. If Elizabeth wanted to put her to death, no amount of arguing by her guardian would dissuade her.

She looked around the small chamber where they had left her to wait. The two guards who had brought her from the Tower had disappeared, apparently unconcerned about the possibility of her escaping. She considered the idea. If she could get out of the palace without being caught, she knew she would be able to make her way to the coast. She fingered the small garnet necklace that had been Lord Wolverton's gift on her last birthday. Surely it could be sold for enough money to buy passage back to Ireland. Once back in her homeland, she'd seek out Bobby and the other outlaw rebels.

She stood up. It was a risky plan, but better than stay-

ing here to wait for Elizabeth to condemn her to death.
Crossing to the door, she opened it and looked cautiously
outside. Not a guard in sight. She took a deep breath and
darted out into the empty hall.

Elizabeth received the Irishmen in her formal throne
room. Niall looked around the gilded chamber, but almost
immediately his gaze was brought back to the woman sitting on the elaborately carved chair at the head of the
room. Once again he was reminded of the curious power
of her presence. Even her posture was regal—back straight
and head high. Her aura of authority seemed to steal the air
from the rest of the room. Niall took a deep breath.

Beside him, Eamon had an uncharacteristic expression
of awe as he looked up at the famous monarch. "God's
teeth, she's beautiful," he said in an undertone.

Niall answered in equally hushed tones. "Nay, 'tis not
beauty exactly. But she takes your breath away, all the
same."

Truly, walking in front of them, turned around and motioned them to silence.

The crowd around them was also quiet as the four men
made their way up to stand in front of the throne. When
they were a few yards from the queen, Truly stopped and
gave a low bow. John, Niall, and Eamon followed his
example.

Niall would normally have smiled to see his brother's
awkwardness at the unaccustomed gesture, but the occasion was simply too serious for humor. Bows completed,
they stood facing the queen, waiting for her to speak.

She took her time examining each of the four men from
head to toe. Finally she gave a half smile and said, "If all
my Irish subjects are as bonny as you gentlemen, mayhap
I should fire my ministers and pay a visit myself."

Truly acknowledged her words with a gallant nod.
"Your Majesty, my fellow Irishmen would be honored. It

will only take completion of the peace negotiations to make such a visit safe for you."

She did not appear pleased with his answer. "Aye, peace, peace! I hear much talk but see no results. And still my soldiers are set upon by brigands every time they venture out to enforce my authority."

Truly's calm expression did not waver. "As we have discussed with your ministers, Your Majesty, there are elements that are still not under the O'Neill's control. But as soon as his representatives sign a firm peace that grants pardons to his men, the remaining holdout rebels will have no support at all among the people."

Niall shifted from one foot to the other as the exchange continued. He'd thought the audience would be concerning Catriona's case, but neither Truly nor the queen seemed in a hurry to address the issue.

Suddenly his head jerked up as he heard her name.

"So the deceitful Mistress Cat is one of these so-called holdout rebels?" Elizabeth was asking.

"Aye, Your Majesty," Truly confirmed.

Elizabeth looked thoughtful, and for some reason, her gaze settled on Niall. Finally she turned to one of the guards who had been standing alongside her chair and said, "Bring her."

The guard bowed, then backed away and disappeared out a small door directly behind the throne. The buzz of conversation from the crowd gradually died as they waited.

Niall judged that it was at least five minutes before the small door opened again. The guard who had left had been joined by two others, and all three held a squirming Catriona, her feet barely touching the ground. One of the men held her around the waist, and the other two each held an arm.

The queen turned around, her lifted eyebrows registering surprise and some displeasure. "I meant for you to escort her, Master Sergeant, not drag her."

The man's face flushed bright as his tunic. "Beggin' yer pardon, Mum, but we did catch the little hellion runnin' away."

Catriona stopped struggling, and her captor set her on the ground.

Elizabeth's expression was hard to read, but Niall thought he saw a glimmer of admiration for Catriona's spirit. "Come before us, Mistress Sherwood," she said, holding out her hand so that Catriona could kneel and kiss her ring.

Catriona did so, then stood facing the queen, her bearing proud. There was no hint of apology in her face. Niall thought that she couldn't have missed noticing him standing with his brother behind Truly Fitzpatrick, but she hadn't so much as glanced his way.

"So, Catriona, they tell me that though you have promised to serve us, you have instead betrayed us," the queen said, her voice frosty.

Catriona's chin lifted as she said, "I have been honored to serve your person, Your Majesty, yet I must serve my country first."

Elizabeth sighed. "You've been one of my favorites, Cat. You have a mind far sharper and a perception far deeper than most of the silly ninnies who serve me. I shall miss you."

Niall felt a chill running up his back. Was the queen about to pronounce her death sentence? Catriona appeared to have the same premonition. She stood stiffly, though her expression was impassive.

"But if we're ever to have peace in that troublesome part of my realm," the queen continued, "we can't have all manner of rebels running around trying to defeat each other, as well as us." The queen looked down at Truly. "Master Fitzpatrick," she said. "You claim that the Irish leader Shane O'Neill wants peace."

"Aye, Your Majesty," Truly replied.

"Yet he cannot seem to find a consensus among his own people."

"Most Irish are behind him in this, Your Majesty. 'Tis only a few rabble elements that have yet to be controlled."

"Indeed." The queen appeared to be lost in thought. Niall's eyes were on Catriona, who stood waiting without a sign of fear.

"It would appear to us, Master Fitzpatrick, that these 'rabble elements' should be Shane O'Neill's problem, not mine. Therefore, I'm giving him this one." She waved a hand toward Catriona.

Truly looked confused. "I beg your pardon, Your Majesty?"

The queen looked past him to Niall. "You—Master Riordan," she said sharply. "Step up here."

Niall, equally confused, climbed the step to stand on the platform where Catriona stood in front of the queen.

"Your Mistress Sherwood is young, and, what's more, she's given me no little amusement in her time here. I've had no better chess partner among all my learned ministers. I'm ill-inclined to chop her head off," she said briskly. "Therefore, it is our decision to send the chit back to Ireland, where she'll become your problem."

Niall could feel the relief flooding his body, but the queen's next words made him straighten up in shock.

"You may extend your gratitude, Master Riordan," Elizabeth said, the words rich with irony. "I'm about to give you a beautiful young wife."

Seven

There was a moment of silence as the queen's words registered with her audience. Then Catriona was the one who spoke. "You may execute me, Your Majesty, but I'll be wife to no man."

The retort brought a full-fledged smile to the queen's face. "Death over slavery, eh, Cat? I have some sympathy for your sentiments, yet regretfully, I must insist."

Catriona looked around as if seeking an avenue to escape. Niall felt an unexpected pang of protectiveness, but his mind was still reeling at the implication of the queen's declaration. Breaching etiquette once again, he spoke. "We could take Mistress O'Malley to Ireland and ensure that she would no longer cause problems for Your Majesty. I don't believe there's any need to, er—" He broke off and looked at Catriona, then back at the queen.

" 'Tis our safety policy, Master Riordan," Elizabeth said briskly. "We have no intention of letting her go back to her fellow rebels to begin plotting again. The Riordans are a powerful family. As your wife, we would expect that she would be closely watched. We would ask for your word on this. 'Tis matrimony or the ax. This is our final decision."

Niall swallowed. His wife? In spite of the fact that Catriona had tricked him, he had not wanted to see her executed. But he'd never imagined that he would be the only means she had of escaping that fate. He'd never even wanted a wife, much less one who was currently regarding him as if he were a slimy toad who had climbed up her silk dress.

"I'll take the ax," Catriona said firmly.

Niall shook his head. She was not only a traitor, she preferred death to the thought of marrying him. Surely even Elizabeth could see that the situation was impossible.

"Aye, we've thought you may," the queen said. "But 'tis not only your head at risk, my dear." She nodded to the guard who once again disappeared through the little rear door.

In a moment he was back with another guard. Between them they held a second prisoner, this time a man. For the first time Catriona's eyes showed fear as she put a hand to her throat and whispered, "Bobby!"

The man was shorter but every bit as robust as Niall. He had a shock of reddish hair that looked matted and dirty. His left cheek was bruised as if from a recent blow. "Don't fash yerself, Cat," the man said to Catriona with a faint smile.

"Are you hurt?" she asked, her voice shaky.

He shook his head. "Nay. As ye do know, my hide's tough. Don't ye let them—"

He broke off as the two guards, at a nod from the queen, pulled him backward out through the door. Elizabeth watched them go, then turned to Catriona. "He's comfortable enough for the moment in the Tower, this lover of yours, but I can as easily send him to Tower Hill to die. It's up to you, my dear."

Niall kept his gaze on Catriona. He had seen just such an expression in the eyes of a hunted doe. Once again, he felt a pang of unwanted sympathy.

Truly Fitzpatrick had been silent through the exchange,

but now he took a step forward. "Your Majesty, I would ask that we make an attempt to find a more reasonable solution. As you say, the Riordans are a powerful family. Cormac Riordan will not be pleased to see his youngest brother forced into marriage with a . . . a—"

The queen ignored him and addressed the two Riordans. "We remember your brother well, gentlemen. He strikes us as a man who would know his duty to his country and to his queen. Give him our regards."

Eamon spoke for the first time. "The Riordan family has always been ready to do their duty, Your Majesty. 'Tis just that marriage is a serious matter. My brother is still young."

The queen gave a sly glance at Niall, then answered Eamon. "Ah, then mayhap you should be the one to marry our Mistress Catriona. It matters not which of you does it, as long as the chit is out of our hair."

Eamon appeared to be considering the queen's words, and Niall felt a sudden rush behind his ears at the thought of Catriona marrying his brother. "Nay," he said loudly, "I'll marry her."

Eamon and Catriona herself turned to look at him in surprise. He continued in a more normal tone. "If 'tis to be, then I should be the one. For the sake of duty," he added.

Elizabeth gave a nod of satisfaction. "Then 'tis settled. The ceremony will be performed on the morrow by our own chaplain. Then you may all be on your way home and we'll be washing our hands of the lot of you. Catriona," she ended, her voice sharp, "do we have your agreement?"

Catriona hesitated a long moment, then said simply, "Aye." The look of fear was gone from her eyes. It had been replaced with a hard glint that, Niall thought ruefully, did not bode well for an auspicious beginning to their union.

"Bella, dear, I'm ever so glad to see you, but if you don't stop crying, I'm going to send you away." Catriona had been pleased and surprised to see her friend when a guard had admitted her to the small bedchamber where Catriona had spent the night after the disastrous audience with the queen. But she'd awakened with an intense throb in her right temple, and her friend's hiccuppy sniffles were not helping the ache.

"I can't help it, Cat. I've been beside myself this past fortnight thinking about you in that horrible place."

Catriona shrugged. "'Twasn't so horrible. The Tower rooms are comfortable enough."

"But there are murderers there and all manner of horrible miscreants."

"I warrant there are, but I wasn't forced to take tea with them."

Bella leaned over to embrace her. "In any event, I'm so relieved that you're out of there. And now you're to be a bride, Cat. I can't believe you're not in a fever of delight."

They sat side by side on the little cot where Catriona had spent a decidedly restless night. *Fever* might accurately describe the state of her head, but *delighted* was the last way she would describe her present humor.

"Don't be a ninny, Bella. I'm being forced into matrimony. 'Tis one of the worst things that can happen to a maid."

Bella stopped crying long enough to look surprised. " 'Tis not as if he's old or a monster, Cat. Niall Riordan is as bonny as they come. And 'tis said that his family has wealth and power back in Ireland. I should think you'd be happy to make such a match, especially considering—" She stopped and frowned. "'Twas ill done of you not to confide in me, you know. I would have kept your secret. Lordy, an Irish lady—who would have thought? Of course, I'm devastated at the thought of you leaving. Mayhap when you get back to Ireland, you'll find a gent as handsome as your Niall and send him down to me."

Catriona listened to Bella's prattling with half an ear. She'd lain awake much of the night trying to find a solution for her predicament. She'd even checked several times to see if they'd left her without a guard again, but every time she'd opened the door a crack, one of the queen's soldiers had been waiting outside.

She could simply refuse to say the words, but the queen had as good as promised that her refusal would mean Bobby's death. Shortly before dawn she'd finally decided that her best course of action would be to go along with the sham marriage. When she was safely back in Ireland, she'd make contact with some of Bobby's compatriots and see what could be done to free him.

"Cat Sherwood, you're not listening to a word I'm saying. Oh, 'tis not Sherwood anymore, is it?" Arabella concluded with a giggle.

Catriona smiled. Bella's giggles were easier to endure than the tears. "Aye, Bella, I'm listening, but 'tis as you say. It's my wedding day. I warrant I have a right to be a little muddled."

"Then you *are* excited!" Arabella exclaimed. "Of course you are! But, Cat, what will you wear? And will there be a betrothal ceremony before the wedding? 'Tis all highly irregular, you know."

"Aye," Catriona agreed. Irregular and not real, she told herself. She would say the words, but they would mean nothing. Still, in a sense this was to be her wedding day, and she couldn't help a little sense of anticipation. "No one will care what I'm wearing, Bella."

"Your groom will care."

"Niall Riordan no more wants to wed with me than I with him. He and his brother simply want to be done with the problem and on their way back home."

Arabella cocked her head as she looked at the plain brown dress her friend was wearing. "You're wrong. I've seen him look at you, Cat. And that was before he knew you were to be his bride."

"Aye, and before I betrayed him and nearly sent him to the gallows."

Arabella waved her hand dismissively. "He'll forget about that. And he'll be interested in how you look, I promise you. Men can't help themselves. They are helpless when confronted with a beautiful female. Their own anatomy betrays them."

Catriona gave another smile at her friend's earthy wisdom but felt a slight shifting in her stomach at the reminder that she would be dealing not only with an unwanted husband but with his "anatomy" as well.

"Be that as it may," she said, "I have no intention of primping for a wedding that I'm being forced into under threat of death."

Arabella jumped up from the bed and shook her head. "You ever were the stubborn one, Cat, but this time I'm going to insist. You're about to be a bride, and I'm determined that you will look like one. Come and let me dress you befitting the occasion."

She held out her hands to pull Catriona up from the bed. Catriona looked up at her friend's eager face and gave a small sigh. "Very well, Bella. First you must promise to get me a powder for my headache. Then you may do with me as you will."

Arabella's efforts had not been in vain. After two weeks in a dank room at the Tower, Catriona felt clean and fresh again, and even she had to acknowledge that her friend had worked miracles in a short time to come up with a wedding outfit that Elizabeth herself may have envied.

The gown was a pearl-colored satin worn over voluminous petticoats. It had a square bodice trimmed with rows of pearls on strips of silver tissue. The open overgown was black velvet, fitted to the waist, and trimmed with white fur.

All four Irishmen—the two Riordan brothers, their fastidious-looking lawyer, and John Black—were already waiting in the chapel when she arrived, escorted by Arabella and two of Elizabeth's guards. Niall watched her with a strange light in his eyes as she made her way down the church aisle. Catriona felt the pounding begin again at the side of her head.

She recognized the minister who stood in front of the ornate silver altar. Elizabeth had kept her promise and sent her own chaplain, Father Humberto, a former Roman priest who had been unable to go back to Rome after supporting Elizabeth's father in his rebellion against church authority.

The Riordans were undoubtedly still Catholic, Catriona realized suddenly. Secretly, she had always considered herself one, too, though she had allowed her guardian to think that he had converted her to the English church. She supposed if she had to endure wedding rites in that church, it was fitting that they be performed by a man who had once served the Holy Father in Rome.

She gave herself a little shake. It was almost as if she were considering this proceeding to be more than the mockery it actually was. She shouldn't care if the marriage were to be performed by the queen's gardener.

"Everyone's waiting, Cat," Arabella whispered from just behind her, and Catriona realized that she had stopped halfway down the aisle.

She drew in a long breath and continued walking. None of it mattered, she told herself again. She was about to be married, but it was nothing but words. To be a true marriage, it had to be of the heart, not a decree from a powerful queen to a condemned prisoner.

Niall knew that he was staring, and that his brother, standing at his side, was watching him in some confusion, but he couldn't take his gaze from her. This was the proud beauty who had tormented his sleep when he had first arrived at court, who had melted into his arms that night at Wolverton House, and who had then tricked him and betrayed him. Within the hour she would be his wife.

"She's a beauty, God's truth," Eamon said in an undertone. "But if you take her to your bed, I'd keep my dagger at the ready under the pillow. If she could stab you with those green eyes, I'd be planning your funeral."

Niall made no reply as his bride approached, followed by her friend Arabella. Though Catriona had betrayed him once, he had no fear about his safety in her company. However, he had no intention of taking her to his bed. She was obviously unwilling. Didn't she already have a lover among her fellow rebels? He'd never had to force a woman in his life, and he didn't intend to start with his own wife.

The chaplain took a tentative step forward and stumbled. John Black reached out to steady the frail old man. For a moment Niall wondered if the priest was capable of lasting out the ceremony.

"You and your bride may approach the altar," the chaplain told Niall, his voice as quavery as his posture.

Niall looked at Catriona, who had stopped some distance from him. She stood stiffly and looked as if she were holding her breath. He stepped forward and held out his arm. After a moment's hesitation, she laid her hand on it so lightly that he could scarcely feel her touch.

"Will there be no one to give the bride to the groom?" the chaplain said, squinting his eyes to look into the gloom of the shadowed chapel.

"Nay," Catriona said firmly.

"I shall do so," boomed a voice from the back of the church.

Catriona took her hand from Niall's arm as all the parties turned around. Lord Wolverton, resplendent in a cloth of gold tunic, strode toward them, filling the narrow church aisle with his imposing form.

"Uncle!" Catriona exclaimed.

"I'd not let you be married without me, Catriona," he said to her. Shouldering Niall aside, he stepped next to her and seized her hand. "I've indicated my displeasure over this match to Her Majesty, but if it is to be, then it will be with my blessing."

Catriona looked puzzled. "Why . . ." she stammered.

" 'Tis kind of you, Uncle, under the circumstances," she ended finally.

"I've tried to fill in as a father to you, child, so 'tis only fitting that I stand beside you as you take a husband." He shot a contemptuous glance at Niall. "Regardless of who that husband should be."

Niall could feel his brother bristling at his side, but he put a cautionary arm across his chest and said, "Leave it be. I'd have this over and done with."

Catriona looked at him. "Aye," she said. "Let's get on with it."

"Please proceed, Father," Lord Wolverton said to the chaplain.

The old man looked around uncertainly at the circle of unhappy faces surrounding him, then cleared his throat and said, "Very well. 'Tis Her Majesty's will, after all." Then he lifted his missal and began to read.

As the English troops had dragged Catriona away from the Valley of Mor, she had sworn on her father's still flaming tomb that she would never rest until Ireland was free of English rule. She tried to keep that oath in her mind, as well as the image of Bobby struggling in the arms of English guards, as she spoke the words that would bind her to a man who was working to destroy everything she and her old childhood friend believed in.

Her groom looked as pained as she by the proceedings. Perhaps once they were safely away from London, he'd be willing to simply let her go about her way. They could forget about this sham ceremony, forget about that night in the orangery, forget that they had ever met.

"This I promise in the name of the Father, the Son, and the Holy Spirit," Niall finished.

It was done. In the eyes of the English church, at least, they were man and wife.

Niall took her hand as they turned to walk along the aisle and out of the chapel. Arabella sat in the front pew of the chapel, crying. Catriona managed a brief smile for her friend.

Her guardian walked just behind them. His appearance had been just one more bizarre thing about this event. She'd never considered her guardian to be a particularly forgiving man. He acted as if the revelation that she had been working against him had never happened. He'd not reproved her for lying to him about the jewel theft.

She turned back to look at him. He was watching the bridal couple with a broad, bland smile.

She gave her head a shake. At least the piercing pain in her temple was easing. "Are we now free to leave?" she asked, turning to Niall.

Her bridegroom shrugged. "I am as much a puppet in this play as you, milady. 'Tis the queen who rules here. But my understanding is that after the ceremony, we were to leave directly for home."

The words sent an unexpected thrill through Catriona. *Home* meant Ireland. How she had longed for the sight of it these past seven years. The idea of once again setting foot on her green homeland filled her with a bittersweet excitement. She'd be returning to her country, but not to her father, not to the Valley of Mor, not even to Bobby, who would be languishing in an English prison until she could find a way to help him.

The final thought strengthened her resolve. She would have to take things one step at a time. The first was to get home; then she would find the Clearys and let them know about Bobby's predicament.

"Home," she repeated. "It has a good sound."

Niall looked down at her, some of the harshness gone from his expression. "You must have missed it these long years as you passed as an English lady."

She nodded. "'Twas not a masquerade of my own choosing. Fate put me on that course. Fate and the English soldiers. Since that time, I've always felt myself alone."

She thought she could detect a glimmer of sympathy in

his eyes as he said, "You'll find Riordan Hall to be a welcoming place. My brother's wife, Claire, will be pleased to have another female in the household."

If she could work out another way to find the Clearys, she might not stay with Niall as far as Riordan Hall, but her curiosity was piqued. "Then 'tis true about the Riordan clan? The household has been mostly male?"

A brief shadow crossed his face. "Aye. Some say 'tis an ancient curse that kills Riordan brides. My brother was one who believed it until Claire gave him a healthy son and seemed none the worse for the process."

They went out the door of the chapel and stopped, uncertain where to proceed. Truly Fitzpatrick came up behind them. "You are free to take your bride and go, Master Riordan," he said. "I'd advise you to leave immediately, since the queen's whims are often short-lived."

Eamon and John joined them, nodding agreement. "If we hurry, we can be well up the Old North Road by sunset," John added.

Arabella darted through the line of broad-shouldered Irishmen and came to throw her arms around Catriona. "I can't bear to have you go, Cat," she said with a sob. "When shall I see you again?"

Standing to one side, Lord Wolverton cleared his throat. "I, too, am grieved to see you leave, my dear," he said to Catriona, "though I understand the necessity for speed. However, 'tis your wedding night. I'd see you spend it in some style."

Once again, Catriona was surprised by her guardian's unexpected generosity. After extricating herself from Arabella's tearful embrace, she said to him, "'Tis kind of you, Uncle, but I hardly think—"

He interrupted her. "No, don't thank me. 'Tis little enough I can do. I've arranged for your party to stay at the Hart's Horn Inn, just north of London. You and your new husband will have quarters to yourself to begin your marriage with some degree of dignity and privacy."

Her husband? Catriona felt her face grow hot. Her thoughts had been on getting through the ceremony, getting free, returning to Ireland, Bobby. Everything but the fact that she would now have a husband with the right to expect everything that that state implied.

Arabella giggled. "Oh, Cat," she said. " 'Twill be your wedding night. Can you believe it?"

Without thinking, Catriona looked over at Niall. The expression in his eyes had shifted from sympathy to something more primal. Her insides began to dance.

In a half-daze she waited while Niall and his brother thanked her guardian for his offer and made their farewells. She endured another of Arabella's embraces and felt her friend's wet cheek pressed against hers. Then her new *husband* took her arm and began to lead her away.

He bent to ask her in a low voice, "Are you ready for the journey, milady?"

She nodded. The pounding in her head intensified. She was ready for the journey, aye. But the wedding night?

Eight

The owner of the Hart's Horn Inn had evidently been informed to expect guests of some importance. The stocky little man greeted them with so many bobs of his bald head that he began to look like a bouncing bandy ball.

His blue eyes twinkled in his ruddy face as he led Niall and Catriona to the room he called his "wedding suite." Truly Fitzpatrick had said his farewells back in London, and John and Eamon had been given their own room in another part of the inn, so Niall and Catriona were alone with the proprietor.

"Nothing's too good fer a foine lady like yerself, mum, and yer foine gent," he told them, "especially on a night like this 'un," he added with a wink.

He stood for a long moment, beaming at the bridal couple, until Niall gave him a coin and ushered him out of the room. "I believe he would have liked to stay," he told Catriona with a brief smile, trying to overcome the awkward feeling of the moment.

Niall would have preferred that he and Catriona had two separate rooms. Everyone knew that the marriage had been forced. It shouldn't be expected that they would have a normal wedding night with everything that event im-

plied. Yet just the thought of what that implied had kept
him edgy all day long. Being alone with Catriona couldn't
help but bring back memories of the last time they had
been alone—in the orangery of Wolverton House.

"I didn't ask if you were hungry," he told her. "Should
I call the man back and ask for a supper to be sent to us?"

She shook her head. "I've no appetite," she said, sitting
on a long bench that stood against the wall opposite the
bed. She put a hand to her temple and rubbed.

Niall frowned. "Does your head ache?" he asked.

"Aye," she admitted. " 'Tis an annoying malady that
comes at times."

He walked over to her. "Wouldn't it be better if you ate
something after all?"

She closed her eyes and continued rubbing. "Nay, I'll
be fine by tomorrow."

Niall looked down at her, frustration mounting. He'd
heard of these kinds of women's ailments, but since there
had been no women in his household, he'd never had to
deal with them. In his experience, pain was something that
came from cuts and bruises after a day of brawling.

"Should I—" He looked around the room helplessly.
"Would some ale help?"

She opened her eyes and smiled. "Perhaps."

With a sigh of relief he filled a mug from a pitcher on
the room's small table and brought it to her. She took a sip
and offered him a smile of thanks.

The brief gesture was enough to send a ripple of unwanted lust to his loins. With some disgust, he returned to
the table, poured a mug of the ale for himself, and drained
half of it in one gulp.

This could be a long night, he considered, glancing involuntarily at the bed. In spite of the fact that she had
tricked him and that she was an unwilling bride, it would
not be easy to lie next to her hour after hour, breathing in
the lemony scent of her, without being disturbed by the re-
actions of his unruly body.

He turned back to her. "Perhaps you should try to sleep," he said, his voice gruff. At the long sweep of her lashes, he added, "Have no fear, milady. I'll not bother you. I'll just bed down yonder on the hearth." Since it was summer, no fire was burning.

She stood to face him. "You have my gratitude, sir. I warrant you have little enough cause to treat me with kindness."

"Aye. Your trickery could have cost me my head. John's, too. But the disaster was averted, and I reckon that I'm glad your head is still attached as well." He gave a weak grin. "Now I'd ask that you call me by my Christian name, since we're legally wed."

She replied with another smile, which did nothing to cool his senses.

She went to the bed and pulled off the puffy coverlet. "Take this, then," she said, walking to hand it to him. " 'Twill soften the stone. Niall," she added.

He took the linen from her arms, his fingers brushing hers, which were icy cold. "You're chilled. I'd best leave this with you after all," he said, handing the quilt to her.

She shook her head and pushed it back at him, then both burst into laughter as they realized the ridiculous nature of their tug-of-war.

"You have it," she said firmly. "I have a wool nightdress that will keep me plenty warm."

He gave up the battle, took the coverlet from her arms, and threw it on the cold flagstone hearth.

She regarded him for a minute more, then walked slowly back to the bed, where the innkeeper had put her satchel. She seemed to be hesitating.

"Did you need something, milady?" Niall asked.

When she turned around, the flush he had seen before had once again crept halfway up her cheeks. "Could I ask you to—er—turn around?" she said.

He nodded and did as she had requested, facing the fireplace. He had only the rustle of silks and the sudden intensity of the lemon scent to tell him that Catriona was undressing. It was a sight he would have enjoyed watching if they had been husband and wife in a true sense. As things were, he would, of course, be enough of a gentleman to let her disrobe in private.

She was taking longer than he expected. The delay gave him time to remember that, as innocent as she seemed, Catriona already had a lover who had doubtlessly enjoyed the sight of her naked body countless times. The thought brought a wave of irritation, but he continued looking only at the dark, cold fireplace.

Finally she said in a small voice, "I'm ready now."

For a brief moment, he thought the words might be some kind of invitation, but he soon realized that she had only meant that she was dressed and ready for sleep. She was already in the bed, a sheet pulled up all the way to her neck.

"Shall I put out the lamp?" he asked.

She nodded. With her slender form sunk into the featherbed mattress and her long hair loose around her face, she looked small and young. Her eyes were impossibly large.

Niall set his jaw and walked over to the table to douse the oil lantern, then made his way in the dark back to the hearth and his coverlet.

"Sleep well, milady," he said.

She didn't answer for a long moment, then finally she said, "I reckon you need to call me by my Christian name, as well. After all, I do owe you a debt, Niall Riordan."

He gave a kind of grunt of acquiescence, then settled down on the hearth to try to sleep.

In his restless sleep, Niall imagined that he was with the rebels again, bedding down in brief snatches in the woods, alert to any possible movement of the English troops that surrounded them. It took several moments for him to realize that the sound he was hearing was not the wind in the trees but soft moans coming from the bed.

He rose quietly and crossed the room. A shaft of moonlight from the nearby window illuminated the bed and its occupant. Catriona was still asleep, but she thrashed about, twisting the sheet around her, as if in some kind of tormented dream. Gently he placed a hand on her shoulder, trying to calm without awakening. But her eyes opened, and she stared up at him without apparent recognition.

"He'll die in there! We must go in for him, Bobby!" she cried.

Niall recognized the name of the man they had said to be her rebel lover.

"You're dreaming, Catriona," he said softly.

She continued looking at him as sense and recognition gradually returned. A tear slid out of the corner of one eye. "My apologies," she whispered.

He shook his head. "No need. I came over because you seemed in some distress."

She nodded and struggled to unwrap herself from the tangled sheet. After a moment's hesitation, he reached to help her. Together they managed to remove the twisted linen, and she sat up, shaking out her disheveled hair.

" 'Tis something that comes over me at times," she said, "though not as often these days."

"You were calling for your—er—friend."

"Aye, he was with me that day." Her eyes glittered in the odd light of the moon. "The day they burned my father alive."

Niall shuddered. "The English?"

She nodded. "I watched my home burn before my eyes with my father still inside. Then they dragged me away before I could even bury his charred body."

"Was it Wolverton?"

"Oh, no. 'Twas the queen's troops. Wolverton agreed to become my guardian once I was back in London. He was my savior, in a way. I warrant he took pity on me."

From what Niall had seen of Lord Wolverton, pity was not an attribute he would ascribe to the man, but he remained silent. He had wanted to know Catriona's story, and she finally seemed inclined to talk about it.

"I've tried to banish my memories of that dreadful day," she continued. "But they come unbidden, usually when I'm asleep."

Her voice was controlled. There were no sobs or shaking of her shoulders, yet tears now flowed silently, making her cheeks glisten in the moonlight. Niall felt an uncharacteristic stab. He sat on the bed next to her and put an arm around her shoulders.

"I, too, saw my father die, but 'twas in his own bed after a tragic fight. I can't imagine the horror you must have felt. And you still little more than a child," he added.

"My childhood ended that day," she said. "Bobby's as well."

Once again, the name of her lover. Niall tried to tell himself that the surge of fury he felt when he heard her say it had something to do with the man being a rebel who was fighting against him. But somehow he knew that it sprang from a deeper, more primitive emotion. The rage he felt had nothing to do with politics. It was sheer jealousy.

She looked smaller and more helpless than she had that night in the orangery. Through the thin wool of her nightdress, he could feel the slender bones of her shoulder, the soft curve of her arm, and the edge of the rounder swell that led to her breast. His breathing quickened.

"'Twas in truth a horror," he said, trying to keep his mind on her story and not her body, nestled tight against him without resistance. "No wonder you hate the English."

"I've tried not to hate," she told him. "But I've sworn to see our country free of them."

He'd had this argument many times with his family and his fellow rebels. He could tell her many things about the toll it had taken on their country to try to end this conflict. He could repeat some of John Black's discourses on the virtue of compromise. He could spend the rest of the night discussing politics. But as she spoke and turned slightly toward him, her unbound breast pressed into his side. The tears had stopped falling, but her eyes were still moist and her lips swollen. Without conscious thought, he bent and kissed her.

After an initial start of surprise, she offered no resistance. Her mouth was soft and pliant under his, and the small moan at the back of her throat was no longer one of anguish.

His left hand went to her breast and simply rested there as he let her nipple grow hard in his palm. Her head fell back against his arm. He stopped kissing her long enough to admire the long stretch of her white neck in the moonlight. Then he moved his kisses there, in the delicate place just under her jaw. Her skin was soft as velvet.

He'd lain down to sleep fully dressed except for his boots, and the heavy clothes prevented him from the closeness he sought, but he didn't want to let her go long enough to disrobe. It might break the sudden, unexpected moonlight spell.

A simple cord was knotted at the neck of her robe. With deft fingers, he untied it to loosen the gown just enough to reveal her breasts. He kissed his way down the slope of her chest and along one full globe until he reached the center nub, which he swirled with his tongue.

She gave a small gasp but didn't move. His own body now throbbing, he put his mouth around her nipple and sucked it in small rhythmic tugs.

After a moment he straightened up to gather her again in his arms. She was sleepy and pliant and willing. And vulnerable, he added to himself. Only minutes before she'd been deep in the memories of unimaginable horror.

Some vestige of conscience forced him to ask hoarsely, "Shall this be a wedding night after all, my beautiful Cat?"

She pulled back a little, looking surprised at the question. Niall's racing body was cursing him for a fool at causing the interruption, but still he paused, waiting for her to give agreement to what it appeared they both wanted. Though it seemed the answer was taking an eternity.

Suddenly, from across the room, there was a creak of the door. Catriona had heard it, too. She stiffened in his arms and pulled her nightdress back up around her neck. In the dim light Niall could see the door slowly begin to swing open. A wave of cold doused all traces of desire. His dagger was across the room next to where he had been sleeping. He pushed Catriona to the back of the bed and whispered, "Lie still."

Crouching low and moving noiselessly, he crept over to the hearth and felt along the stone until his hand touched the cold steel of his knife. The door was halfway open, and he could see shadowy figures on the other side. There were at least two of them.

A quick glance at the bed told him that Catriona was following his orders. She appeared to be sleeping. He looked around. The moonlight through the window lit that side of the room, but the part of the room where he knelt by the fire was in darkness. He considered shouting to try to arouse his brother and John, but he knew that they had been taken to another part of the inn and would probably not hear his calls in time to be of any help.

Fear closed his throat for a brief moment, but he swallowed it down and forced himself to focus. The intruders were now entering the room. He let out a relieved breath when he saw there were only two of them. Two he could handle. He'd had a lot of practice over the years fighting both Cormac and Eamon at once when they'd decided it was time to go after their baby brother.

They were creeping closer to the bed. Each appeared to have an upraised dagger. Wisely, Catriona continued to feign sleep. As soon as both were turned with their backs to him, Niall sprang into action. He jumped at the one nearest to him, hitting him at the back of the waist with both feet. Though he still had no boots, the blow was strong enough to knock the man down. Then he turned his attention to the other, who had now turned toward him, knife raised.

Niall thrust upward with his dagger, hoping to hit the man in the chest, but the intruder ducked to one side and the blade struck his arm instead. By now the man he had knocked to the floor had recovered and was dragging at him from behind. Niall kicked at him with one leg while parrying the blows of his companion.

He thought he could feel his foot smash against the fallen man's throat, and a terrible rasping cough told him that he'd done damage. But the assailant in front of him with the knife was a formidable opponent. Every time Niall attempted a strike, he was able to dodge. Niall hadn't been able to wound him since the first cut on the arm.

He glanced behind him to see that the man on the floor was still disabled, and the brief distraction was enough for his attacker to get a hold on his right arm and slash the knife across his left. Niall could feel the sting, and the warmth of gushing blood, but he ignored both and kept his mind on the fight.

Behind the intruder, Catriona stood up on the bed and picked up a pillow. Just as Niall's attacker was closing in for another strike, she brought the pillow crashing down on his head. The blow did not stagger the man, but it surprised him enough to make him lose his hold on Niall's arm. Niall seized the opportunity to come up from below with a swift thrust that hit the man just under the breastbone. For a moment, all action seemed to freeze as the attacker stiffened and Niall held the knife steady within his attacker's midsection, fighting the swift nausea that had always overcome him in battle when hand-to-hand combat turned lethal.

Behind him, the other assailant jumped to his feet, still breathing in terrible wheezes, and ran from the room.

"He's getting away!" Catriona exclaimed, jumping from the bed as if she were about to take off after the intruder.

Niall pulled his knife out of his victim and let the man slide to the floor, then caught her around the waist before she could run. "Let him go," he told her. "He still has his weapon. We'll be sure this one's done for, then I'll get Eamon and John to help me search for him."

Catriona stopped and looked down. The man who had attacked them lay lifeless at Niall's feet, a dark circle of red slowly seeping from his middle. The back of her throat filled with bile. All at once she realized that her nightdress was also soaked with blood where Niall's arm had seized her.

"You're hurt, too!" she cried.

Niall swayed but stayed on his feet. "Aye," he agreed. "I warrant I need to stop this bleeding before I faint on you."

Catriona's voice became calmer. She put an arm around him and eased him to the bed. "Is this man dead?" she asked, looking down at the attacker without flinching.

"Aye."

"Then you sit right here. I'm going to fetch your brother and Dr. Black."

Eamon and John had shown no mercy in their interrogation of the innkeeper at the Hart's Horn, but after an hour with the man, they concluded that he was telling the truth when he said that he had no knowledge of the attack on his important guests. He was sure that Lord Wolverton, who had made the arrangements, would be equally distraught to see that his plans for a proper wedding night for his ward had gone awry.

"Could Wolverton himself have been behind it?" Eamon asked as the three men and Catriona sat in the room John and Eamon had shared at the inn. Niall and Catriona had abandoned their quarters while the apologetic innkeeper dealt with the cleanup.

Catriona looked distressed. "Lord Wolverton would have no cause to do such a thing. And it makes no sense.

Why, he came to the wedding to give me away and give us his blessing."

It was midmorning, but they had decided that they would delay resuming their journey until Niall had regained his strength and they had found some answers about their midnight intruders.

"None of the queen's ministers were very friendly to us or our cause," Niall said. "Any of them could have sent the attackers."

John stood and walked over to where Niall was resting on the bed. "I'll change your bandages again, lad," he said.

Niall waved him away. "I'm fine. 'Twas no more than a scratch."

"Scratches kill if the poisons set in, Niall. Sit up and show me your arm. Doctor's orders."

Reluctantly Niall let John tend to him while they continued to discuss possible motives for the midnight attack. No one could seem to come up with a solution. The peace negotiations were already on hold, and if someone wanted a further delay, it would have made more sense to wait and attack the new emissaries that would be sent once Niall and John reported back to the O'Neill.

Niall winced as John tightened the bandages around him again. He knew that he was lucky to have John's medical skills available, but he didn't like being fussed over like a babe with a nursemaid.

"Did you send to the palace for Truly?" he asked Eamon. His brother nodded.

As if his words had conjured him, the door opened and their lawyer strolled into the room. "And now what have you boys gotten yourselves into?" he drawled. He was dressed in yellow silk from head to toe.

Eamon's eyes widened as he took in the man's attire, but he answered with a rueful smile. "It seems that Niall's idea of a wedding night was almost as bad as Cormac's."

By now everyone in the Midlands knew the tale of Cormac abandoning his bride on her wedding night and the disastrous chain of events that set in motion.

"'Twas no idea of mine," Niall said firmly. "But I'd give a small fortune to learn exactly whose idea it was."

"Why don't you ask your bride to answer that question?" Truly said.

Every man in the room turned his gaze to Catriona, who merely looked puzzled at the lawyer's remark.

Truly waited until the pause had grown dramatic, then he said to Niall, "I warrant the brigands were here to kill you and rescue your bride."

"That's nonsense!" Catriona cried, indignant.

Niall nodded agreement. "I think 'tis a bit farfetched, Truly."

Truly looked around the room with another dramatic pause. "Not farfetched at all, my boy. Her lover escaped from the Tower yesterday. I warrant the attacker you sent running was none other than Bobby Brosnihan himself."

Nine

Alger Pimsley's knobby knees, encased in violet silk hose, shook violently. He'd been listening to Lord Wolverton's ranting for more than an hour and the powerful nobleman's fury showed no signs of abating.

"How many men were sent to do the job?" Wolverton roared. "Not enough, obviously. Do I not have legions at my disposal?"

Pimsley shifted his aching feet and answered meekly, "If you recall, sir, you had said it was important that none of the men could be connected with your household, and that—"

"Then you should have raided the stews of the waterfront for an army of brigands. All I wanted was the matter over and done with—my lovely ward and her new husband dead and buried. Was that so much to ask?"

"My lord, I've already disciplined the captain who was in charge of the raid. The chap who ran away has been sent off to sea, and, of course, the other is dead."

Wolverton rose from behind his big oak desk and walked round it to tower over his lackey. His tone had changed from bellowing to silky. "Does any of that help me get rid of the problem, Pimsley?"

"No, milord."

"And how long after my ward reaches Ireland do you think our secrets will stay buried?"

"I don't know, milord." Pimsley's voice had become a squeak.

"Then we'd best ensure that she's taken care of, hadn't we, Pimsley?" Spittle from Wolverton's mouth splattered against Pimsley's face as he said the name.

"Aye."

"Quickly."

"Aye, milord."

Wolverton gave a growl of disgust, then walked past his aide and out of the room.

Catriona knew with utter certainty that the man who had fled in the darkness had not been Bobby. If it had been, she would have sensed it somehow. She would have felt his presence. And, in any event, a sneak attack in the dark would never be Bobby's way. Of course, if the men had come to rescue her, that was a different story. Bobby might have sanctioned such a plan.

She didn't know these men he had joined up with—the Clearys. They might be ruthless enough to come in the dead of night with knives drawn. She simply couldn't know.

The attack had come just at the moment that she was about to surrender herself to the passion that seemed to spring unbidden every time Niall touched her. She couldn't decide if the interruption was a good or a bad thing, but she supposed for her peace of mind, it was just as well.

She didn't want to respond to her new husband's caresses. As Bobby had told her, if Niall was on the side of peace, he was her enemy, as surely as were the English. She needed to keep her mind on her duties and forget about how it had felt to feel his hands on her, to watch in the moonlight as his mouth tugged at her bare breast. The sensations had been beyond belief. But they were not for her.

The men had left her alone. There had been an awkward

silence after the lawyer's revelation about Bobby's escape. Then both Eamon and John had suggested that she be moved to another room while they discussed their plans.

Niall had not said a word. He'd simply watched her, his dark eyes angry and hurt. She'd wanted to defend herself, but with doubt in her own mind about the involvement of Bobby and the Clearys, she didn't know what to say.

It had to be well into afternoon, but still no one came, even to offer her food, though there was a pitcher of ale on the nightstand by the bed. They had locked her in. She'd established that shortly after she'd been left there. And the room had no windows that could provide a possible escape route.

If Bobby had engineered last night's attack to rescue her, he would try again. If he did, she hoped that this time it would be without violence. Niall might be her enemy, but the thought of seeing him hurt made her throat burn.

Dispirited, she flopped back on the bed. Perhaps they had already ridden away and left her here, she thought. After last night the Riordans might have decided to wash their hands of her. Perhaps English troops were on the way to take her back to the Tower.

She gave herself a little shake. Speculation would serve no purpose. Niall might be angry with her, but somehow she didn't believe that he would abandon her to the mercy of the English. Not after what had almost begun between them last night.

"Swounds, Riordan, she's your wife. I warrant you're the one to say what will become of her." Truly Fitzpatrick's usually unflappable demeanor was suffering from the early-morning summons.

"'Twas Elizabeth who made this devil's bargain," Eamon answered for Niall. "What will she have to say for the arrangement now that my brother is fighting off assassins?"

Truly shook his head. "Elizabeth wants to be rid of the

problem. She has more pressing matters of state at the moment. The Spaniards are threatening again, and the Dutch are raiding the ports in the north. The 'Irish Problem,' as she calls it, has been shoved aside. She'll not thank us for bringing it back into the forefront."

"So we just ignore what's happened?" Eamon asked.

Truly looked at Niall. "Are you afeared to continue on with the girl, Riordan?"

"Nay," Niall answered quickly. He was certain of that much, at least. It would take more than a knife scratch on the arm to frighten a Riordan. He was less sure of the rest of it. If the intruders had, in fact, come to rescue Catriona, did he want to hold her against her will? Elizabeth had essentially paroled her to the Riordans, making them responsible for her behavior. But if the man who fled had been her lover, did he want to keep her from going to him?

"We should send her straight back to Elizabeth," Eamon said.

John frowned but said nothing.

Niall hesitated a moment, then said, "We'll continue the journey. Royal blackmail or no, she's my wife. I'll not send her back."

Eamon shook his head, but Niall noted that John appeared to be relieved. Niall had decided that the older man held some kind of special fondness for Catriona, though, strangely, this hadn't engendered the same kind of jealousy as the thought of Catriona's rebel lover.

Truly clapped his hands. " 'Tis settled, then. You gentlemen can be on your way as soon as Niall feels well enough. I'll have the authorities continue to investigate last night's attack, and if they learn anything, I'll send word, though I'm not counting on it. Attempted theft in an out-of-the-way inn is hardly likely to inspire much attention."

"Could it have been simply a case of robbery by common thieves?" Niall asked, holding a glimmer of hope. The three looked at him without speaking. After a moment he grinned weakly and said, "Aye, I know. 'Tis not likely."

Truly turned to John to give him some last instructions, and Eamon walked over to Niall. "You'll not let this girl muddle your thinking, will you, brother?"

Niall gave a rueful shake of his head. "You may be the older and wiser one, Eamon, but someday I'll see how clear your thinking stays when they toss you into bed next to a wife the likes of Catriona."

Eamon smiled. "Never fear. I intend to leave the wiving to you and Cormac."

Niall slid aside the bolt and opened the door. Catriona appeared to be in the midst of a peaceful sleep. He took a deep breath. Apparently the day had not proved as trying for her as it had been for the rest of them.

He walked across the room, not bothering to soften the sound of his boots against the wood floor, but she didn't awaken. When he reached the side of the bed, he looked down at her and his irritation softened. She looked pale and her eyes were hollowed with dark circles. None of this could have been easy for her. She'd been imprisoned for more than a fortnight, forced to marry against her will, taken away from her home by near strangers, and then the attack.

Even if one of the intruders had been her lover, Niall was almost sure that she hadn't been aware that he was coming. After all, she had helped him by bashing the man he was fighting with her pillow.

Niall was exhausted, too. He was tempted to lie down beside her on the soft bed and sleep for a week. But he'd agreed with his brother and John that it would not be wise to stay in the inn another night. Eamon had already left. He was to travel quickly home to take news of all the events to Riordan Hall. John, Niall, and Catriona would follow at a more leisurely pace, giving Niall time to properly tend to his wound. But they wanted to be well away from London and further trouble before they stopped to rest.

He'd have to wake her. He leaned over and shook her

shoulder lightly. She stirred, but didn't open her eyes. It took a second little shake before her eyes opened. She gave a sleepy smile that died immediately as she remembered where she was and under what circumstances.

"My apologies, milady, but we must leave," he said.

She sat up, her expression sober.

When she didn't speak, he said, "If you'd care to freshen up, I'll return in ten minutes."

She nodded.

He turned and started toward the door but stopped as she said, "'Twas not Bobby."

Slowly he turned back to her and waited.

"That man last night who ran—'twas not my friend, Bobby," she repeated.

Even the name grated. "How do you know? We were in the dark."

"I—I just know. If it had been Bobby, I would have known."

Of course, she would have known the man who was her lover.

When he continued watching her without comment, she added, "I can't tell you if the men involved were Bobby's friends. Perhaps 'tis true that they were coming for me. But I swear I had no knowledge of it. Nor would I have sanctioned such an attack had I known."

Niall's arm throbbed, he was bone weary, and instead of going to bed, he had to set out on the road so that he would not risk murder in the night by unknown assailants. All of which served to make his answer more harsh than he had intended. "I reckon I'd be the last person you'd tell if you had known about it."

She looked indignant. "I swore to you—the word of an O'Malley. I can give you no better bond."

He gave a grudging nod. The truth was, he did believe her, but he couldn't tell if his judgment on the issue was entirely keen. It was difficult to think clearly when that faint lemony scent kept wafting toward him, reminding him of all the sensations he had felt the previous evening before they had been interrupted.

"Will you be wanting the ten minutes or do you come with me now?" he asked.

"Do you believe me?"

"It matters little what I believe, milady. We are tied together by royal decree and politics. Such things as trust and sentiment must give way to duty."

"Then you intend to continue this charade of a marriage, even though you think I may have tried to have you killed last night?"

The weakness was returning. He'd been on his feet too long. If they could get started, at least he'd be able to sit on his horse. "I don't believe that you tried to have me killed. Let that be an end of it. I'll return for you in ten minutes, and we leave immediately."

"For Ireland?" she asked.

"Aye, for home."

Then he spun around on a wobbly leg and left the room.

Catriona had little memory of the short crossing that had taken her away from her homeland after the death of her father, but she vowed she would remember every moment of the voyage back. She'd stood on the rail of the ship and watched the horizon without moving until the first sight of the gentle rolling green told her that she was about to set foot on the land she had dreamed of for so many long years.

She'd talked little with her companions. Niall's arm had turned feverish and John had been tending him regularly. She had the feeling that neither one was sure that she hadn't had a part in the attack back at the Hart's Horn. But none of it seemed to matter. The important thing was that she was going home.

They'd landed in Dublin at midday, but John had insisted that they take lodging at an inn rather than continuing the journey. Niall was looking sick, his skin sallow and moist. Catriona had readily agreed. She was in no hurry to arrive at Riordan Hall. She expected a cold welcome from a household of people who no doubt all suspected her of trying to kill their kinsman.

"My apologies, milady," John had told her as they'd walked the short distance from the wharf to a small dockside inn. "We'll have to lodge all three in the same room. I need to be near in case Niall takes a turn for the worse, and I can't take responsibility for leaving you by yourself."

She'd nodded a vague agreement, looking around eagerly at the bustling Dublin waterfront. The fishermen who dragged their boats up the sand called to one another in a familiar, lilting burr. The young lads who scrambled about the end of the pier picking up the mussels brought in by the high tide had the ruddy cheeks and the bright eyes of the lads she had grown up with. She took in a deep breath of salty air. She was home.

"Are you listening, lass?" John asked. "We'll stay here only as long as Niall needs to recoup himself. A day or two at the most."

She looked over at the older man with a smile. He'd been particularly kind to her the entire journey, and she was grateful. He had little enough reason to befriend her. Her actions at Wolverton House had put him in prison as well as Niall.

"I appreciate your concern, Dr. Black," she said. "I'm content to wait here as long as necessary for Niall to regain his strength."

The doctor nodded and pushed ahead of her to where two boys from the dock were carrying their things. Two more had already led their horses from the ship to the stable just up the block. Niall had wanted to go with them to be sure that his big bay mount, Cinnabar, was properly cared for, but after a brief attempt to climb the steep cobblestoned street, he allowed Catriona and John to persuade him that the horses would be fine.

Catriona walked alongside him to the inn. He appeared to be making an effort to concentrate on every step.

"Will you be all right?" she asked. "Shall I fetch someone to help us?"

He shook his head curtly. "John's right. I need a night's rest. Then I'll be fine."

Though he had professed to believe her denial of any knowledge of the attack at the Hart's Horn, he had scarcely spoken to her during the journey. There had been no resumption of the lovemaking that had begun that night. For one thing, they'd not been alone together. John had been with them constantly, insisting on regular stops to bathe Niall's wound and change the bandages.

" 'Tis the only way to ward off the poisons," he'd said. "I've seen it in battle. When the wounds are kept clean, they heal rather than fester."

Niall seemed to find the delays bothersome, but he didn't argue with the older man. She was aware that both men were edgy, on the alert for trouble. Niall had taken a pistol from his travel bags and had it primed and ready.

At times Catriona wondered what she would do if Bobby suddenly appeared and did, indeed, attack them. Somehow she just couldn't picture it. If Bobby found them, she was sure that she could talk both men out of any violent action. Still, Niall's pistol made her jumpy.

"Does your arm ache?" she asked him. The look of tired indifference on his face made her feel cold. She shivered as a breeze blew up from the water behind them.

He shrugged. "It nags. Like a broken tooth before it's pulled."

"John says it should heal cleanly if you take care of it."

"Aye, I'm lucky to have his care, though he nags, too." She was pleased to see one of his crooked smiles, even briefly.

"It will be good to rest."

"Aye," he agreed. Then he lapsed into silence.

They reached the inn, and she waited while John made

arrangements for lodging for the three of them. The only room available had one bed, and she knew that though Niall was now swaying with fatigue, he was too much a gentleman not to give it to her.

As she mounted the narrow stairs to the second floor behind John, she said to him in a low voice, "Doctor, you must make Niall take the bed. He's weak and needs a good rest. I'll do very well on the floor."

John turned around and smiled. " 'Tis a brave lass you are, Cat O'Malley. I'll try to convince him, but the Riordans are a stubborn lot."

As it turned out, by the time Niall had climbed the second flight of steep stairs, he was in no condition to argue. He stumbled as they entered the room, and John, without asking, simply led him to the bed and eased him down on it.

Niall closed his eyes and appeared to lose consciousness.

"Has he fainted?" Catriona asked.

John put a hand on Niall's forehead to test the temperature of his skin. "I believe he's simply fallen asleep. He's still weak from the blood loss."

Catriona watched for a minute. Niall's chest seemed to rise and fall in peaceful slumber. "Well, then, we'll let him rest." She pulled off her cap and gloves and deposited them on the room's small table, then sat next to it on a stool.

John looked from her to Niall, hesitating. Finally he asked, "Would you be all right here alone with him? I've an errand to run. You'd have to promise me not to try to leave while I'm gone."

Catriona was surprised but touched by the older man's trust. She was exhausted from the journey as well, and the idea of attempting an escape now was not in the least appealing.

"Aye, I'll stay with him," she said. "I'll be here when you return."

"Word of an O'Malley?" he asked with a grin.

She smiled back at him. "Aye."

"I hope 'twill not be too tedious. If Niall awakens, be sure he has something to drink."

"Don't worry, Doctor. I'll be a good nurse. In the meantime, I'll—" She looked around the bare room with a slight frown. "Would that I had one of the books from Whitehall. 'Twas the best part of living at the palace."

John appeared to consider for a moment, then he walked over to the little stand where the boy from the dock had put his bag. He reached into it and pulled out a small leather volume.

"You may read this if you like while I'm gone," he said, handing it to her.

"You travel carrying a book?"

" 'Tis"—he paused, searching for the words—" 'tis something of a lucky talisman. I keep it with me always."

"I shall take good care of it, then."

He nodded, then turned to leave. "I should return before supper, but if you need anything, call the innkeeper. The door will be open," he added with some emphasis.

She answered him with a smile, then he turned to leave.

For a moment, opening his eyes to look up at a rough-beamed ceiling, Niall had no idea where he was. He was on a bed, but he couldn't remember arriving there. Then he turned his head and saw Catriona perched on a stool next to the bed. She was engrossed in a tiny leather volume that Niall recognized as the book John sometimes studied and guarded as jealously as a mother with old-maid daughters. He'd asked his friend about it, but John had never offered to show it to him. How did Catriona get it?

With sudden panic, he looked around the room. John was nowhere to be seen. "Where's John?" he asked loudly.

Catriona jumped a little at the sound of his voice. "Oh, I didn't see that you had awakened," she said, closing the book.

"Where did you get that?" he asked suspiciously.

Catriona looked annoyed. "I didn't steal it, if that's what you're implying. John went to do some errands, and he gave me this to read while I waited for you to wake up, though if I'd known you were going to be so grumpy, I might not have agreed to the plan."

"He never gives that book to anyone," Niall said, sounding every bit as grumpy as she had accused him of being.

"Well, he gave it to me."

She was glaring at him, and he gave a reluctant laugh. "Perhaps he considers you a mite prettier than he does me," he conceded.

Her expression softened. " 'Tis poetry," she told him. "Mostly love poems."

"I'll be damned."

"Perhaps I shouldn't have told you."

"Nay, 'tis just—John has never seemed one for romance. He likes ladies, well enough, but just for—" He stopped and flushed. After two years at court Catriona had little trouble imagining what he had been about to say.

"On the contrary," she argued. "Dr. Black seems to me like the most romantic of gentlemen."

Niall looked amused. " 'Tis what he wants the ladies to think. But he gives his heart to none of them."

"He must have given his heart to someone," Catriona protested.

"What do you mean?"

She held up the book. " 'Tis written here at the beginning: 'To my own true love—Forever, John.' "

Niall looked puzzled. "I know that he has never had a wife."

"Maybe he had a sweetheart who died. That would explain why he has the book and not she."

"Let me see," Niall said. He sat up in bed and swung his feet to the floor, wincing as his hand pressed into the mattress.

"Is your arm bothering you?" she asked.

"I reckon 'twill be awhile before I'll be able to take Eamon and Cormac two falls out of three."

Catriona frowned. The doctor had said he'd be back by supper, but since Niall had fallen directly to sleep, his bandages hadn't been changed since they'd gotten off the ship. "Perhaps I should look at it," she suggested.

Niall looked doubtful. "When did John say he would be back?"

"It could be a couple more hours." With sudden decision she got up and went over to the bed. "Come on," she said. "Let me help you off with your tunic and we'll have a look. I can at least change the linen."

Niall was reluctant, but she brushed aside his objections and proceeded to help him out of his shirt and unwrap the bandages with what she fancied was all the efficiency of a professional healer. After his initial hesitation, Niall cooperated with her administrations, and even seemed to be grateful.

They were still involved in the process when the door opened and John Black came in. He looked surprised to see Catriona fussing about a half-naked Niall, the two apparently engaged in friendly conversation.

"I see you two have made good use of my absence," he said. There was a little twinkle in his gray eyes.

Catriona flushed and backed away from the bed. "Niall's arm is aching, but I see no redness. Now that you're back, I'll let you finish the bandaging."

John walked over to Niall and took a look. "It appears that you were doing just fine without me," he said. His expression turned thoughtful as he looked from Catriona to Niall and back to her again. "In fact," he said slowly. "I was about to impose on you even further and ask if you would be willing to continue tending my friend tonight."

"All night?" Catriona asked.

"Aye, I—" John paused. "I've not yet concluded my business, and it might take me until the morrow."

Catriona looked over at the bed. If John was gone all night, it would leave her alone with Niall in these small quarters.

"Can it not wait until after we reach home, John?" Niall asked.

Once again Catriona could swear she could see a glint in the older man's eyes. "As I said, 'tis pressing, Niall. What about it, lass, are you willing to help me by continuing as nurse for a bit longer?"

John had been kind to her, and if he was asking as a favor, she had little choice but to agree.

"Aye," she said. "I'll take care of him."

Niall frowned. "What is this all-fired important business of yours, John?"

" 'Tis a private matter, Niall. One you may learn of someday but not now. Surely 'tis no hardship, lad? All you have to do is lie in your bed and mend. And I've provided you with the prettiest nurse in all Ireland to tend you."

Niall and Catriona exchanged glances, both helpless to argue against the older man.

"So be it, then," Niall said finally. "But don't tarry."

John looked from one young, frowning face to the other and gave a benevolent smile. "I'll be back before you have time to miss me."

Ten

No hardship, John had said. Yet Niall felt he'd done few things more difficult in his life than lie without response as Catriona tended him, her cool hands smoothing back the hair that had fallen over his forehead, her fingers gently pressing against the upper part of his arm, brushing against the side of his bare chest to check for fever.

She nodded with satisfaction. "I feel no sign of fever in your skin," she said.

"Nay, 'tis not the skin that's fevered," he answered with a rueful grin.

She pulled her hand away, flushing. She was sitting next to him on the bed, her leg touching his hip. She moved to slide away from him. "Do you need the bandage changed?"

The blush and the tightness of her voice gave her away. She was feeling their nearness as surely as he was. Yet since John had left, she'd only spoken to him regarding his care, and then she'd kept the conversation brisk and impersonal.

He reached for her hand. "My bandage is fine. My arm is fine. I need no water, or towels or food or sleep. I need no nurse, nor yet a mother."

Her flush deepened, but she did not try to pull her hand out of his.

"So let us just talk, milady wife. Tell me how it feels to be back in your country after so long away."

He congratulated himself for having chosen just the right question. Her face softened and a light shone in her eyes. She let her hand rest in his as she answered, "I knew I'd come back someday. In London Lord Wolverton kept telling me how lucky I was to have been rescued from the savage land of my birth and brought to civilized England. I never argued. I simply bided my time, knowing that one day I would be home, and all those years of simpering courtiers and two-faced ladies would be like a bad dream."

"Yet you seemed happy enough at court."

"There were some good people. In spite of everything, I sometimes found myself admiring the queen. And, of course, Bella was a sweet friend."

"Were there no men at court you admired?" Niall asked with sudden curiosity. She didn't appear to notice that once again their legs were touching on the soft mattress.

She gave a grimace. "Nay." She looked out the window of their room where they could see a view of the harbor in the distance. "None of Elizabeth's courtiers could compare to my memories of the O'Malleys and the other men of our clan."

Niall smiled briefly. "You'll get no argument from me that an Irishman can outfight an Englishman with one hand tied."

She turned back to look at him. " 'Tis not just fighting. So many at court call themselves noble, yet the men I remember from the Valley of Mor were more noble in so many ways. They would rather starve than steal from the poor. They would rather die than lie to a friend."

Niall wondered if she was thinking about her rebel lover when she talked about the men of her homeland, but he pushed the thought away. "Aye," he agreed. "Values are simpler here, it would seem. You will find many such men when we reach County Meath."

Her smile was bittersweet. "Which may make my reception there even more uncertain. Your brother has gone ahead and will surely tell them of my deception against you and John. They will have little enough reason to like me."

"They are men of honor," Niall answered carefully. "Yet they also understand what it is to act for a cause one believes in. Whether or not they think your cause was just, they will acknowledge your right to fight for it."

She was looking at him with an odd expression. "Does that mean that you have forgiven me for the wrong I did you?"

He hesitated. When he thought of how easily he had been duped that night in the orangery, how he had considered her response to his kisses to be genuine, he still felt anger, but at this moment as she waited for his answer, her eyes wide and concerned, he realized that he had forgiven her.

"Aye, my clever Cat. Though my pride may yet be sore from being tricked by a girl, and I may expect some ridicule on the subject when I reach Riordan Hall, I warrant I've forgiven you."

Now there was no reservation in her smile. "I'm glad."

They looked at each other for a long moment, and both seemed to suddenly become aware that their hands were still clasped. She pulled her hand slowly out of his grip.

Niall looked over at the door of the room. "When do you suppose John will return?" he asked, his voice altered.

Catriona stood and shook out her skirts, then walked around the edge of the bed to look out the window. "I don't know. Does he often go off like this?"

Niall frowned. "Nay."

"I trow he'll be along shortly. You should try to sleep. He wanted you to rest."

"I think I shall," Niall said. He turned on his good side

and closed his eyes. He was not the least bit tired, but
putting an end to the conversation would give his racing
body a chance to calm.

"Sleep well, then," Catriona said softly.

"Aye," he murmured, then forced his shoulders to relax
and his breathing into an even pattern. Within minutes he
realized that sleep would not be as difficult as he imagined.

When he opened his eyes, the shutters on the small window had been closed and the lantern on the table was lit.
Catriona was seated at the table, once again looking over
John's volume of verse. When he stirred, she looked up
and smiled. "So you've decided to wake up," she said.

His mouth felt stale and dry. "How long have I slept?"

"All afternoon. I imagined you might sleep until the
morrow, but if you're awake, I'll have a look at that arm."

He blinked the haze from his eyes. " 'Tis night again
and John hasn't returned?"

She cleared her throat and reached for a folded paper on
the table beside her. "He's sent word that he'll be delayed
even further."

"How much longer?"

Even across the room, he could see the sweep of her
lashes. "Two or three more days."

Niall sat bolt upright. "Three days!"

She rose from her stool and walked over to hand him
the paper. He read quickly. It was a simple note from John
apologizing for the delay and saying that he expected to return in two to three days. He provided no explanation.

Niall looked up at Catriona, who tilted her head and
said, "It would appear that you and I will be spending more
time by ourselves."

Niall felt a surge of anger at his friend. "Where the devil
can he be? I'd thought to be off to Riordan Hall by now."

Catriona sounded a little wistful as she looked around
the room and said, "This is not such a bad place to tarry
awhile. I could see a roaring fire in the taproom below

when I went out to the garderobe. And there were all kinds of savory smells."

Niall put aside his anger as he realized that his companion had spent the day shut up with nothing to do but watch him sleep. "Have you eaten nothing?" he asked.

She shook her head.

He swung his feet to the ground, shook off the dizziness that showed he hadn't entirely recovered from his weakness, and stood. "Nor have I, I reckon, unless I dined in my sleep." He walked over to the basin to splash water on his face. "Then the first thing is to find some supper. We'll worry about what to do after that."

"Do you intend to set out for Riordan Hall without him?"

Niall looked at her over the top of the towel he was using to mop off his face. She'd taken off her cap and her hair was loose, slightly disheveled, framing her face. As she waited for his answer, her lips were slightly open, full, and moist. Once again he felt the gnawing in his middle he'd seemed to live with ever since he'd taken Catriona's hand and said the vows. It was simple wanting, he told himself. Normal male lust. Yet it felt like nothing he'd ever known with the women in his past.

He'd fought it all the way from London, but now he was wondering why. She was his lawful wife. She'd had lovers before, or at least one lover. And the previous day, before they'd been interrupted by John's return, he'd seen the telltale signs. Why should he struggle against giving in to something that it appeared both wanted?

"Nay, we'll wait for John here," he said slowly, throwing the towel aside. "What's the hurry, after all? You and I will just have to figure out a way to entertain ourselves until he gets back," he added with a crooked grin.

If she read any of the obvious undertones in his remark, it wasn't apparent. She merely looked back at him with her cat-green eyes and said brightly, "Aye, we will. Mayhap in the morning we can take a stroll along the pier, if you feel up to it."

"My nap this afternoon was remarkably refreshing. I feel I'm up to almost anything," he added, raising his eyebrow.

Once again she made no response to his attempt at innuendo. With a polite smile, she nodded, then turned toward the door. She played the innocent well, Niall thought. He himself felt like a randy stripling on his first visit to Carmen, the village woman who had first introduced many Meath lads to the arts of sexual pleasure.

He watched her from behind for a moment, eyes lowering to the gentle sway of her hips as she started down the inn stairs.

Catriona may be experienced, he reminded himself, but she was no village whore. He'd do well to take a deep breath, will his thudding heart to slow down, and get himself under control so that he could go to supper and give his bride the proper wooing she deserved.

For the life of her, Catriona couldn't understand why she felt so heady. Perhaps she'd forgotten the strength of Irish ale, she thought ruefully, looking into the nearly empty mug she was drinking. Was it the warmth of the huge fireplace that made her cheeks burn, or was she tipsy? Or was it something else entirely?

She looked across the table to where Niall was watching her. He'd not shaved during the journey, so his face had a new growth of beard that shadowed the strong lines of his jaw. It made him look older. With his long, straight nose and thick dark brows, he could be some Celtic warrior of old, fierce and commanding. But his dark eyes danced in the firelight as he watched her.

"Tell me more about your family," she requested after a pause in the conversation had grown awkward. "I know that Cormac is the oldest, then Eamon. Do you have other brothers?"

"Nay. My father took three brides, and each one died giving him a son. After that, he had no more heart to marry again."

"So you boys were raised without a mother."

"Aye. 'Tis said we're a rowdy lot, but much of that has changed since Claire arrived. She's trying to civilize us," he added with a grin.

"I warrant she's equal to the task if your brother is so much in love with her."

"Aye, that he is."

" 'Tis a wondrous thing they say, being in love."

Niall shifted in his chair. "I've heard it can be both wondrous and miserable. Cormac and Claire passed some fair amount of agony before they could be happy together."

"Have you ever been in love?" She'd wanted to ask the question before, but the moment had never been right. Now she found herself holding in a breath as she waited for his answer.

"Nay. In truth, I've never seen much point to the notion. It brought little enough happiness to my father and proved fatal for his brides."

"Childbirth is the risk every woman takes on willingly," she said. "That is, if 'tis her *choice* to wed." Even as she made the statement, she regretted the reminder about the circumstances of their marriage, but Niall didn't seem to notice.

"Aye, women have a hard lot. We men claim bravery for facing a foe on the field of battle, yet our women at home risk death without a murmur each time they give birth."

Catriona smiled. "I intend to make a bit of a murmur should my turn ever come."

He returned her smile, then both looked away as once again the realization came that they were, in fact, husband and wife. It was his baby she would be expected to have. All at once the thought didn't seem so odd to Catriona. For seven years she'd sworn that a regular life was not for her.

When she'd refused Bobby's love, she'd been convinced that such a love was not meant for the likes of her. She'd lost her father and her birthright, and she'd intended to spend the rest of her life dedicated to righting that wrong.

Now, suddenly, she was sitting across from Niall Riordan in a seaside inn contemplating having his baby. The idea was so remarkable that it left her quite without breath.

He seemed to be having similar breathing problems. There was a catch in his voice as he asked softly, "Shall we go up to our room?"

Sometime while she had been lost in his dark eyes, he had taken hold of her hand. He stood now, pulling her up with him.

The heat in her cheeks flared. She swayed slightly. She *was* tipsy, she decided. Her legs felt weak, and it seemed as if the only thing keeping her upright was the arm he had slipped around her waist.

"Shall I bring the ale?" he asked, motioning to the pitcher on the table.

She shook her head. "I believe I've already had too much."

He leaned toward her and said in her ear, "You had barely a glass, *a stór*. I believe we're both intoxicated, but 'tis not from the wine."

A stór—treasure. She'd not heard the endearment since the olden days. It seemed to release something that she had been trying to hold tightly inside her. She felt a tear trickle from the corner of her eye.

Niall looked down and saw it. "What's the matter?" he asked, alarmed.

She shook her head and tried to gulp the tears down as she answered, "I'm fine. Perhaps just overwhelmed by being home again."

Niall looked around the tiny taproom. The only other customers had long since left, and the boy who had brought their dinner was nowhere to be seen. Bending slightly, he lifted her easily and settled her in his arms, dropping a light kiss on her nose.

"Oh, no!" she protested at once, squirming and putting a hand on his bandage. "You'll open the wound."

He gave a husky laugh. "What wound, *a stór*? The only thing I feel is your softness nestled against me." Once again he whispered in her ear. " 'Tis a sweet torment, love. One I believe it's time to end. Tell me you feel it, too."

She stopped resisting and became very still. His face was inches from hers. "I feel it," she whispered back.

He gave a quick nod, then turned to carry her up the stairs.

The truth was, his wounded arm did throb as he placed her gently on the big bed. Sweat had broken on his brow from the long climb up the stairs. But none of it mattered.

He smiled down at her. "Shall I douse the lantern?" he asked.

She nodded. He would have preferred making love to her in a room ablaze with light, but he was sensitive to her modesty. Though he probably wouldn't have made the offer if he hadn't seen the full moon shining in brightly through the narrow inn window.

His hands trembled. Perhaps still from weakness? he wondered, willing the shaking to stop. She'd made no move to disrobe. In fact her eyes looked up at him with something resembling apprehension. He frowned.

"I won't hurt you," he said a bit defensively.

She didn't reply. Was she thinking of her rebel lover? Was she reluctant to give herself to another while Bobby Brosnihan wandered free, perhaps still attempting to rescue her from her forced marriage? The notion dulled his sympathy but, oddly, fueled his desire.

Ignoring the stabs of pain in his arm, he pulled off his tunic and undershirt, leaving his chest bare as he lay beside her on the bed and drew her into his arms. "Don't think," he commanded. Then he began to kiss her.

Catriona could no longer deny what was happening to her. As Niall had said, it wasn't the ale. If she was drunk, it was with him—the male scent of him, the feel of his soft lips, and the rough rasp of his whiskers. He plundered her mouth, leaving her weak and breathless and utterly aware of every inch of her own skin.

When he moved to one side to begin removing her clothes, she helped him in a heady daze that allowed no room for embarrassment or doubts. In that moment, in this bed, she was his. She would follow wherever he led her on this wondrous path of new sensations.

In a few moments she was naked, and reason erupted long enough to make her wonder where Niall had learned so much about women's clothing if he had been raised among men. But the thought was quickly drowned as he began to kiss her again, this time letting his kisses trail along her throat and down her breasts.

He lingered there on first one, then the other. She laced the fingers of one hand through his thick dark hair as she watched him tease her nipples into hardened peaks. When he looked up to smile at her, his face had changed. His eyes were narrowed, his nostrils flared. Something in his expression sent a surge straight to her private female place. As if reading her body, he moved his hand there. She felt sudden warmth, and then something more as he began to stroke her.

His fingers found an exquisite spot that made her moan and arch involuntarily. He chuckled and moved to kiss her mouth again. "My Cat is purring," he murmured. "Methinks she likes that."

She could only nod in response as the stroking continued and an odd restlessness began to build. She couldn't seem to lie still. Her thighs moved against each other and she lifted her bottom to press herself against the invading fingers.

Niall's voice was hoarse as he moved over her and said

against her cheek, "Your body speaks for you, *a stór*.
You're warm and wet and ready for me."

Then his fingers were replaced by his stiffened penis.
He moved into her gently, but he was thick and dry, and
she gave a gasp of surprise and pain at the unaccustomed
stretching.

He pulled out and looked down at her, his face suddenly
ashen. "You're a virgin," he rasped.

"Aye. Naturally." His surprise confused her until she remembered suddenly that when they had appeared before
the queen, Bobby Brosnihan had been labeled her lover.
Niall had evidently believed the tale. "Aye," she said more
firmly. "I've bedded with no man."

He looked so dumbfounded that she almost felt sorry
for him.

"I'd thought . . ." he stuttered. "I'd thought . . . they
said you were lovers."

She lay back against the bed with a sigh, all the heat
draining from her body. "If you mean Bobby, nay."

He was silent a moment, then he asked softly, "Did I
hurt you?"

"Nay."

He laid his forehead on her chest. "I could have given
you more time. I thought you'd already—"

After a moment's hesitation she put a hand on his hair.
Her initial irritation over his assumption that she had had a
lover was subsiding. The interruption had cooled her ardor,
but there was still a vague feeling of wanting that was beginning to grow stronger again. But he was making no
move to resume their lovemaking.

"'Twas not unpleasant," she said after a long pause.

He lifted his head and looked into her eyes. Slowly a
glint of humor lit them. "I daresay 'tis not the highest com-
pliment I've ever been paid."

She smiled. "I mean even at the end. The beginning was
much better than 'not unpleasant.'"

"I'm glad to hear it." His tone was dry, but the light was still in his eyes.

Still he did not resume his attentions, and after another long pause, she asked with a touch of irritation, "So do you have a policy against bedding virgins?"

He gave a surprised laugh. "I've never had occasion to formulate a policy one way or another. The, er, opportunity has never presented itself before."

She frowned. "Are you thinking that it would be disagreeable?"

The glint in his eyes had turned mischievous as he said with mock seriousness, "I'd be willing to risk it."

She tried to keep from smiling back at him. She'd always thought a woman's first time should be a solemn occasion, and she'd been told to expect discomfort, and even pain. Yet at the moment all she could feel was that odd restlessness between her legs. "Well, then?" she prompted.

In an instant he had scooped her up again, this time putting her on top as he lay flat on the bed. She could feel the hard ridge of him riding against the tender part of her body as he started kissing her again. His lips then brushed each of her breasts.

In only moments the restlessness below had become a dull ache, and she found herself moving rhythmically against him, looking for some kind of release to the building tension. He pushed her half upright, then grasped her hips to arrange her directly over him. "You're in control, sweetheart," he told her, lifting her onto his shaft. "Just take as much of me as you like."

But she would have no half-measures. Moving her legs to each side of him, she rocked gently until she could feel his fullness deep inside her. The sensation was odd, but not painful. He drew her hand down to touch where they were joined and her fingers found the same sensitive spot his had rubbed earlier. As her rocking movement continued, she heard him groan. He was watching her, his eyes hooded. Just when the tension seemed almost unbearable, waves of feeling burst through her. Niall seized her hips and held her steady while incredible surges pulsed from him and radiated throughout her middle. She clutched his hands and held on while her body shook with their shared climax.

As the waves subsided, she collapsed on top of him as if all the bones had suddenly been pulled from her body.

"You're crying!" he said, gathering her in his arms.

She shook her head, then realized that her cheeks were wet where they touched his chest.

"Are you all right?" he asked, concerned.

She gave a weak laugh. "Aye. Though I know not how people do this kind of thing on a regular basis. I feel as if it will be a week before I can move."

" 'Tis the aftermath, *a stór*. I predict you'll be moving just fine in a few minutes."

She felt incapable of shaking her head to disagree with him. "At least a week," she mumbled.

In the course of their lovemaking, they'd jumbled the bedcovers. He reached down to bring up a blanket to cover them, then held her in silence for several minutes. "Feeling better?" he asked finally.

"Mmmm."

"Truly, are you well? We've done no harm?" he insisted.

To her surprise, she was suddenly once again quite capable of lifting her head. "Harm? Nay. Was it not done right?" she asked.

"Sweetheart, it was the most right I've ever known, but I warrant 'twas vigorous for a first time. I just want to be sure that you're suffering no ill effect."

She laid her head back on his chest and considered, moving her miraculously recovered legs against him. "If there were ill effects, they've yet to let my head know about them."

He pulled her up to give her a solid kiss. "I'm glad," he whispered. Then his mouth softened and lingered.

After several moments she pulled away and asked softly, "What about your arm? Did it suffer ill effects?"

As an answer he gave her a squeeze with the limb in question. "I believe you've just invented a new cure, my beautiful nurse."

She giggled and rolled against him, noticing as she did that the lower part of his body was once again fully erect. Her eyes widened. "Should this cure be performed more than once? I mean, in order to be sure it will have permanent results."

He gave her bottom a gentle swat. "I thought you were going to be incapable of moving for a week."

"I've had a rather remarkable cure myself."

His expression was doubtful. "I don't think 'tis a good idea to overdo when you are . . . when you are not accustomed."

Following some age-old instinct, her hand went to grasp the stiffened part of him and began to move back and forth. "So be it, then," she said with feigned indifference. "If you're no longer interested . . ."

He resisted for mere seconds, then with a growl, flipped her over and moved on top of her. "Just don't blame me on the morrow," he said, his voice already husky.

She smiled up at him with a saucy smile. "Why sirrah, don't you know what they say? We cats have nine lives."

Eleven

When she awoke, Niall was propped up on one elbow, watching her. Through their small window, the sun was already high in the sky. She stretched sleepily.

"My Cat has finally decided to awaken," he said.

She smiled. "How's your arm this morning?"

He leaned over and kissed her nose, then said in a low voice, "Cured. How is your . . . er . . . how are you?"

"I'm—" She wrinkled up her nose as she tried to think of the right words. "I'm happy," she said finally, though the words seemed far too pale to describe how she felt. How could she explain that last night in his arms she had found a sense of belonging that had been missing since that horrible day in the Valley of Mor? She'd lain awake much of the night feeling the warmth of him beside her and realizing that she now belonged to him, body and soul. She, who had thought she would never again belong to anyone or anything.

"'Twas wondrous," she concluded.

"Aye." There seemed a slight reservation to his agreement.

"Is anything wrong?" she asked.

"Nay, 'tis just—" He stopped.

She pulled out of his arms and sat up. "Just what? Are you sorry we made love?"

He looked up at her, his expression sober. "I'll never be sorry, but what about you? Were you pledged to this man—the one they called your lover?"

She sank back down on the bed, relieved and secretly pleased. Niall was jealous. That's what had put the scowl on his face. "Bobby has been my best friend for as long as I can remember," she told him. "When the English soldiers took over my family estate and killed my father, he risked his life to stay with me and try to keep me safe. I owe him much."

"Do you love him?"

She did love Bobby, in her own special way, but she didn't think it was something that she'd ever be able to explain to Niall. "Nay," she said simply.

He was silent for a long moment, then he leaned over and kissed her again on the bridge of her nose and the tip of her chin. "I'm glad. And, yes, last night was wondrous. If I didn't feel guilty for how, um, vigorous we were, I'd scoop you up and start in all over again."

She smiled and gave another leisurely stretch. It was true, she did feel a few odd twinges here and there from the unaccustomed activity, but nothing that was painful. "I wouldn't mind," she said, trailing a finger along his bare chest.

He rolled over her and jumped out of bed. "I'll not be tempted, minx," he scolded. "We're going to get up and go downstairs for a proper breakfast like a respectable old married couple."

The notion sounded almost as delicious as another round in bed with him. He stood looking down at her, waiting. He was naked except for the bandage around his arm. For the first time she could see his body in the full sunlight. The light hair on his broad chest tapered into a darker vee over his flat stomach that led to the thick thatch surrounding his manhood. His thighs were hard and sinewy. She felt her stomach give a lurch at the sight.

"I'm not hungry," she said with a slight pout. "And people with wounds need a lot of sleep."

He grinned at her, fully aware of her careful survey of his body. Then he turned to collect her clothes from where they had been thrown the night before and threw them on top of her in the bed. "Up with you, slugabed!" he ordered. "If you hurry, we may watch the fishermen coming in with the morning's catch."

She pushed the heaps of silks and linens off her face and with some reluctance swung her feet to the floor. Niall had begun putting on his own clothes, but he stopped as she stood up, as naked as he. His tone had changed as he said, "Ah, sweetheart, you could tempt the devil himself with a body like that." His clothes half on, he pulled her roughly against him and kissed her, this time deeply and hungrily.

For a moment she let herself melt into his arms, then she pushed on his chest and stepped away, snatching up a petticoat for protection. "Fie, sir. A lady offers herself only once in a morning. Now you've piqued my curiosity to see those, er, *fish* you were talking about."

She started to dress herself calmly while Niall looked on with a rueful expression, the bulge in his hose revealing his frustration. "I believe you may be right about needing to rest this arm," he ventured.

She laughed, lacing up the front of her bodice. "Then pray do so. The bed is all yours." She walked over to the basin and splashed water on her face, then quickly drew a comb through her tangled hair. He stood watching her, still without dressing. When she was finished, she turned toward the door. Over her shoulder, she gave him a saucy smile and said, "I shall be down in the taproom. I've discovered that I have an appetite after all. In fact, I just may finish that entire roast the landlord had on the spit last night."

•   •   •

Catriona scanned the waterfront, hungry to take in all the sights of her newly regained homeland. As Niall had suggested, they'd first gone down to the pier to watch the fishermen bringing in their baskets of mussels and squirming lobster and nets full of silvery herring. Then they'd wandered up the banks of the River Liffey, where vendors of all sorts were selling their wares from colorful carts.

Catriona couldn't remember when she had been so happy. She had certainly not felt this carefree since before her life in the Valley of Mor had been shattered. And she couldn't remember ever before feeling this giddiness. With Niall's hand clasping hers as naturally as if they had been lovers for years instead of just one night, she felt as if she could burst into song at any moment.

"The catch has been good this year," Niall was saying. "So has the farming. Perhaps after all the years of trouble we'll finally have some prosperous times. The menfolk can leave their fighting and go back to their homes to raise their families. 'Tis the way things should be."

Bobby Brosnihan and the Clearys would not share the sentiment, Catriona knew, but she was too content to think about war and politics today. "What are the blue ones?" she asked, pointing to a small boat brimming with slippery, slimy fish that glinted blue in the sunlight.

Niall looked in the direction of her hand. "They're mackerel. We'll get some salted ones to take with us to Riordan Hall. Molly will fix them into a chowder."

"Molly?"

"Our cook. When I was younger she rarely produced anything more than salt pork and potatoes, but since Claire's arrival, she's turned into a regular genius in the kitchen."

"Your brother must be pleased to have brought home a wife who could bring such changes to your household."

"Aye." Niall grinned. "Claire's turned my fearsome brother Cormac into a pussycat. But I don't think Molly's improved cooking had anything to do with it."

Since Catriona had felt very much like purring with contentment all morning long, she understood exactly what Niall was meaning. She squeezed his hand. "So before Claire, your brother was fearsome?"

Niall shrugged. "I warrant all the Riordans had a bit of a reputation. We had no women to rein us in, and our father always thought competition was a good thing. We've been known to start a brawl or two on a Saturday night."

"But now Cormac has decided there are more pleasurable ways to spend his evenings."

"Aye, though with another babe on the way, he may find that he and Claire have little time for such pursuits."

"They say babies bring their own special pleasures."

Niall frowned. "Aye, but 'tis something I'd just as soon leave to my brother to experience."

A breeze drifted up from the water, smelling of salt and fish. Catriona dropped Niall's hand and hunched her shoulders against the sudden chill. She herself had never thought about having a family, but last night had changed that. She and Niall had not just made love. They very well may have created a child inside her. Yet now he claimed that he wasn't interested in children. Of course, he had been coerced into marrying her. It hadn't been for love. It was her own fancy that had put those notions into her head last night. She'd been lulled by the firelight and the warm ale into thinking that they could be like a normal couple, falling in love with each other, planning a future together.

Niall had been alone in an inn with a willing woman. What else would he have been expected to do but take advantage of the moment? He was, after all, one of the formidable Riordan brothers. His brother had found happiness in love and a family, but it didn't appear that Niall was interested in following his brother's example.

"Are you cold?" he asked.

She looked out at the sea that had grown black and choppy. "Aye, there's a sudden chill."

He seized her hand again and rubbed it between his.

"Your hand is like ice. We'd best go back to the inn." His lips cocked in a crooked smile. "I'm feeling a bit tired myself. Mayhap 'tis time for a nap."

She did not mistake his meaning, but all at once the idea did not seem as appealing as it had when she had awakened that morning. "Aye, let's head back," she said. "Perhaps there will be some news from John."

There had been no word from John, and by the time they had sat together through a mostly silent supper, Niall was feeling thoroughly out-of-sorts with his friend and with the world in general. How could John have left him alone with an unpredictable, capricious female who one moment seemed like a veritable goddess of passion and the next a total stranger?

Unlike the previous evening, Catriona had drunk little ale. The firelight had not seemed to dance in her eyes. It was almost as if everything that had occurred through their long, sensual night together had not been real.

At one point he had reached for her hand across the table, but she had pulled it away. By the time they had climbed the steep inn stairs to their room, he was ready to forget about John and leave directly for Riordan Hall.

"If we hear nothing from John by noon tomorrow, I think we should start on our way," he said.

Catriona was taking off her cap at the little nightstand. She turned and looked at him in surprise. "He did say two or three days."

"Aye, but I'm tired of waiting. We'll leave word here and he can follow later."

"You sound angry." She turned away from him and picked up the brush to comb out her hair.

Not angry, confused. No one had told him that along with the pleasure, falling for a woman brought with it uncertainty and complications and even fear. He had been horrified by the sudden realization as they walked along the pier that their lovemaking could result in Catriona facing the very event that had killed so many young Riordan brides. And if that notion alone weren't enough to give him pause, she had suddenly changed her demeanor, for no apparent reason. It was as if the cold north wind had come in from the Irish Sea to blow away all the warmth they had shared.

He sighed. "Nay, I'm not angry, except perhaps a bit with John. He shouldn't have left us for so long without discussing it first."

"We don't know what has delayed him. His business may have been important."

"Aye," he acknowledged. She was brushing out her hair in long, even strokes. It had a lustrous red sheen in the dim light of the lantern. He could remember the feel of it sweeping across his chest. His heart sped up a beat. "But I suppose I could stand to wait here one more day."

She turned around, her expression dark. "You could stand it, Master Riordan? How generous of you, when I'm sure 'tis such a burden to be here with me."

"I didn't mean—"

"I didn't notice you complaining last night when you brought me to this bed, when you were taking off my clothes and . . . and . . . doing . . . things. . . ."

Her face had grown red with indignation, but the tears gathering in her eyes told another story. Niall crossed the room in three long strides and took her in his arms. "Don't cry, *a stór*," he murmured. "Forgive me. I didn't mean to sound as if I didn't want to be here with you."

The tears had begun to slide down her cheeks. "'Twas what you said," she accused with a gulp.

"Nay, 'twas not." He began kissing the tears away, one by one, tasting the saltiness of them, feeling the soft skin of her cheek against his lips. The resulting surge of lust combined with tenderness was like nothing he had ever before experienced. "I thought John was wrong to leave us, but now that he's gone—" He stopped kissing her cheeks and took her chin in his hand to force her to look at him.

"He could stay away for weeks if we could just be like this—you here in my arms."

There was a blaze of joy in her cat-green eyes. "I thought you were regretting what happened last night. On the pier today when we were talking about—"

He didn't let her explain. Instead he bent his head to take her mouth in a kiss that left no doubt about precisely what he wanted. "Are you finished with your hair?" he asked hoarsely.

She smiled up at him, nodding. "Unless you'd like to brush it for me?"

"Later," he said. "At the moment, I'd like to see it wrapped around your naked body."

She responded by offering her mouth for another kiss. By the time they broke apart, both were breathing more heavily. Catriona's cheeks were flushed.

"Shall we leave the lantern on tonight?" Niall whispered, pulling her toward the bed.

The knock on the door made them both jump. Niall uttered a swift oath and barked, "What is it?"

There was a moment of silence, then they heard John's voice. " 'Tis I. Shall I go away?"

Niall looked at Catriona, then walked over to open the door. John entered, then paused, surveying the flushed young couple with an amused glance. "I see you two have managed well enough in my absence."

Niall frowned. "First you disappear without a fare-thee-well, then you appear without warning, just at the wrong time."

The older man shrugged an apology. "It's nice to know that I wasn't missed. How's your arm?"

"The fever's gone, I think," Catriona answered for him. She appeared to be struggling to sound as if nothing were out of the ordinary.

Niall walked over to her and put a deliberate arm around her waist. "She's a better nurse than you, my friend, and more dependable."

"I warrant she is," John said, regarding the couple with a fond smile. "Lucky for you."

"Aye," Niall agreed. "Now mayhap you'll tell us what was so important that made you run off."

"You'll know in good time, Niall. But I'm afraid I've come back to tell you that I must leave once again, this time for a longer trip. I'll be sending you and your bride on to Riordan Hall by yourselves."

"My brothers are expecting you," Niall protested. "Cormac wanted a report from both of us about the peace negotiations before he meets with Shane O'Neill."

John waved his hand. "I'll be sorry to miss out on the homecoming, Niall, but you don't have to worry about reporting anything to the O'Neill. I'll be meeting with him directly. He's helping me with an investigation of sorts."

"This mysterious *business* you've been about?" His friend's secretiveness made Niall feel oddly offended. He and John had worked together with Elizabeth's counselors, and he'd felt that he was doing an important job for his country. The disaster at Wolverton House had put an end to all that, but he'd at least expected to be consulted on how the peace efforts should proceed. "Well, then," he said after a moment. "We should get some sleep so that we can leave early in the morning."

John gave a nod of satisfaction. For a moment, Niall wondered if the wily doctor had deliberately made him angry so that he wouldn't inquire further into the nature of the business that was preventing him from accompanying them to Riordan Hall. "I assume you'll let us know what becomes of you, Doctor," he said with a slight edge to his voice.

"As I said," John answered with a bland smile, "you'll hear about my business soon enough."

Niall had to be satisfied with that as John refused any further explanation about his activities.

"I should give you back your book, Doctor," Catriona

said. She walked over to the table to retrieve the little volume and handed it to him. "The poems are beautiful."

John smiled but said nothing as he took the book from her and tucked it inside his jacket.

"Let's take another look at that arm," he said to Niall. Grumpily Niall submitted as his two companions redressed the wound. John pronounced that it was healing well and praised Catriona's nursing talents. She gave him the kind of happy smile that Niall himself had not seen since she had turned distant earlier on the pier, which heightened Niall's irritation with his friend.

"Are you ready, then, Niall?" John was asking.

"Ready for what?" Niall snapped, rubbing his arm, which ached from John's prodding and the rebandaging process.

"For sleep. I've just been saying that I've arranged a room for the two of us tonight. Lady Catriona will finally have some privacy."

"Er . . . I'd thought . . ." Niall paused, then looked over at Catriona, who gave him a brief, noncommittal smile. John's interruption had definitely broken the spell of their earlier kisses, but he couldn't tell if she was regretting the doctor's suggestion that Niall sleep elsewhere. Finally he said, "Very well, then. I trust you'll sleep well, milady."

"You gentlemen, as well," she murmured.

"We'll come by for you at dawn, Catriona," John said and once again was rewarded by a warm smile.

Niall turned to follow him out of the room. "I swear, old man, if you start in snoring like a wounded bear tonight, you'll sleep in the corridor."

John laughed but didn't bother to answer.

Niall seemed ill-tempered as they started out the next morning toward Riordan Hall. Catriona was not sure if his ill humor was due to irritation with John or with her, or if he was bothered about something related to the imminent homecoming. She'd made a brief inquiry, and had asked if his arm was bothering him, but he'd given her short, vague answers and lapsed back into silence.

By midmorning, however, he appeared to relax as he began to point out familiar landmarks. He was obviously happy to be nearing home.

"This is Tara Hill," he told her as they reached a windswept series of mounds.

Catriona had heard of the mystical seat of ancient Irish kings all her life, but she'd never seen it. The site itself looked unremarkable, but she felt a chill up her neck as they rode past. "There's not much left of it, is there?" she observed, looking around at the scattered stone ruins.

Niall grinned. "Just the ghosts," he said.

The chill turned into a sudden shiver. "Do you think there are such things?"

Niall pulled up on Cinnabar's reins and turned to survey a small brownish hill that was the center of the ancient site. "Oh, they're here," he said. "The shades of our ancestors. I fancy they linger here waiting for their descendants to bring peace to this land so that they can finally get on with the eternal rest they've been promised."

He spoke with a smile, but Catriona felt there was a seriousness behind his words. "Perhaps they have to keep watch over this place until all the foreign English invaders have been driven from it."

Niall's smile faded. "If so, then many more good men will join them in the hereafter before the thing is done." He pulled his horse around and started moving again. "We'll be at Riordan Hall in a couple of hours," he said brusquely.

Catriona regretted her impulsive remark. Just when Niall had seemed to be warming up, she'd had to mention their differences. It was as if he had once again closed a shutter between them. They rode most of the rest of the trip in silence.

Finally they reached a set of stone pillars on either side

of a rutted road. "This is where we turn into Riordan Hall," Niall told her.

They turned their horses up a raised pathway that was bordered on each side by a grassy bog dotted with colorful wildflowers. "Spring is a pretty time to be arriving," Niall said, his tone reflecting pride in his home.

In the distance she could make out the house itself. It was made of gray stone and had the look of an imposing medieval castle, complete with turreted towers. "Riordan Hall?" she asked, pointing.

He smiled broadly. "Aye. 'Tis my home."

He hadn't said that it was now also *her* home, but she returned his smile and told him, " 'Tis a beautiful place. You've a right to be proud."

The road took them directly to the front door of the manor, but as they approached, Niall veered off along a path that led up a hill toward the stables. His mount, Cinnabar, seemed to know the way. At Wolverton House Catriona would have dismounted from her horse at the door and expected a stable lad to appear to retrieve it. Uncertain, she let her horse follow Niall's up the hill.

As they approached the huge stable, a burly young man came out. From his clothes, he looked to be a servant, yet Niall leaped from his horse and clapped his shoulders in a hearty embrace.

"Welcome home!" the stableman said, returning Niall's embrace with enthusiasm. Then he turned to Catriona and, pulling on his cap, murmured, "Welcome to Riordan Hall, milady." He seemed to know who she was. Of course, Eamon would already have apprised the household of her arrival. No doubt he had also added his own opinion about her and the actions that had landed Niall in prison.

"This is our stableman, Aidan Shaw," Niall said, offering his arms to help her dismount. She slid into them, and he released her immediately and turned back to the stableman, who had taken Cinnabar's bridle and was giving the horse a careful scrutiny. "He looks none the worse for the journey," the man said. "Saints preserve, all the way to London and back."

Niall gave Cinnabar a pat and agreed, "Aye, he's served well for the long trip, as usual. Cormac's horse may be swifter, but there's not a surer mount in our stables than my Cinnabar."

"I'll no argue ye that 'un," Aidan agreed with a smile.

Both men seemed to have forgotten Catriona's presence. "How's the foaling?" Niall asked the stableman. "And did Old Grey make it through the winter?"

"One thing at a time, Master Niall. I've taken good care of yer domain, never fear."

"I know you have, Aidan. 'Tis why I was able to leave with a clear conscience."

For several minutes Catriona waited as the two men entered into a detailed discussion of the state of Riordan Hall's livestock. Finally, just when she was beginning to grow irritated, Aidan took Niall's arm and said, "Ye'd best see to yer lady, sir."

Niall looked around as if surprised to see her still standing there. "Oh. Aye," he said. "We'll continue this later, Aidan."

The man nodded and gave another pull of his cap. "Pleased ter meet ye, milady," he said.

"Aidan's the best there is with horses," Niall told her as they walked down the hill toward the house. There was an enthusiasm in his tone that she couldn't remember hearing before.

"You appear to work well together."

"Aye," he said with a deep, contented laugh. "Cormac may be the head of Riordan Hall, but I'm master of the Riordan stables."

"And you're happy to be home," she said.

Niall looked down at the house, then back up the hill where Aidan was standing by the stable door, watching them. "Aye," he answered softly. "I'm happy to be home."

As he spoke the big double doors of the mansion burst

open and two men came barreling out. She recognized Eamon, and there was no mistaking that his companion was the third Riordan brother, Cormac.

Niall dropped her arm and took off running to meet them. This time instead of an embrace, the greeting more resembled some kind of wrestling match. From Catriona's vantage point, it appeared that Cormac was attempting to twist his brother's head off his shoulders.

She continued walking toward the melee at a sedate pace. As she reached them, Eamon straightened up and bowed stiffly. "Welcome to Riordan Hall, Lady Catriona," he said. His tone was formal without any of the warmth they'd been given by the stableman.

"We're pleased to be here. 'Twas a long trip," she answered a little uncertainly, then turned to meet the head of the powerful Riordan clan.

Cormac Riordan regarded her without a smile. His face resembled Niall's but was more guarded. She did not expect a smile to light it as easily as it did his younger brother's. After a moment of awkward silence, Niall said, "This is Catriona, brother. An O'Malley of the Valley of Mor." There was no mention of wife or wedding, though Catriona was sure that Cormac had had the story from Eamon.

"Welcome, Catriona O'Malley," Cormac said finally. His voice was deeper than Niall's, but had the same mellow timbre.

"Thank you," she said. Her throat was dry after the long ride.

Cormac regarded her gravely for another long moment, then he turned back to Niall. "So my baby brother has returned from the great court of Elizabeth. We're waiting to hear your tales." He clapped Niall on the back and turned him to walk up the stairs. "Molly is this very moment preparing your favorite pot pie for supper."

Twelve

"She's my wife, Cormac. She deserves a place of respect in this household. Granted, the thing was done by order of the queen, but nevertheless, the vows were said." Catriona had been taken to a bedroom by one of the servants and Niall had joined his brothers in the big manor library for a pint of hot ale before supper.

He'd seen his brother's reaction to Catriona's arrival, and he'd seen the look of hurt and confusion in her eyes. He was confused himself, and unsure of what this marriage meant for either him or Catriona, but at the moment she was his wife. He wasn't about to let her be insulted or ignored by his family.

Cormac's thick eyebrows drew together in a scowl. "The girl tried to have you killed, Niall. Twice."

"First she lied to send you to prison, then she had her lover try to murder you in your sleep," Eamon added.

Niall blew out a puff of air. "She lied to me, aye. But I'll swear that she knew nothing of the attack at the inn. If 'twas her . . . if 'twas Brosnihan who came for her, she was not part of the plot."

Cormac and Eamon exchanged a glance. Eamon

shrugged and said to his older brother, "I told you. He's besotted."

Cormac stood from the bench by the fire where he'd been sitting and went to stand over Niall. Laying a hand on his brother's shoulder, he said, "Listen, baby brother. We men are an accursed lot. Sometimes when a female comes along to addle our brain, we lose all good sense and reason. The girl's a beauty, I'll admit—"

Niall interrupted, throwing his brother's hand off angrily. "I'm not your baby brother anymore, Cormac. I'm a man grown. Old enough to plan my own life and make my own mistakes, if need be."

"A marriage with no consummation is not valid in anyone's eyes," Eamon interjected calmly. "All you have to do is go explain the situation to Father Brendan, and he'll see to an annulment. Then the thing will be done. Your little wildcat can go find her rebel lover and wreak what havoc she may."

Niall's eyes were dark. "The consummation of our marriage is no one's business, especially not a meddling old priest."

"Bloody hell," Cormac said with an exasperated click of his tongue.

Eamon looked confused for a moment, then realization dawned on his face. "You *have* bedded the wench."

Niall was silent.

Eamon added an expletive to match his older brother's.

Cormac had begun pacing the room. "Don't tell me you think you're in love with this girl, Niall. Surely you can't believe she loves you, after everything that's happened. You can't be that much of a bloody fool."

Niall looked up at his brother. "I seem to remember calling you something very similar when you fell in love with Claire, in spite of the fact that her brother had killed our father."

That left his oldest brother silent, Niall noted with satisfaction, but Eamon had not given up.

"Do you intend to put guards around Riordan Hall in case her rebel friends decide to visit again and cut all our throats? Think of little Ultan and Claire expecting another baby any time now."

Niall felt a twinge of conscience. It was true that by bringing Catriona home, he was involving his entire family in a problem that was not their concern. But before he could reply to Eamon, Cormac spoke.

"Eamon, you've yet to discover that sometimes love turns men into fools. And there's not a bloody thing anyone short of God can do about it."

"I'm just saying that having her here puts us all at risk," Eamon argued. "And for what? A treacherous rebel who—"

Cormac held up a hand. "As long as Catriona O'Malley is peacefully seeking refuge in this household, she is welcome. Personally, I won't be likely to trust a single word coming from her lovely rebel mouth, but that will be Niall's problem, not ours. She's his wife, until he decides to remedy that unfortunate state of affairs."

A slight rustling sound made all three men turn their heads toward the doorway, where Catriona was standing. Even from across the room, Niall could see that her jaw was set, her eyes dry. "Your manservant told me that you were ready to go in to supper," she said with brittle dignity.

Niall winced. He didn't know how much of their conversation she had heard, but she must have heard Cormac's last remark. If she had suspected from the initial greeting that she was not exactly welcome at Riordan Hall, she surely must be convinced of it now.

He jumped up from the bench and walked over to her, extending his arm. "Aye, 'tis past time, and I can assure you that nothing you ate in London will rival Molly's pot pie."

She hesitated a moment, then said, "For seven years every bite I ate on English soil was tainted. I would have exchanged the most sumptuous court meal for a diet of plain boiled cabbage, if I could have been back home."

Then without taking Niall's proffered arm, she turned and walked down the corridor toward the dining room.

Catriona was determined not to let the icy welcome she had received break her spirit. After she was taken to England, she'd had a lot of practice being among strangers who were not particularly happy to have her in their midst. And she'd had a lot of practice never letting any of them see her pain.

There had been moments—back at the inn in Dublin—when she'd hoped for a happier stay at Riordan Hall. She'd even allowed herself to imagine that she and Niall might overcome the events in London and explore the possibility of being together as a true couple. Certainly the magic they had found together in that small bed must have some meaning.

Yet since they'd reached his home, Niall had seemed almost as cold as his brothers. He had left her almost immediately to join Cormac and Eamon in a conference that, from the little she had heard when she arrived at the library doorway before supper, was mostly a discussion on how they could best be rid of her.

The evening meal had been awkward and full of long silences. Except for Niall's brothers, no other Riordan kin joined them at the gigantic dining table. Cormac's wife, Claire, was also gone. He'd explained that she was away on one last visit to her family before her condition prevented further travel, but Catriona suspected that her absence might be another sign of the displeasure of the household over the arrival of Niall's unwanted bride.

Niall's boasts about his cook's pot pie had been justified, but Catriona found it difficult to eat more than a few bites. As soon as she felt that she'd spent a decent amount of time at the table, she rose and excused herself, pleading fatigue from the long journey.

Niall stood along with her. "I'll be up shortly to be sure you have everything you need," he said.

His words did not indicate whether he planned to be sharing her bedroom. In her current humor, she was not sure that she wanted him there. "I'm sure I'll be fine," she answered coolly.

She was certain that it was Niall's bedchamber that she'd been shown to before dinner. She'd found the saddlebags that contained her few belongings already there. At some point she'd have to figure out how to get some clothes, since she'd been in the same travel-stained riding dress since leaving London.

Bella had promised to try to send a trunk with the belongings she could collect from Whitehall and Wolverton House, but Catriona had no idea how long that would take. As she took off the dirty dress, she wondered if she dared ask Cormac to lend her one of his wife's frocks.

Her dinner with the three Riordan men had made her curious about this paragon of a woman whom Niall spoke of with such reverence. How had she felt when she had first come to this all-male household? Had her reception been warmer than Catriona's?

She held her dress to her nose and sniffed in disgust. If they weren't inclined to lend her one of Claire's dresses, she swore she'd take something of Niall's tomorrow from the big chest in the corner of the room. She'd sooner wear hose and a male tunic than spend another day in this filthy garment.

A bath would be nice, she thought with sudden longing. During her childhood at the O'Malley estate, she'd been used to bathing regularly in the stream, even during the coldest months. In England she'd developed the habit of regular indoor bathing, much to the amusement of many of her friends. Now she'd not been able to take a true bath since her imprisonment in the Tower.

There was a knock on the door; then it opened and Niall entered the room. He stopped when he saw her standing in her shift and petticoats. "Er—I came to see if you needed anything," he said.

She was irritated that he had essentially abandoned her at their arrival, and she had intended to be cool and indifferent, but there was something about being together in a room with him half-dressed that brought back some of the sense of intimacy they'd achieved the other evening in the inn. Unwillingly, she found that her breathing had heightened.

"You ate little at supper," he said. "Are you sure you are quite well? Can I bring you anything?"

She hesitated a moment, then asked, "Would it be possible . . . is there such a thing as a bath basin available?"

Niall looked surprised at the request, but he said, "Of course. My father always said that a clean body stayed healthier. Odd idea, but we grew up that way."

She gave a sigh of relief. "I would ever so much appreciate a wash," she said.

Niall grinned. "And were you needing someone to do the washing?"

She laughed. Now that she was alone with him again, away from the dour looks of his brothers, she found it hard to sustain her anger. "Nay, I think I can handle the washing myself. I just need the water and"—she glanced over to the bench where she had thrown her dress in disgust—"and tomorrow I may need something to cover myself, for I refuse to put that on again until it's had a good airing."

"Of course, forgive me for not thinking of it. I'll ask Cormac about getting you something of Claire's until we can have some clothes made for you."

Before she could stop herself, she asked, "Will I be here long enough for that?"

He frowned. "What do you mean?"

Suddenly self-conscious about standing in front of him half-naked, she went over to the bed and pulled a blanket around herself. "I believe your brothers, at least, are hoping that I somehow disappear."

Niall didn't deny her charge. " 'Tis none of their business. I'm the one who married you, remember?"

"Aye, and I also remember that you were forced to do so by the queen. We're not in England anymore. I doubt Elizabeth cares what we do from here on. You could simply let me go."

"Is that what you want?"

She waited a long moment before answering. The truth was, she was no longer sure what she wanted. "What I want is a bath," she said finally with a tired smile.

Niall seemed willing to let the more serious topic drop. She was sure that he was as tired as she. More so, since he was recovering from his wound. "A bath you shall have, milady," he said lightly. "I'll have some hot water brought up to you directly."

As he turned to leave she said, "Wait, are you coming back? That is, I wondered"—she flushed—"this is your room, is it not?"

"Aye, but I can sleep with Eamon."

"Oh."

He started toward the door, then hesitated. "Or I could stay here. That is, if it would make you more comfortable not to be alone in a new place."

She had been alone in dozens of new places over the past seven years, but she found herself saying, "I'd like you to stay."

A spark smoldered in his eyes, but it was quickly banked. "Fine. I'll send up the water and give you time to bathe, then I'll be back." He cast her a final look that made a pulse beat at the side of her throat. She stood without moving while he left the room and closed the door behind him.

Sweet St. Anne, she said to herself. What is wrong with me? I'm with people who distrust me, in a house where I'm not welcome, in a marriage that was neither sought nor desired. I have no idea what has happened to my best friend. I know nothing about my future—where I will go or what I will become. And all I can think about is that tonight once again I will lie in Niall Riordan's arms.

• • •

Niall paced one final time across the library, then headed up the stairs to his room. He probably hadn't given her enough time to finish her bath, but the mere thought of her wet and naked had him so aroused that he found the waiting intolerable.

But if the thought of it was disturbing, the reality was even more so. She made no move to cover herself as he opened the door. He felt his loins tighten at the sight of her seated in the small basin. Her breasts were wet and gleaming in the lamplight. She'd washed her hair, which hung in dripping ringlets around her shoulders.

She gave a slightly embarrassed smile. "I've tarried," she said, "I'm sorry. It felt so good to be clean again."

"Nay, don't apologize. Take as long as you wish. Would you like me to leave?"

She shook her head. He closed the door behind him and started walking toward her. "Do you mind that I'm looking at you?" He wondered if he'd be able to take his eyes off her if she answered in the affirmative.

"As I recall, you've seen this before. Or did I dream that night?"

He reached the side of the basin and looked down at her. "If 'twas a dream, then I shared it with you."

They exchanged tentative smiles. Somehow it seemed as if everything outside of these four walls was forgotten—their past history, his brothers' misgivings, even the fact that her former lover had tried to kill him. None of it mattered, at least not to him, but he needed to be sure that she felt the same.

"I fear my brothers were not as welcoming as they could have been," he said.

Her smile faded. "I can't blame them. They have no reason to trust me." She drew her knees up against her chest and huddled over them, covering most of herself from his view. Instantly he regretted bringing up the subject. He should have followed his first instincts and simply taken her in his arms.

"It matters not whether they trust you. You're my wife."

She looked up at him. There were beads of moisture on the tips of her lashes and he couldn't tell if they'd come from the bath or tears. "But we're not truly wed, are we? I was forced on you. And now I'm being forced on your family. They're suspicious and resentful, and it's only natural. What do they know of me? What do *you* know of me?"

At that, he waited no longer. He reached down and picked her out of the water, soaking his own clothes in the process. Then he marched with her over to his bed. When he had laid her on it, he stood back and began to strip his clothing. She turned her face away until he said, "Cat, look at me." When she slowly turned back toward him, he said firmly, "To answer your question, aye, you are truly my wife. We did not come together in the way we both may have imagined for our marriage bed, but we are fair and truly wed by law and by God."

Now he was as naked as she. He lifted her with his good arm to pull back the bedcovers, then placed her back on the bed and slid in next to her. "We are wed, Cat, and I intend to spend the rest of this long night reminding you of the fact."

Her anxious expression began to change to one of surprised pleasure. "All night?" she asked, her voice suddenly low and sensual.

He grinned. "Until you tire of me."

She drew her full lower lip slowly through her teeth. "Aren't you weary after the journey?"

"I was until I walked into this room and saw you in that tub."

"And that"—now she returned his smile—"that woke you up?"

"Aye."

"I'm still wet," she protested as he began to move over her.

Her skin was soft and slightly damp. "Aye," he said. Then he placed his hand over the tight wet curls between her legs and teased her with his fingers.

She was wet both outside and inside her feminine folds. In just seconds he could see the telltale flush to her skin as she closed her eyes and moaned in pleasure. "Ah, my passionate Cat," he whispered. "Your mind may question it, but your body knows that we are man and wife."

She opened her eyes and drew him down for a kiss. "I never knew it was possible to feel such things," she whispered.

"Sweetheart, we've barely begun." He took her hand and moved it to his aroused body. "You can tease me, too, if you like," he said, showing her how to please him.

For a few moments she seemed to forget about herself as she curiously learned the feel of him, but before long Niall could no longer endure the sweet exploration. He pinned her back on the bed and began to kiss her mouth. She accepted his kisses and returned them. Her legs fell gently open, and the movements of her hips told him that she was as eager as he for a more complete union.

He entered her gently, still afraid of hurting her, but she grasped his hips and urged him more fully into her. Soon he forgot all need for caution as he drove into her again and again. Finally he felt her stiffen and cry out just as he reached his own climax and came pouring into her.

It was several moments before he could move. He feared that his weight might be too much for her, but he didn't have the strength to roll away. Their skin seemed welded together.

"Now there's a proper welcome to Riordan Hall," he said finally.

He could feel her low chuckle against his chest. "Aye," she agreed.

"I'm going to flatten you," he said. "I'll move."

But her arms came around him and held him in place with surprising strength. "I like the feel of you on me."

He lay still for several more moments, then he slowly pushed himself to one side. The minute they were separated, he felt a strange sense of loss. Immediately he pulled her back and snuggled her in his arms. "That's better," he said, resting his chin against her soft hair.

"Mmm," she murmured.

His body floated in a deeply satisfied lethargy, but even in the midst of his satisfaction he felt a slight misgiving. He'd wanted to ask her more about the rebel Brosnihan, the man she'd called her "best friend," but the moment had never seemed right. He wished he could forget he'd ever heard of the man. Catriona may have loved her rebel, he told himself, but she had not given herself to him. That part of her she had shared only with Niall.

He lifted his head to give her a soft kiss. Her eyes were closed, though she gave a dreamy smile. "Do you want to sleep?" he whispered.

She opened her eyes. "You said we've only begun."

He laughed. "Aye, *a stór*, but your beautiful eyes refuse to stay open. There's no hurry. We'll have many long nights to experience all the pleasures of our bodies. Go ahead and sleep."

"Will you be here with me?"

"Short of a fire, nothing will get me from this bed tonight. And, at that, it would have to be a very big fire," he added with a grin.

"I'm glad." She snuggled into the crook of his shoulder. "Let's sleep for a spell, then. Later we can, you know . . . when we wake up . . ."

Her eyelids fluttered closed and her breathing became even. As Niall watched her for several long moments, his chest tightened with some kind of raw feeling that he couldn't remember ever experiencing. It wasn't entirely pleasant. It was at once warm and wonderful, but also frightening. For the first time since he was a boy, tears welled into his throat.

Was this what it was to love? Was this the thing his father had felt three times . . . and lost three times? All at once Niall understood something of the sadness that had always seemed a part of Ultan Riordan.

He looked down again at Catriona, sleeping peacefully in his arms. Was the happiness of love worth the devastation of losing that love? His father had lived many years alone, and Niall had always thought Ultan Riordan had decided that the answer to that question was no. Now, unexpectedly, it seemed that Niall was about to find out the answer for himself. For whether he willed it or not, he had fallen in love with his wife.

Alger Pimsley's face had turned the same puce color of his new-fashioned waistcoat. "Do you mean to tell me that you simply let them go?" he asked the two men who stood scraping their feet on the floor in front of him.

"Yer Lordship, no one told us we was ter follow them clear out of the country. By the time we reached the coast, they'd already made off in a boat to Dublin."

Pimsley closed his eyes and took a deep, calming breath. "Which means by now they're safely ensconced in Riordan Hall, and we'll have the entire Riordan clan to deal with in any attempt against them."

"I reckon," said the older of the two men, looking pleased to be able to agree with his superior.

Pimsley opened his eyes. "Lord Wolverton wanted this matter settled quickly and without scandal. He wanted it to look like a simple robbery, which is why he sent your group of men to do the job."

"I reckon," the man agreed again, his expression growing less certain.

"If they're at Riordan Hall, we'll have to change the whole plan." Pimsley's voice was calm, but his hands were shaking. "Do you know how it makes Lord Wolverton feel when his plans are thwarted?"

This time the man made no answer. His companion looked frightened.

"It makes him angry," Pimsley continued in the same tone. He looked around the antechamber as if searching for something he could throw.

Finally the hired man spoke again. "I could take the boys over to that Riordan place and do 'em in there, if ye like. 'Twas just that no one told us to follow them across the water."

Pimsley appeared to be considering the offer. "How long would that take?" he asked.

"I'd have to get the boys together again. When we got back to London, most of them took off fer a visit to the stews." The man hitched his pants. "A man gets to itchin' after a trip, don't ye know?"

Pimsley regarded the two characters with a look of utter distaste. "On second thought, I believe Lord Wolverton would be loathe to trust you gentlemen a second time. If we're to take on the Riordans, I fear the approach will require a bit more finesse."

"We woulda slit their throats purty as you please if we'd only caught the buggers," the man defended himself.

Pimsley's eyes narrowed to black slits. "I'm sure you would have, Timlock, but the fact is you didn't catch them, and therefore I would suggest both you and your friend here take yourselves as far away from London as possible before Lord Wolverton finds out what miserable weasels you are and decides to cut your heads off."

The eyes of Timlock's companion bugged out of his face. "Let's get outta here, Barty!" he whispered frantically.

Timlock looked as if he wanted to make one more attempt to defend himself, but as his friend continued tugging urgently at his sleeve, he gave up.

Pimsley watched as both men scrambled out of the

room. Then he picked up an ornately sculpted gold bell from his desk and rang it. Within moments a page appeared and bowed in front of him.

Pimsley sat with his elbows on his desk, tapping together the tips of all ten fingers. "I need you to go to Wolverton House and find out when Lord Wolverton is free to see me," he told the boy.

"Very good, milord. Shall I relay a message regarding the subject of the meeting?"

Pimsley stopped tapping and brushed an imaginary speck off the silk of his ballooned sleeve. "Aye, it may be good to prepare him before he sees me. You may tell him that it appears it has become necessary for us to go to Ireland."

Thirteen

Life at Riordan Hall was far from perfect. Catriona had the feeling that not only Niall's brothers, but all the other Riordan kin who lived around the estate and the entire staff of servants (some of whom were distant kin, as well, she learned) were wary of the young woman who had so disrupted their young kinman's life.

Niall couldn't seem to convince them that his marriage was no longer an imposition, even though it should have been obvious to everyone that the newlyweds could hardly wait each night to leave the dining hall and retire together to Niall's roomy bedchamber. It was certainly known that in the fortnight since the couple had arrived at Riordan Hall, they hadn't appeared for the morning meal once and often were not seen emerging from the bedroom until almost midday.

Yet the suspicious glances and the whispers continued. Niall had urged her to pay no attention. "The Riordans are a stubborn lot," he told her. "But they'll come 'round in time."

So Catriona had tried to ignore the chilly atmosphere and concentrate on the huge and incredible thing that had

happened to her. She was in love. With each passing day
and each erotic night, she became more convinced.

She finally understood why she had never been able to
respond to Bobby in the way he had so obviously wanted.
She loved Bobby, but she hadn't been *in love* with him.
Not in this giddy, exhilarating, surprising way. It seemed
as if she and Niall couldn't get enough of each other. When
he rode off with his brothers to deal with some matter on
another part of the Riordan lands, she thought of nothing
else until he was with her again. It was exhausting, in a
way. Yet wonderful.

Still, she wondered if she shouldn't be doing something
more to make herself part of the household. Cormac's wife
was still away visiting her family. Though Catriona would
never presume to take over her role as mistress of the
household, she decided that it might be considered proper
for her to visit the kitchens and see that things were proceeding smoothly during Claire's absence.

Since her arrival, Catriona had barely seen Molly, the
Riordan cook, but she had been introduced to the round little woman, and Catriona decided that if anyone on the estate would warm to her, Molly would seem to be a good
candidate.

Niall and Catriona had come downstairs late, as usual,
and Niall had scrounged some bread and cheese for a late
breakfast. Then he and his brothers had ridden out before
the noon meal. Catriona was not the least bit hungry, so she
decided to seek out Molly and tell her not to worry about
setting food in the dining hall until the men returned in the
evening.

She found the cook kneading a ball of dough. Her
plump arms were covered with flour up to her elbows and
a fine mist of white covered the front of her hair, adding to
the natural gray that was already showing.

The cook looked up in surprise as Catriona entered.
"Good morrow, milady," she said, glancing at her hands

with some consternation. "Forgive me for not . . . I'm just in the middle here."

Catriona rushed to reassure her. "Please continue, Molly. I've not come to interrupt your labors. I just thought I'd tell you that the men have ridden out, so there's no need for dinner this midday."

"Aye," Molly said. "I packed some food afore they left. I'd not let them go without it. They need their sustenance. They're big lads."

Catriona smiled. "Aye, that they are."

Molly had not resumed her kneading. She appeared to be waiting for Catriona to speak.

"I, ah, I also thought I'd ask you if there's anything you need," Catriona said after a moment. "Anything that needs discussing, since the Lady Riordan is not at home."

"No, mum. The Lady Claire always plans well for her absences. She's a wonder, she is."

Catriona had heard so much about the virtues of his brother's wife from Niall that she had begun to feel a slight resentment. She hoped that Molly couldn't see through her falsehood when she said, "I'm looking forward to meeting her."

"Everyone loves her," Molly said firmly with a meaningful glance at Catriona. Then she finally began punching her dough.

Catriona watched her for a moment, then impulsively said, "The truth is, Molly, I'd like to be able to help. I mean, how will people get to know me and accept me here if there's nothing for me to do?"

Molly looked over at her, a skeptical expression on her face. "What do you mean by help?" she asked.

Catriona shrugged. "I'll do anything. Cooking, gardening, airing the linens. Whatever needs doing."

She could see Molly glancing sideways at her attire. Niall had brought her a couple of Claire's dresses to wear until the village seamstress could finish some new ones. Today she was dressed in a pink organdy that, even Catriona could recognize, was more fit for the parlor than the kitchen.

"I don't have my own clothes," she explained. "But I could use an apron . . . or . . . I'll just be careful. Please, I'd really like to help."

Molly stopped kneading and met Catriona's gaze. After a moment she smiled, then slapped the ball of dough into the bowl and extricated her fingers. Ignoring the dough clinging to her hands, she turned around and pulled a rough linen overdress off a peg on the wall behind her and held it out to Catriona. "This should cover that pretty dress. Do ye know how to punch bread?"

At Catriona's nod, she pointed to the end of the table where two other bowls sat covered by towels. "The rye should be about ready," she said. "Ye can start in on that."

Catriona took the dress and tied it around herself, feeling a little hum of happiness. The cook's acceptance might be conditional, but it was a start. And now she'd have something worthwhile to keep her occupied until she could see Niall again.

She walked over to the bowls and peeked under the covers. One ball of dough was white, the other brown. She re-covered the white and picked up the brown.

"The white is for pastries," Molly told her. "I'd thought to make some raisin honey tarts. They're Master Niall's favorites. If ye like, after ye finish the bread, ye can roll them out fer me." This time Molly's smile was without reservation.

"I'd like that very much," Catriona answered. Then she plunged her hands happily into the sticky mass of dough.

Niall looked surprised when he entered the small kitchen building to find his wife chatting happily with Molly.

"What conspiracy are you two beautiful ladies brewing?" he teased, walking over to the fireplace grate and peering into the big kettle that Molly and Catriona were jointly stirring.

Molly giggled. "The only beauty here is yer wife, Master Niall, and the only lady as well."

"Molly's my new teacher," Catriona said brightly. "I'm learning about what it takes to feed a houseful of brutes like you and your brothers."

Niall cocked an eyebrow. "What tales have you been telling her, Molly?"

"No tales, Master Niall, just the truth. How every farmyard in Meath would be bare of pigs and every field bare of wheat if we'd of let you boys eat yer fill when ye was agrowin'."

"Ah, Molly." He leaned over to give the little cook a kiss on her sticky cheek. "You did love it, as I recall. Come now, if you're into truth-telling. You miss those days, don't you? You're a bit sorry that Claire came along to civilize us."

"The Lady Claire and age," Molly replied. "Thank the Lord for both, for I swear ye'd have eaten the house itself if yer father hadn't kept a strong hand."

Catriona was enjoying the exchange. She'd been fascinated all afternoon by Molly's stories of the three Riordan brothers as they grew to manhood. It gave her a whole new perspective on her new husband. She'd been robbed of those final growing-up years in her own household, but obviously the Riordans had had a happy childhood, though a rowdy one without the influence of a mother.

"It appears I'd best take my wife away from here before you have her convinced that she's wed a monster." Niall tried to make his expression serious, but there was a twinkle of humor in his eyes.

"Supper's nearly finished anyway," Molly said. "I thank ye fer yer help, milady."

"Your 'boys' may be grown, Molly, but 'tis still a formidable task to feed everyone," Catriona told her, removing the overdress Molly had given her. "I can come again on the morrow."

Molly looked a little uncertain. "I'd not want to burden ye—"

" 'Tis no burden," Catriona assured her quickly. "I'd like to come, if you'll have me."

Molly looked at Niall's face. He smiled and nodded.

"Very good, milady," she said. "Yer welcome in my kitchen whenever ye please."

Catriona's heart was light as Niall put an arm around her waist and they strolled out of the kitchen. "You sounded happy there with Molly," he said.

"Aye, she's a sweet woman."

"You wouldn't think she was quite so sweet if you could have seen how she slapped our hands when we tried to sneak tarts off the cooling rack."

Catriona laughed. "It's a wonder the poor woman survived through it all. But I did enjoy the afternoon. It was good to be doing something useful."

Niall leaned over to kiss her briefly. "I've been selfish these past few days, keeping you to myself. I should have spent more time introducing you to the rest of the household."

"I haven't minded that you wanted me for yourself," she said, accompanying the words with an arch smile.

He gave her a playful swat on the behind. "Don't start with me, minx, or I'll need to spirit you off to my room again before supper and we'll have the household buzzing."

"They already are, I fear. I'm not sure that most of them like the fact that I'm your wife. Your brothers have not yet softened."

"It just needs time, Cat. Don't get impatient. Molly likes you, I can tell. Once she begins to champion your cause, the rest will soften."

"I hope so."

The sun was beginning to sink in the west over the stable buildings, turning the landscape golden. "We have half an hour before dark," Niall said. "Would you like a quick ride?"

She didn't know if her words had made him feel guilty about her inactivity or if he was trying to distract them both so that they would forget about the big bed waiting for them back at the house. But either way, the idea of a ride across the hills in the twilight sounded heavenly.

With the sun rapidly descending, they hurried up the hill to the stables and hastily saddled their mounts. Niall's horse looked a bit disgruntled at being saddled once again after a full day's outing but made no protest as they headed out the stable door and up the path.

"This is called Scota's Hill," Niall explained, "after the ancient goddess. We used to joke that Scota was the only female ever to last at Riordan Hall."

"But then Claire came."

"Aye." He smiled at her. "And now we have you."

His words warmed her. After the afternoon with Molly, she was feeling that though it might take a while, she *could* become a part of this household. They had crested the hill and Catriona stopped for a moment to look at the rolling countryside stretching out in front of them. "You live in a beautiful part of the world, Niall," she said softly. It was not as beautiful as the wooded valleys of the Valley of Mor, she thought with the familiar pang, but it was Ireland. She was beginning to feel that this place could be the kind of home she'd yearned for all these long years.

"Shall we have a race?" Catriona asked, looking down the hill. It felt wonderful to be up on a horse again, though on the long trip from London, she'd sworn she wouldn't want to ride for a year.

"Nay, 'twould not be fair. Your mount is fresh. Cinnabar and I have already been out all day."

Catriona leaned over to pat the dappled mare Niall had chosen for her to ride. "Isn't it always the way, girl? Men will have any excuse not to be shown up by a woman."

Niall had reined in his horse next to her.

"If we ride over that smaller hill yonder, will we come—" she continued, but stopped speaking as Niall waved his hand as if to urge her to silence.

Puzzled, she tried to follow the direction of his gaze to see what he was looking at. In the gathering darkness all she could see were hills dotted here and there by clumps of bushes and stone shepherd shelters.

"What is it?" she asked in a low voice.

"The bushes are moving," he whispered back.

She looked down the hill and squinted, but she didn't see even branches moving, much less entire bushes.

"Are you sure?" she whispered.

"Wait here," he said tersely. Then he nudged his horse and started moving down the hill.

Catriona watched uneasily. They were home, on the vast Riordan estate. Surely they didn't need to worry about danger here. As Niall descended the hill, she became less certain. If there was someone lurking below in the dark, it was foolish of Niall to ride down alone. The farther away he rode, the more nervous she got. Finally she yelled, "Niall, wait!" and kicked her little mare into action. The horse plunged down the hill, but before they could go more than a few yards, Catriona reined up and watched in horror as the dark bushes did indeed spring to life. At least a half a dozen mounted men rode out from behind them and moved toward Niall.

All at once it was as if she were back in the Valley of Mor, watching as a tragedy unfolded below that she was helpless to avert. She opened her mouth and screamed.

Suddenly there were hoofbeats up the hill behind her. She turned in the saddle to see Cormac and Eamon and several other men crest the hill and start down. They thundered past her without a glance, heading toward Niall. Knowing that her entry into the melee would only cause more difficulty, she kept her mount still and watched helplessly as the rescuers neared the place where the intruders had surrounded Niall. Someone fired a pistol, and suddenly the invading riders turned and fled, leaving Niall reeling in his saddle, his horse stumbling.

The Riordan brothers and their men ignored the fleeing riders. They dismounted around Niall and caught him as he fell from his horse. Catriona started down the hill. By the time she reached them, Niall was lying on the ground. "Is he—?" she gasped.

Niall's head was in Cormac's lap. He turned to look up at her and said, "My brother's alive, no thanks to you and your colleagues."

"They wouldn't . . . I don't think 'twas—" She stopped. The truth was, though she didn't believe that Bobby would be a part of such behavior, she couldn't be that sure about the Clearys. By all accounts, they were desperate men. Desperate enough to attack an unarmed man in the darkness? She simply didn't know.

She dropped to her knees beside Niall. "I'm fine, Cormac," he was saying. "The blackguards hit me in the head, which as you know is the hardest part of me. Though I'd not like to think what may have happened if you hadn't come along."

Catriona took his hand, but he pulled it away.

"What were you doing out on the hill?" Niall asked his brother.

Cormac pointed to one of the men who had accompanied him. It was the stablemaster, Aidan Shaw. "Aidan saw you two ride out and, thank God, had the sense to come tell me."

"Yer brothers have worried that they never caught the ones who slit yer arm back in London, Master Niall," the stableman explained. "I'd orders to keep watch."

Niall looked chagrined. "I don't like to think that I need caretaking, but I reckon this time 'twas fortunate you all came along."

"Let's get him up, Eamon," Cormac said, ignoring Catriona, who was still kneeling beside Niall. Eamon reached around her and together the two brothers helped Niall to his feet. He swayed a moment, then stood straight.

"He shouldn't be moving so fast," she said. "We must be sure that he's not been hurt, that nothing is broken."

Eamon looked down at her. "I believe we can take care of our brother, milady."

Aidan Shaw was looking at Cinnabar. "The bastards have gone and broke the leg," he said, his voice taut.

Niall walked uncertainly over to his horse. The upper part of the right front leg was bloody with a deep gash. A cracked white bone glistened through the opening. In the twilight Niall's face looked like a hard mask.

"Give me your knife," he said to Cormac.

His brother shook his head. "Take my horse and go back to the house. We'll deal with this."

Niall rubbed his hand along Cinnabar's muzzle. "Nay. I'll do it."

Without another protest, Cormac pulled a long hunting knife from his belt and handed it to his brother. Niall looked up at the indigo blue of the twilight sky and took a deep breath. "Smooth trails, old friend," he said softly, then he grasped Cinnabar's mane and drew the knife swiftly along his throat. The big horse crashed instantly to the ground.

Blood covering the front of his tunic, Niall dropped Cormac's knife on the ground and turned his back on the dead animal.

"I'll take Niall back on my mount," Eamon said, steering his brother toward his stallion.

Niall said nothing as he mounted behind his brother. He still had not looked at Catriona.

"Go back to the house," Cormac told them. "We'll clean up here, and see if the brigands left any clues." He turned to Catriona. "I don't suppose you would tell us if you recognized any of them."

Catriona was taken aback by the question. "It was getting dark. I couldn't see," she said, then realized that the answer did nothing to make her sound less guilty.

Cormac nodded as if her reply had been what he expected. "You'd best ride on back to the house, as well," he said curtly. None of the men remaining offered to help her mount, so she pulled herself up on the little mare and started up the hill.

By the time Catriona reached the stables, Eamon and Niall were nowhere to be seen. A stable boy took her horse, and she made her way down to the main house. She'd expected to see the two brothers in the front parlor or perhaps in the dining room ready to eat, but they were in neither place. A quick look in Niall's bedchamber revealed that he was not there, either. She went back downstairs and found one of the servants who was setting the table for supper.

"Where are Master Niall and Master Eamon?" she asked the man.

He answered politely enough, but there was unmistaken hostility in his eyes. "They've taken Master Niall to the master suite, milady. To Lord Cormac's bed."

To bed? "Then he *is* hurt?"

"I wouldn't be able to tell ye, milady."

"But you say they've taken him to bed?"

"Aye, milady."

With a nod of thanks she left the man and rushed up the stairs to the north wing of the house where Cormac shared the big master suite with his wife. How badly had he been hurt? she wondered. And why hadn't they taken him to his own bed?

The bedchamber door was open. She walked to the doorway, then hesitated. Niall was lying on the big bed but appeared to be awake. Eamon sat on a high stool at his side.

She cleared her throat, then asked, "Are you hurt?"

Both men turned in her direction but neither spoke.

After a long awkward moment Niall said, "Nay."

"He fainted," Eamon corrected.

"I did no such thing."

"You would have been laid out flat on the flagstone in front of the door if I hadn't held on to you."

Niall looked at Catriona. "Eamon's a mollycoddle. He insisted I lie down. They clipped me across the forehead and it's made me a little dizzy. But 'tis nothing."

She took a few steps into the room and could see a red welt across his temple. As he spoke she searched his face for some sign that he did not hold the attack against her, as his brothers obviously did, but his expression was inscrutable.

"I believe you should listen to your brother," she said. "Rest for a while until you're sure you've come to no greater harm."

"He'll not leave this bed tonight," Eamon said. "I'll see to that."

"I could stay with him," she offered.

Eamon shook his head. " 'Tis not necessary. I intend to be here."

"I don't need anyone to sit with me," Niall protested.

His answer did not reject her offer specifically, but she had the feeling it was directed against her. His dark eyes held none of the warmth she had grown accustomed to seeing these past few days. Just this morning they had been laughing together in their bed, naked and intimate as people can only be when they have shared their bodies with each other. Now he was speaking to her as if she were a distant and unwanted neighbor who had come to make an offer of help.

The notion irritated her suddenly. "I'm his wife," she said firmly. "I should stay with him."

"I don't intend to be insulting, milady," Eamon told her, "but I'd not feel comfortable leaving you alone with him."

She looked at Niall, expecting him to refute the implication of his brother's words, but he remained silent.

Eyes stinging, she stepped back from the bed. "Very

well," she said stiffly. "If you need me, I'll be in our . . . I'll be in Niall's bedchamber." Then she turned and left the room.

The sky outside the bedroom window had finally begun to brighten. It was still barely dawn, but Catriona threw off her covers and rose from the bed. The night had seemed endless. If she'd slept at all, it had been fitful and brief. The events of the previous day had given her one of her headaches, and lying alone in Niall's bed would not help her get rid of it.

She'd often found that the best cure for the megrims was a walk in the fresh air. She doubted anyone would miss her at this time of day, so she quickly dressed and made her way downstairs and out the side door. Then she started climbing Scota's Hill. She cast a wistful glance at the stables as she passed. Would she and Niall ever go riding together again? she wondered. Their ill-fated ride the previous evening seemed to once again have spoiled the trust that had begun to grow between them.

With sudden resolution, she started walking more quickly up the hill. Perhaps if she went back to the scene of the attack, she would find something to help the Riordans discover the identity of the intruders.

It was obvious that his brothers thought the encounter had something to do with her. Niall most likely shared their opinion. And the truth was that she herself could not be sure that the attackers were not somehow connected to Bobby and the Clearys. Yet the idea seemed farfetched. She'd heard nothing from Bobby since his escape. If he were near, he would surely have contacted her.

At the top of the hill she paused. The sun was rising through a morning mist. Its light hadn't yet reached the lower part of the hill where the riders had come out of the bushes. She looked down at the foggy landscape. At least today none of the bushes appeared to be moving.

Slowly she moved down the hill, looking around on the

damp ground for any sign of the previous day's struggle, but everything looked normal. As the sunlight hit the top of the hill and began creeping toward her, she made her way from one clump of bushes to the next, peering intently. She wasn't sure what she expected to find, but something, somehow, had to serve as proof that Bobby had had nothing to do with Niall's attack.

Still there was nothing. She looked back up to the top of the hill. She'd already descended beyond the point where the riders had emerged yesterday, and she could see nothing the entire length of the hillside.

Giving up the quest with a sigh, she started walking back. The household would be waking up, and her absence would be noticed. If she hurried, she could arrive in time to help Molly with the morning meal. Somehow she had the feeling that the friendly cook would stand by her, even if the others were against her. She sped up her pace, her head bent toward the ground so that she could keep a sure footing over the rough terrain.

Suddenly her elbow was grabbed from behind, spinning her around.

"Don't cry out, scamp," said a voice.

It was Bobby. Catriona, her heart sinking, closed her eyes and let herself be pulled into his embrace.

Fourteen

"*Ah, Cat, 'tis* good to see ye," he said fervently. "I was sick with worry. When I saw ye for just that instant at that wretched palace, ye looked so pale and sad. I wasn't sure how I'd find ye after all that's passed."

"I've worried over you, too, Bobby," Catriona said, though she realized with a pang of guilt that her lifelong friend had been in her thoughts much less than he deserved these past few days.

Bobby took a step back and studied her. "Ye're looking none the worse for the ordeal. Are ye well?"

She ignored his question and asked, "Where have you come from, Bobby? Are you with the Clearys?" She feared she already knew the answer. There had been a number of attackers the previous evening. If Bobby had been responsible, he hadn't acted alone.

"Aye, with the Clearys and the other patriots, though there are fewer and fewer each day, it seems. Many seem to have lost faith in the cause of liberty."

She looked away from the intense look in his blue eyes. "Mayhap 'tis because it comes at too high a price."

He was silent a long moment, then said softly, "No price is too high to pay for freedom."

She turned her head to look at him. "Truly, Bobby? Is all this worth it? Just to stop a woman from claiming that she's queen of all of us? Is it worth dying for? Is it worth becoming a hunted animal who travels in the dark and attacks innocent victims?"

His eyes narrowed. "What's got into you, Cat? Did your stay in an English prison take away your heart and your soul?"

He looked away from her. She felt the sting of his words, but she wasn't sure how to answer.

When he looked back, his expression had hardened. "Or was it something else that took away your heart? Is that the way of things?"

She looked up the hill. The sun was almost full in the sky. People would be stirring, perhaps traveling this way. "We shouldn't stay here—" she began.

Bobby seized her shoulders and spun her to look at him. "Damnation, Cat, tell me! What is it that's changed you? Is it Riordan?"

This time she didn't avoid his gaze. "I wed him, Bobby," she said. Tears welled in her eyes.

Bobby's face softened, and he pulled her back into an embrace. "I heard, scamp," he murmured in a soothing tone. "But 'twas a forced marriage—no fault of yers. I've come to take ye from here. Ye'll never have to see him again."

Her tears came in earnest, and he stroked her hair. "Has he hurt ye, Cat?" He held her away to look into her eyes and asked more sharply, "Has he? I swear if he's hurt ye, I'll slit the bastard's throat."

Catriona pulled herself out of his arms and took a deep breath. "He's not hurt me, Bobby," she said. "Nor do I want you to make any further attempts to harm him. You'll have to tell your friends—"

His expression was puzzled. "What do you mean, further attempts?"

"Such as the attack last night. Were you there with the rest of them?"

He looked at her as if she had taken leave of her senses. "Cat, I have no idea what ye're spoutin' off about. I know nothing of any attack."

Catriona looked around her. "Last evening, on this very hill, Niall and I were riding when we were attacked by masked riders."

"And ye thought it was I?"

"Well, I . . ." She stumbled for the words. "Aye, after the attempt to free me at the inn, everyone just assumed—"

"What inn?"

She knew at once that his bewilderment was genuine. A wave of relief flooded through her. "You had nothing to do with either attack?"

He shook his head. "Nor do I know what in the devil yer talkin' about, Cat. What I do know is that ye seem mighty interested in protecting a turncoat rogue who is working for the bloody queen of England."

"He's not a turncoat, Bobby, and he's not working for the queen. He simply sees things differently than we do."

"And ye want to protect him."

"Aye."

"Why, Cat?" he asked very softly.

She lifted her chin. She'd hurt Bobby before, and each time it had been like a stab to her heart, but somehow she knew this would hurt more than anything she'd ever said in the past. "I love him, Bobby," she said.

He winced. She could see that he was struggling to keep his voice calm as he said, "Cat, ye've had a tough time. The prison and all. I should have come for ye afore this, but it was a devil's trick gettin' out of England this time. I can understand how ye might have looked to someone else for protection, especially if the bloody traitor was nice to ye. But I'm tellin' ye that 'tis over. Ye're comin' with me."

"To where, Bobby?" she asked. "To live in the woods?

To fight a losing battle against a queen who already appears ready to give us most of what we're asking? Why should we care who claims sovereignty over Ireland? Aren't we free to live the way we please? To build our homes and raise our families in peace?"

Cat had completely forgotten about guarding against being seen as they stood facing each other. Out of the corner of her eyes, she could see two village boys round the top of the hill and head down the east side. They glanced at the two people who were standing and arguing farther down the hill, but they didn't seem unduly interested and continued on their path without stopping.

"You can't stay here," Catriona said urgently.

Bobby's expression had changed from sympathetic to angry. "Why? Because yer *husband* might come looking for ye? Are ye worried he might suffer some hurt if he gets within reach of my dirk?"

"I fear someone is ahead of you on that score," she snapped. "He lies in bed recovering from the two wounds he's received since we were wed." She paused. In her concern to make her case to Bobby, she'd momentarily forgotten what he'd said earlier. "We've been attacked, Bobby. Twice. If you were not responsible, then who was?"

Bobby gave a sullen shrug, obviously still angry. "Who knows what enemies he may have?"

"Could the Clearys have been behind the assaults without your knowledge?"

"There are no Clearys within fifty leagues of this place. And, if truth be told, Cat, the Clearys are not as united as once they were."

He appeared reluctant to make the admission, but Catriona heard it with relief. Maybe the attacks had had nothing to do with her after all. Perhaps, as Bobby had said, they had been made by some enemy of the Riordans.

"I came alone to fetch ye," Bobby added. "It never occurred to me that I would need help convincing ye to come. I didn't think ye'd ever need reminding about what they did to yer father at the Valley of Mor. Maybe I was wrong."

Catriona closed her eyes briefly. Then, remembering once again where they were, she yanked on his arm and pulled him behind a large clump of bushes. When they were safely out of sight of the top of the hill, she turned to him and said, "I'll never need reminding of that, Bobby Brosnihan, as you well know. But I need time to think."

"Think about what, Cat? Either you are ready to stand up against the English or not."

" 'Tis not that simple."

"Aye, 'tis exactly that simple. What's not simple is the spell this Riordan seems to have put on ye. Surely ye don't think he loves ye, Cat? After everything ye did to him? And you a rebel without a fortune or a name? If he's being nice to ye, 'tis for the same reason men have been nice to women since the beginning of time."

She was silent.

"Ye've not given yerself to him, have ye, Cat?" There was a note of desperation in Bobby's voice. When she didn't answer, he turned away and muttered, "Christ almighty."

She realized that from Bobby's perspective, everything that she and Niall had experienced over the past two weeks could have a different interpretation. Was she herself sure of what it had all meant? She knew her own feelings, but did she really know Niall's? He'd seemed ready enough to turn against her last night.

She gave a deep sigh. Perhaps her vision of a life with a loving husband at Riordan Hall had been a fool's illusion. Perhaps Bobby was right and her place was with him. But she couldn't leave without letting the Riordans know that the intruders had not been part of the outlaw rebel group. They needed to know that they should be looking elsewhere for the culprits.

"I need time, Bobby," she said again.

"Time for what?" He spat out the words.

She put a hand on his arm. "It may be hard for you to understand, but I must go back."

"Shall I wash my hands of ye, then, Cat? Shall I go away and never see ye again?"

The misery in his expression as he looked at her gave her heart a wrench. This was Bobby, her lifelong friend, the only one who had stood by her in good times and bad. "Nay, I don't want you to wash your hands of me," she said finally. "I have to go back, but only to get some things straight. Then I'll go away with you."

There was a blaze of hope in his eyes. "That's me girl," he said. "We'll go find the Clearys, or if they've given up the fight, we'll find other brave men who will fight to the death before they let our country be ruled by the bloody bastards who killed your father."

"Aye," she agreed wearily.

He seized her hands and squeezed them. "I knew ye were still a true Irish," he said. "How long will these things take? When shall I come for ye?"

She thought for a moment. "Tomorrow at dawn."

"Here?"

She looked around at the windswept hill. Riordan land. She didn't belong here. "Aye," she said. "I'll meet you here this time tomorrow."

"Catriona can't control what her former friends do," Niall told his brothers with a scowl. He was sitting up in Cormac's bed, feeling mostly back to normal except for a slight headache, but Cormac had ordered that he was to spend the day resting, and they'd refused to bring him his clothes.

"Niall, you're deluding yourself," his older brother answered. "If they were 'former friends,' they wouldn't have come for her, would they?"

"Cormac's right," Eamon added. "You may think you

can trust the lass, but I believe the last time you had such trust, you ended up in the Tower."

"That was different. It was before—" He paused. How could he explain to his brothers the closeness he had experienced with Catriona over these past few days? It was a feeling so rare and so new that he could hardly explain it to himself. It wasn't just their long nights together, though that intimacy had made him feel nearer than he had ever felt to anyone. But over these past few days he and Catriona had revealed more to each other than their bodies. Eamon was right; he had been fooled by her in London, but that time now seemed worlds ago.

Immediately after the attack the previous day, a few lingering doubts had surfaced, but he'd had the night to think about it, and he would stake his life that Catriona held no responsibility in the incident.

"She knew nothing of this attack," he said firmly.

Cormac shook his head. "Love," he snorted. Eamon nodded a grave agreement. "I can see I'm wasting my words trying to convince you," Cormac continued. "But will you promise me to be on your guard? You've been wounded twice since you linked up with this girl. The third time they just might finish the job. And while I may think you're a stubborn fool, you're my brother, and I'd like to have you around to play with my grandchildren."

Niall welcomed the sudden opportunity to change the subject. "Speaking of children, does that wife of yours ever intend to come home and let me see my little nephew?" Cormac's son, Ultan, now two years old, had been named for their father and was a favorite of both his uncles. "If she doesn't come soon, the next Riordan might be born at her father's house. 'Tisn't fitting for a Riordan to be born in the house of an O'Donnell."

"It worked well enough the first time," Cormac reminded him with a smile.

"Aye, it did." He smiled back, relieved to have turned his brother's thoughts to something other than Catriona.

But his relief was short-lived. "So do I get that promise?" Cormac asked.

"What promise?"

"That you will be on guard, and that you will not trust that lovely and possibly treacherous new wife of yours."

"I have nothing to fear from Catriona. I'd stake my life on it."

"You may be doing just that," Cormac replied angrily, giving a punch to a pillow he'd been tossing in the air. "Come along, Eamon," he told his brother. "Let's get out of here and let this lovesick fool rest."

Catriona walked slowly back down the hill to Riordan Hall. She veered to give a wide path around the kitchen buildings, not wanting to run into Molly. By now everyone on the estate undoubtedly knew of the second attack on their beloved Master Niall. She couldn't really blame them if they looked on her with suspicion. She was an outsider who had been responsible for Niall's imprisonment.

Would even Niall believe her after this second attack? And what would he say when she told him that Bobby was here on the estate, that she had met with him that very morning?

There was no one in the big front hall when she entered the house, and she was relieved that the house seemed almost empty as she made her way up to the north wing to the master bedroom suite. As expected, she found that Niall was still in Cormac's bedroom. He was sitting up in bed, naked, arms crossed, with a scowl on his face. He looked up in surprise as she opened the door and entered the room.

"How are you feeling?" she asked.

"The buggers have stolen my clothes," he grumbled.

His comment was not at all what she'd expected, and she laughed in spite of herself. "Your brothers? I suspect they had their reasons," she said.

"They're a couple of mollycoddles."

She walked over to the bed and looked at the scrape on his head. It looked less sinister than it had the previous evening. "You do look better," she admitted. She put her hand gently on the welt.

"I'm fine," Niall said, but he winced and brushed her hand away.

"I'm sorry about—" She paused, searching for the words. "I can understand why you might be thinking that I've caused you trouble. You've been wounded twice—"

He interrupted. "Wounds will cure. I've a tough hide. 'Tis the loss of Cinnabar that hurts the most."

"Aye. He was a fine mount."

"He was a good friend." Niall's lips tightened, but after a moment he said in a lighter voice. "No doubt he's now enjoying his just reward, galloping through the Elysian fields."

She smiled. "No doubt," she agreed.

He made a move to get up from the bed, then grimaced and put a hand to his head.

Catriona looked at him with concern. "Your brothers are right, Niall. Another day in bed would do no harm." She had to tell him about her visit with Bobby, but first she wanted to be sure that he was well enough for the discussion.

She stood at the edge of the bed looking down at him, and suddenly there was a look in his eyes that she recognized from their past fortnight together. It made a hollow at the pit of her stomach.

"Aye," he said slowly after a moment. He seized her hand. "A day in bed might not be such a bad notion after all."

She flushed and tried to pull her hand away, but he held her firmly. "Nay, 'tis not a good idea," she protested. "You aren't recovered—"

He yanked gently on her hand, making her sit down on the bed beside him. Then he let go and began to trail his fingers up and down her arm. "Aye, my sweet nurse, I'm ill with fever," he teased. "Verily, I'm burning. Can you feel it?" He took her hand again and drew it gently over his stiffened penis.

Catriona's mouth had gone dry. "But we can't—" She looked around the room. "We're in your brother's bed-chamber . . . and . . . and you've been wounded and . . ."

Suddenly he lifted her up and drew her across his lap. "Have you come to cure me or to talk me to death?" he murmured against her mouth as he began kissing her.

"Niall, there's something I need to tell—"

"And still she talks," he said with a sigh. "I see I'm going to have to be more convincing." Then he flipped her over onto her back and lifted himself over her. Looking down with mock surprise, he added, "Why, you're still dressed, sweetheart. We can't have that."

He began nuzzling her neck and teasing her with little licks of his tongue as he proceeded to rid her of every piece of clothing. By the time he had flung her brief shift to the floor, she was flushed and could feel the telltale moisture between her legs. All thoughts of Bobby and the attack and everything beyond the boundaries of Cormac's huge bed left her.

He lay propped on his elbow at her side and traced a path from her chin to her stomach and back. "I've not yet broken fast today, my beauty, so beware, for I swear you are beautiful enough to devour."

"You should eat something." She started to sit up in protest, but he pushed her down again.

"Hush," he said. "All I want is you." Then for a moment it seemed as if he *would* devour her as he took her mouth in a long, liquid kiss that went on and on until Catriona felt it all the way to the tips of her fingers. She moaned approval. Niall finally pulled away and smiled down at her.

"That was the first course," he said, his voice a little altered. "But I've hunger still." Then he moved to her breasts. First he teased each of her heightened nipples with the tip of his tongue, swirling around them until they ached for stronger pressure, which he finally gave her, suckling first one breast, then the other. The pull was firm, yet not painful, and Catriona writhed with pleasure as the sensations streaked through her midsection and pooled in her loins. She reached a hand down to her own woman's place as if to capture the vibrations there and keep from exploding.

Just when she thought she could bear it no longer, Niall left her breasts with a final teasing kiss to each rosy peak and said, "Now for the main course."

He slid along her body and before she even knew what he was intending, he had opened her with his thumbs and was lapping the swollen nub between her legs. He eased her legs apart to gain fuller access, then gently sucked. Catriona gasped at the intensity of the feeling.

He stopped for a moment and lifted his head. His dark eyes were hooded and glazed. "Is this all right, sweetheart?" he asked.

She nodded, unable to speak, and he lowered his head to continue his erotic laving. In what seemed like seconds the explosion came, wracking her lower body with waves of feeling. Niall wiped his mouth with his hand and looked up with his crooked grin. "I reckon a man could not ask for a better way to break the fast," he said.

Catriona was still too stunned to be able to muster a smile, but she held out her arms to welcome him as he moved back up and kissed her. Pressed between their bodies, his erection felt enormous. In spite of the climax she'd just had, she found herself wanting to feel it within her. She arched slightly and reached her hand down to enfold him.

With a pleased smile, he helped her guide him inside. When they were joined, an uncontrollable urge to cry came over her. He felt so right there. She could forget everything else in the world if she could just stay here like this. She loved this man, she realized with a sudden intensity. She opened her mouth to tell him so, but just then he began to thrust, and his movement took away her words. She joined him in the age-old rhythm, working faster and harder until they each stiffened and shuddered with completion.

Their bodies were damp from the exertion. Niall lifted his head and gave a weak smile. "Lord, my Cat has turned into a lioness."

She smiled back at him. "I believe it was the breakfast that did it."

"Aye, they do say that a good breakfast prepares one for what's to come."

She was too exhausted to laugh. Her cheeks were still wet from the tears she'd shed, and, as the damp skin of her body cooled, she was remembering what she had wanted to tell him in the heat of their lovemaking. She could no longer deny it. She was in love with him. This was why she'd felt so sad about the thought of going away with Bobby. This was why she could never leave Riordan Hall, no matter how much Niall's brothers distrusted her. She loved Niall, and if she left him now, it would be like leaving behind a piece of her heart.

Niall had collapsed on the bed beside her, a contented grin on his face. "Ah, sweetheart, whoever is attacking me might as well not bother, for much more of this and I'll be finished in any event."

She frowned at the mention of the attacks. Should she tell him now about Bobby? she wondered. Instead, she asked, "Are you feeling well? Mayhap we overdid things. I shouldn't have let you convince me."

He pulled her into his arms and pulled a blanket over them. "I don't remember giving you a choice, sweetheart," he said.

"Your brothers—"

"Don't worry, I'll tell them it was all my fault. I'll explain that once I saw your lovely white body naked underneath me, I couldn't resist—"

She gave a little giggle. "You'll tell them no such thing, Niall Riordan."

"I suppose not," he agreed with a sleepy yawn.

"But now you must rest," she urged.

"Aye, I reckon we both could use a little nap. You'll not be telling me that you had much of a rest last night."

"Nay."

He tucked her head under his chin. "Then go to sleep, my little lioness."

His own voice was thick, and in just moments his breathing became deep and regular. Catriona watched him with a little frown of worry. He'd barely recovered from the blood loss after his arm wound when he'd suffered this new attack. Perhaps the exertion of their lovemaking had not been good for him. Though it had certainly been good for her, she thought with a contented smile, nestling down into the bed. She couldn't ever remember feeling so deliciously satisfied.

She reached her fingers up to trail idly through Niall's dark chestnut hair. How was it possible to get so comfortable with another person's body in just a few days? she wondered. It was as if they had been together always. And always would be.

Her heart gave a lurch. Tomorrow morning at dawn Bobby would be waiting for her at the other side of Scota's Hill. She remembered his words—that she didn't belong with the Riordans, that Niall did not truly want her as a wife. But all the doubts he had sown had been forgotten as she and Niall lay in each other's arms.

Perhaps she wouldn't have to tell Niall about Bobby at all. Maybe by now his brothers had found the real attackers and the danger would be past. Tomorrow she'd go explain to Bobby why she couldn't go away with him. By Bobby's own admission, he had been in love with her himself. She couldn't expect to make him understand the feelings that she had for Niall. But she would have to try. She would meet him at dawn, but only to tell him that she had found her home at Riordan Hall.

•   •   •

Lord Wolverton leaned back on the bench and lifted his booted feet to rest on the railing in front of the fire.

The pale-faced innkeeper wrung his hands in anguish. "I don't have enough food in my entire larder to feed all your men, milord. But I've a nice roast that I can bring out for you and this gentleman, here." He made a vague gesture toward Alger Pimsley, who sat at the other side of the fireplace.

Wolverton's reply was pleasant. "What's your name, my good man?"

"Finbar, milord."

"Finbar, the roast will do nicely for a start," Wolverton said, his tone still soothing. "But I suggest you quickly find a solution for feeding my men, as well. They get surly when they're hungry."

"But, milord, there must be forty of you, and I wasn't prepared—"

Wolverton stuck one of his feet toward the man. "Rid me of these boots, Finbar, my friend."

"Aye, milord."

With some amount of tugging, the innkeeper managed to pull off the nobleman's long boots, and Wolverton put his feet back on the rail with a sigh of contentment.

"When my men are hungry, they've been known to burn entire villages to the ground," Wolverton continued with a bland smile. "And they usually like to see one or two of the inhabitants roast along with the blaze. It amuses them."

The lump in the innkeeper's throat bobbed wildly as he stammered, "I . . . I . . . I could go into the village and see what I can find."

"I suggest you do, Finbar," Wolverton said.

"We don't have the provisions for an extended campaign," Pimsley said after the innkeeper had scurried away, leaving the two Englishmen alone in the taproom.

Wolverton scowled. "This wasn't to be an extended campaign, you fool. If your chosen group of soldiers had taken care of the job the other night as they should have, we'd be on our way back to England."

"Now the Riordans will be on their guard. We may have to mount an open attack."

"Which would mean breaking the queen's truce," Wolverton replied in disgust. "You are determined that I end up in the Tower, aren't you, Pimsley? But I swear, before they cut my head from my body, I'll see you hang on Tower Hill."

"If we do it right, we could keep anyone outside of the Riordan estate from knowing that the attack had been by English soldiers. Once the thing is done, we could make it look as if it had been just another fight between warring clans. It's been going on for centuries in this country."

Wolverton pursed his lips as he looked into the roaring fire. "You may be right," he said thoughtfully. "How many men are on the Riordan estate?"

Pimsley leaned forward eagerly. "Counting all the various kin and servants, there may be three dozen. But some are older. And we would have the element of surprise."

"We need to get on with it, before this miserable village runs out of food. Besides, I've the devil of a tooth." He touched the side of his jaw. "I think 'tis the bloody cold of this place. I want to go home."

"Just give me a couple more days to map out the layout of the Riordan estate, find out where they store their weapons and so on."

Wolverton continued looking into the fire. Finally he said, "Of course, we'd have to be sure that this time there are no witnesses left. If I'd just finished the matter at the Valley of Mor, we wouldn't have to be here at the ends of the earth trying to get rid of our little heiress. But she was such a pretty thing. I've always liked pretty things, Pimsley."

Pimsley seemed to be weighing his words. "Well, the deed was done. Her pretty face bought the girl a few more years of life. But now, unless you want your illegal seizure of O'Malley lands exposed to the queen, we've no choice but to get rid of her."

"Aye, and the Riordans along with her," Wolverton said, rubbing the side of his face. "God *damn* this tooth!"

"A few more days and we should be rid of the lot of them, milord—the girl and the Irish rebels who've taken her in." Then he, too, leaned back and put his feet up on the rail with a sigh of contentment.

Fifteen

"How can Niall continue to believe the deceitful baggage?" Eamon asked impatiently. "I'd thought he'd come back from London with more sense, but he seems to have returned as stubborn as ever."

Cormac took a sip of ale. The two brothers had come to the dining room for midday dinner, but neither one had much of an appetite. "It's called love," he answered. "And I don't envy him the affliction."

Eamon smiled. "You managed well enough in the end."

"Aye, but that was because I fell in love with a woman who was honest. Our families were the problems."

"And the curse," Eamon reminded him with a grin.

"Aye." Cormac didn't return the smile. Though his fear of the ancient curse had diminished with the birth of his healthy son, he remained uneasy, especially now that Claire was facing another childbirth.

"Perhaps things will work out for Niall as well."

Cormac put his mug down and stood. "I doubt it. Even if she has no knowledge of the attacks, we know for a fact that the wench tricked him in London. I don't trust her."

Eamon rose to his feet. "I should take him up some

food," he said, piling some slabs of beef on a plate and topping it with a piece of bread.

"Aye, I'll go with you and see how he's faring after his meeting with her."

Eamon picked up the plate of food and Cormac poured a mug of ale. Then the two brothers made their way up the stairs and into the north wing toward the master's chamber.

Cormac opened the door cautiously. "He may be asleep," he explained to Eamon.

He peered into the room for a long moment before Eamon asked, "What is it?"

Cormac closed the door gently and turned around to his brother with a grimace. "The wretched wench is there in bed with him."

"Catriona? When did that happen?"

Cormac shrugged. "I don't know, but from what I could see, they were both sleeping and neither one appeared to have much in the way of clothing."

Eamon looked up at the beamed ceiling with an exasperated sigh. "I reckon he's forgiven her again for nearly getting him killed."

"I reckon," Cormac agreed glumly.

Both brothers were silent for a moment, then Eamon looked down at the plate in his hand. "What about dinner? Niall hasn't eaten. Wouldn't you think he would be hungry?"

Cormac gave him a sideways glance. "Certain things take precedence over food, Eamon, as you may discover someday."

"What should we do?" Eamon asked.

"I'm tempted to go in and drag them both out of bed, then pound on Niall until he comes to his senses," Cormac told him.

"Sounds like a good plan to me," Eamon agreed.

"You'll do no such thing," said a firm, female voice just behind them.

Both brothers whirled around. Cormac shoved the mug

at Eamon, spilling ale all down his brother's linen doublet, then he threw his arms around the new arrival and lifted her entirely off her feet. "Ah, how I've missed you, lass," he said.

Eamon looked down at his soaked chest with some dismay, but he added, "Welcome home, Claire. You're just in time to try to help us rescue Niall from the clutches of a wicked wench who's cast some kind of spell on him and made him lose his senses."

Claire O'Donnell Riordan was a striking woman with coal black hair and lively blue eyes. At the moment her hair was disheveled from her ride, and her eyes were brimming with love as she looked at her husband. But her words carried some admonishment. "It sounds to me as if Niall has fallen in love, and you boys resent not being the center of your little brother's attention."

Suddenly Cormac remembered his wife's condition and put her gently back on her feet. " 'Tis serious, sweetheart. The girl's a spy and a sympathizer of the outlaw rebels."

"She's the one who had Niall sent to the Tower?" Claire asked, incredulous.

"Aye." Both brothers answered at once.

"And now they're in our bed together? How did this come to be?"

" 'Tis worse than that. He's married the baggage."

Claire's blue eyes widened in surprise. "It appears a few things have happened in my absence. I warrant we'd better go down to the parlor so you can tell me from the beginning."

"And my son?" Cormac asked, looking over her shoulder down the hall.

"He's coming in the cart with Fiona. I rode on ahead. I was suddenly"—her face reddened—"anxious to see you," she finished.

Neither spoke for a moment. Eamon looked from one flushed face to another, then cleared his throat. "I reckon I'd best go see if the guards have been posted," he said loudly. "Cormac, you can fill Claire in on all the developments."

Cormac's gaze was on his wife, and he looked as if he hadn't heard a word his brother had said, but he nodded and said, "I'll speak with you later."

Eamon rolled his eyes and turned to leave.

As his brother disappeared down the hall, Cormac lifted Claire, more gently this time, into a tender embrace. "I *have* missed you, my love," he murmured.

She moved her hand between their bodies to his stiffened manhood and said archly, "So it would appear."

"Not just for that," he protested.

"I know, but—" She went up on tiptoe and nipped the lobe of his ear, then whispered, "Fiona and Ultan will be along in an hour, and then your son is going to want your attention the rest of the day."

Cormac looked at the door of their bedroom with a scowl. "It would appear that our bed is currently occupied by my little brother."

Claire tipped her head and murmured, "Then that would make Niall's bed empty, would it not?"

He turned back to her with a slow smile. "Aye, my clever wife. You were ever a good one to solve problems."

Niall was ready to throttle his older brothers. He'd butted heads with them in the past when they'd tried interfering in his life, always assuming that they knew more than he, but this time they were going too far. Catriona was his wife, and as such she was going to be a member of this family and this household. He was tired of listening to their suspicions and accusations.

At least now Claire was home. Niall hadn't yet seen his sister-in-law. By the time he'd awakened from his nap, it had been late afternoon, and Claire had already taken little Ultan away to feed him supper in the nursery. Now Niall and his brothers were waiting for her in the front sitting room so that they could go in for the evening meal.

Niall had debated awakening Catriona, but as he'd watched her in Cormac's bed, he'd decided to let her continue sleeping. She'd had circles of fatigue under her eyes and her face was pale. None of this had been easy on her, either, he'd reminded himself. And his brothers' continuing suspicions didn't help.

He stood up and began to pace the woven carpet Claire had brought from O'Donnell House in her continuing campaign to bring some gentility to the formerly rowdy Riordan household.

"What can we say to convince you?" Eamon asked. "It's obvious you're in love with the girl, but that doesn't mean you have to abandon all good sense."

"I don't object to our protecting ourselves," Niall argued, trying to remain calm. "Post your guards, if you like."

"We already have," Cormac said grimly.

"Fine, then. I'm just saying that whatever these attacks are, I don't think Catriona has anything to do with them, and I'll not have you treat her like a criminal."

"Niall, she's already been judged a criminal. If it weren't for the whims of a sentimental queen, she'd have a permanent residence in the Tower of London, instead of here where she can make you forget all reason every time she gets you near a bed."

Niall gave an inner groan as he looked up and saw Catriona standing quietly in the doorway. Following the direction of his gaze, both his brothers turned their heads.

"Good evening, gentlemen," she said, her chin raised. She still looked tired, but her expression held a beauty and a quiet dignity that made Niall's heart twist.

Neither of his brothers returned her greeting. Niall reached his hand out to her. "Come in, sweetheart. I'm just trying to convince my lughead brothers that I don't need to fear you attempting to murder me in my sleep."

She looked from Cormac to Eamon, then walked forward and took Niall's hand. "Have you succeeded?" she asked with a brief smile.

" 'Tis not you we fear, milady," Cormac clarified. "But it would seem that you have some very dangerous friends, and, even though he can be bothersome at times, Eamon and I are too fond of our brother to let him be butchered by a bunch of misguided rebels."

"I think you should look elsewhere for the culprits. Are there no enemies of the Riordans who might be perpetrating these attacks?"

"Enemies who would ride as far as the outskirts of London to attack Niall in a wayfarer's inn?" Eamon asked. " 'Tis hardly a likely notion."

"We've worked hard to seek peace, milady," Cormac added. "And we seemed to have achieved it until you came into our brother's life."

Niall gave her hand a sympathetic squeeze. "They may be right, sweetheart. No one's blaming you, but this Brosnihan fellow may have recruited some of his friends for the deed. We can't be sure—"

Catriona pulled her hand out of Niall's and folded her arms in front of her. " 'Twas not the rebels," she said quietly.

Niall frowned. "What do you mean?"

"My friends were not responsible for these attacks. Not the one yesterday, nor the one outside of London. You must look elsewhere for your suspects."

Cormac lifted his head with interest. "How do you know? Do you have some information about the attackers?"

She shook her head. "Nay, I have no idea who they were. I only know they were not the Cleary rebels."

"Could they have been other comrades of Bobby Brosnihan?" Cormac persisted.

"Nay. Bobby had nothing to do with either attack."

The three brothers exchanged looks.

"How do you know?" Cormac asked again.

Niall felt a sudden chill, much like the one he had felt back in the entrance of Wolverton House when they'd pulled the jewel out of his bag. "How can you know that, Cat?" he asked softly.

She bit her lip, hesitating. Finally she said, "Because he told me."

Niall took a step back. A dull pain where he'd been hit in the head suddenly grew sharp. "When?" he asked, his throat dry.

"This morning."

This morning. Just before she'd come to his bed and let him make love to her. Out of the corner of his eye Niall could see his older brother's grimly smug expression.

"Where was he?" Cormac asked.

"We need to get the men out looking for him immediately," Eamon added.

"Nay!" Catriona cried in alarm. "He's done nothing to any of you."

Niall felt a tightness inside his chest. Nothing made sense. He looked at Catriona, whose eyes were full of anguished pleading for the man she had said she didn't love. The man who had conveniently appeared at Riordan Hall the day after Niall had been set upon by armed men.

Earlier that day, when he'd had Catriona in his arms, he would have sworn on his father's grave that his wife was as much in love with him as he was with her. Now he felt as if he couldn't be sure of anything. His world had turned upside down.

"I beg you, Niall," Catriona said, "leave him be. Bobby is here alone. I had no idea that he was anywhere near until we met this morning. It's the first time I've seen him since they brought him out that day at the palace. I swear it."

He wanted to believe her, but logic and his brothers' looks of scorn told him that her story was not credible. "Today is the first time you've seen him?" he asked. "What convenient timing. Just in time to proclaim his innocence in yesterday's attack."

"He didn't come for that. He knew nothing of the whole incident."

"Then why was he here?"

"He came to fetch me. He means no harm to you. He says I belong with my own people."

"The Clearys are not your people," Niall pointed out.

"Nay, but Bobby is, and some of the folks who escaped the raid on my father's estate joined the rebels after the Valley of Mor was taken. There are probably many old friends with them."

Niall gave his head a slight shake, wishing his mind did not feel so fogged. "If his only mission was to fetch you, why didn't you go with him?"

Even now, with every strain of reason telling him that his brothers were right about her, he found himself holding his breath as he waited for her answer.

She glanced briefly at his brothers, then answered, "I had no choice. I owed it to you. I had to tell you and your brothers that the Clearys were not involved in the attacks. You have another enemy that you don't suspect."

Niall looked away, disappointed. What answer had he been expecting? A declaration that she had stayed because she was in love with him? She had either stayed out of some sense of responsibility, perhaps to assuage her guilt for the trouble she had brought into his life, or else his brothers had been right about her and she had stayed to help Brosnihan carry out his mission.

Cormac had evidently decided that she had been given enough time to explain herself. He stepped between Niall and Catriona and asked sharply, "How do you know you can believe Brosnihan?"

"I'd know if Bobby were not telling me the truth. He came alone to take me away, that's all. The Clearys aren't even in this part of the country."

"She's lying, Cormac," Eamon said. "No one else has a motive to attack Niall."

"But she did come back here," Niall argued. "She could have just left with him."

Cormac shook his head. "I don't pretend to know what the scheming wench is up to, but I'm not about to let my home and family be threatened again. Let's get on with it and find this Brosnihan."

Steeling himself to ignore Catriona's pleading eyes, Niall nodded agreement. "I'll go out with you to look for him."

Cormac appeared to be about to refuse his offer, but then he nodded and said, "Good. The more men we take, the sooner we'll find him."

"What about her?" Eamon asked, tipping his head toward Catriona.

"She'll be placed under guard," Cormac answered.

Just then Claire appeared in the doorway. She looked immediately at Catriona, who stood miserably in the center of the three men. "I don't think guards are necessary, husband," she said calmly. "I shall keep the Lady Catriona company until you men return."

Cormac turned toward her angrily. "You have no idea what—" When he saw his wife's determined expression he stopped and drew in a deep breath. "Very well," he said after a moment. "But I shall be leaving men here at the house in case you need them."

Claire walked up to Catriona and put an arm around her waist. "We shan't need anyone," she said. "I intend to feed this poor girl."

Once again Cormac appeared to be about to argue, but in the face of his wife's calm insistence, he gave up.

Catriona shot a grateful look at Claire, but tried one more time to dissuade the men. "Finding Bobby will avail you nothing," she argued. "I've told you—he's alone, and he's not the one who attacked you."

"Then perhaps while we're out looking for him, we'll happen upon these mysterious *other* assailants," Cormac said dryly. "In any event, we'd best be about it before there's no daylight left."

Niall could sense that Catriona was waiting for him to speak, but he was too taken aback by her revelation to know what he wanted to say to her. In the end, he simply gave her a curt nod, then followed his brothers out of the room.

After hearing so much about Claire's perfections since she had arrived at Riordan Hall, Catriona had expected to feel a degree of resentment when she finally met the woman, but as they sat together at the big dining table, Catriona instead found herself liking her new sister-in-law immensely.

She'd never known anyone quite like Claire Riordan. Though she was obviously devoted to her husband, the powerful head of the Riordan clan whom Catriona had found to be mostly suspicious and taciturn, she had not been afraid to stand up to him. Cormac had not even attempted to argue when Claire had adopted that firm tone. Yet as he had left them earlier, he had given his wife a glance that was so warm and intimate—and so full of *love*—it was almost as if the couple had shared a kiss right there in the middle of the parlor.

The brothers were similar in appearance, and Catriona had seen some of that same smoldering warmth in Niall's eyes before they had tumbled together into his high bed. But she'd not seen the love. That part had been missing.

She tried to concentrate on what her companion was saying. Claire had insisted that they sit down to supper as if everything were normal. But things were not normal, Catriona reminded herself. Her husband and his brothers were this very moment out hunting her very dearest friend. Though she knew Bobby would resort to violence only under pressure, he was armed. Who knew what would happen if he was confronted by the entire group of Riordan men? He could be killed. Or he could kill one of them. Either prospect was unbearable.

"I vow 'tis difficult, Catriona, but you should try to eat a little something. Just a piece of this nice mutton to give you strength," Claire urged.

Catriona shook her head and pushed away the pewter plate. Plates had replaced trenchers in the Riordan household—another of Claire's innovations, she'd learned. She looked over at her pretty sister-in-law. What would it be like to live here, accepted and loved? she wondered. Everyone on the estate from the lowliest servant to the master himself seemed to adore her. She sighed. Claire *belonged*. That was the difference. Catriona herself would never find such acceptance among these people.

"It's grown dark. How long have they been gone?" she asked.

Claire shook her head. "You know men. They'll stay out as long as it pleases them with little thought for those who might be at home worried about them."

"Do you think they've found him?"

"Your, er, friend?"

"Aye, my friend," Catriona answered firmly.

"He's truly not your lover, then? This Bobby?"

"Nay, he's not my lover, nor has he ever been."

Claire looked thoughtful. "But Niall thinks that he was."

Catriona flushed, but she answered directly. "Niall of all people knows that Bobby was never my lover."

"Ah," Claire said with a slight smile. "Then 'twould seem that you and Niall have not remained entirely indifferent to each other."

Catriona's flush deepened. "Nay, we have not."

Claire leaned forward and put her hand on Catriona's arm. "Are you in love with him?"

The idea was so new that Catriona had barely admitted it to herself, yet there was something about the young woman sitting across the table from her that made her want to confide her feelings. "Aye," she said. "I love him."

Claire sat back and pursed her lips. "Yet there would appear to be a few details to be sorted out."

Catriona gave a rueful smile. "I think you could say that."

With a dismissive wave Claire said briskly, "Don't fret yourself, sister-in-law. When two people are in love, entire mountains can be moved. Cormac and I are enough example of that."

Seeing them together, it was hard to imagine that Cormac and Claire had ever had a single problem, though she'd heard some reference made to a bride curse that had caused some difficulty when they had first wed. "Do you mean the Riordan curse?" she asked.

Claire gave a little laugh. "That was part of it. By the saints, we had to defeat the ancient druid hex, resolve a family feud, win over his brothers, change the course of the war with England, and various other details before Cormac and I could settle into this relatively peaceful existence you see today."

It was encouraging to think that Claire, too, had had difficulties yet had eventually found happiness. "How did you manage to do all that?" she asked.

Claire's whole expression softened. "Love finds a way," she said.

Catriona's throat tightened. Love may be able to move mountains, but she had no evidence that Niall loved her. He himself had admitted that she'd brought nothing but chaos into his life. She gave Claire a brittle smile. "You and Cormac are lucky."

"Aye, we are."

Suddenly a tiny bundle of flying feet and arms barreled into the room. Claire turned in her chair and held out her arms as her son jumped into her lap and planted a messy kiss on her cheek.

Claire wiped her face with the side of her hand, then

took a cloth from the table and dabbed at her son's mouth. "I see you had your pudding tonight," she told him.

"Ultan ate all his puddin', Mummy," he said proudly.

"I see that you did, sweetling," Claire said as she continued to clean his face. "Now give greetings to your Aunt Catriona."

Ultan's smile faded as he turned shyly toward Catriona and bobbed his head, mumbling, "Aunt Catri-tri-o."

Catriona smiled. "Aunt Cat. How would that be?"

"Cat?" the little boy asked, brightening. "Like Boots?"

"Aye, Cat like your little Boots," Claire agreed as she finished the face cleaning and scooped him into a hug.

"That's a funny name," Ultan said with a giggle.

" 'Tis my nickname," Catriona told him. "Since the full name is a little hard."

Now that his mother had finished washing his face, she could get a clear look at him. He was a Riordan, no doubt about it. His eyes, in miniature, were the same intense black. His hair was dark and wavy. He even had the beginnings of a crooked grin, just like his father and uncles.

"He's beautiful," she said to Claire.

She smiled, happily rocking the child slightly in her arms. "Aye. We hope this next will be a little girl."

Ultan was staring at her. "You have eyes like Boots, too."

"Aye, sweetling, your aunt's eyes are green like your cat's, are they not?" Claire gave a slightly embarrassed laugh as she turned to Catriona and said, "I hope you don't mind. Children are very observant, I've found."

Catriona shook her head. "Don't apologize. He's charming." She found herself envying the other woman as she watched Claire playfully tickle her son and kiss his little nose. Ultan responded with delighted shrieks, but obediently slipped off her lap and took his nurse's hand when she came to get him for bed.

When prompted, he turned to give his new aunt a goodnight hug. Catriona leaned down and let him put his chubby arms around her neck. She felt the downy skin of his cheek brush hers as he lisped, "Do you want to see Boots?"

"Tomorrow you may show Boots to Aunt Cat," his mother answered. "For now it's off to bed."

Both women watched as his nurse, Fiona, led the little boy out of the room and up the stairs. "In truth, you are a lucky lady, Claire," Catriona observed softly after a moment.

"Aye," Claire agreed, her eyes shining.

The sound of commotion in the front hall broke their reverie. "Come," Claire said, jumping up. "The men are back."

Sixteen

Catriona followed her out to the hall, where all three brothers were just coming in after dismissing the men who had been riding with them.

"What happened?" Claire asked. "Did you find him?"

Catriona waited anxiously for the answer.

Cormac stepped forward to give his wife a quick kiss on the cheek. "Nay. We found neither Brosnihan nor any wandering bands of"—he cast a sarcastic glance at Catriona—"*brigands* who might have taken it in their heads to attack my brother."

"So now what?" Claire asked as her husband slipped an arm around her.

"Now I go say good night to my son," Cormac answered. "Morning will be time enough to resume the hunt."

"You intend to go out again?" Claire asked.

"Aye," Cormac answered. "We'll find the blackguard. 'Tis only a matter of time."

Catriona looked at Niall, who avoided her gaze.

After a moment of silence Cormac said, "Well, then, it's off to bed with everyone. We'll start again early."

Claire left her husband's side for a moment to walk over

to Catriona and give her a brief embrace. "Remember what I said," she whispered. "Everything will work out." Then she went back to Cormac and they both turned to walk up the stairs.

Eamon said, " 'Tis a fine enough night. I reckon I'll sleep out with the men. Morning will come soon enough, and we'll be out on the road again."

Niall was still not looking at Catriona. As Eamon started to leave, he said, "Wait, I'll join you."

Catriona bit her lip but said nothing.

Eamon looked uncertainly from his brother to Catriona, shrugged and said, "Suit yourself."

Then without a further word to her, Niall followed his brother out the front door.

After staying in bed much of the afternoon, Catriona knew that sleep would not come easily, not with her mind still whirling over the events of the day. She'd started the day at dawn with Bobby on Scota's Hill, convinced that her place was with him and with whatever members of her father's estate she might find with the outlaw rebels. Then sometime during the course of those hours in bed with Niall, she had come to realize that what she had with her new husband was something too precious to lose, no matter how noble the cause.

Now as she sat by the embers of the nearly dead fire in Niall's bedchamber, she was once again full of doubt. What she had told Claire had been the truth. She loved Niall. But in spite of what Claire had said, some mountains love could not move. Or at least not a one-sided love. Claire and Cormac had been able to accomplish all they needed to reach their current happy state because they *both* had wanted it.

She remembered the way Niall had avoided her eyes as he had left earlier to sleep outside with his men, rather than join her in their shared bedchamber. They'd be off early, they'd said. To hunt down Bobby.

She drew her knees up to her chest and hugged them, rocking back and forth, ignoring the tears that streamed down her cheeks. "Oh, Niall," she whispered. "Why didn't you come upstairs with me? Why won't you listen to me about Bobby?"

She wasn't sure how long she sat there, letting the misery wash over her, but finally the tears subsided, and she began to feel a determined calm. Though Claire had been kind to her, the Riordans had made it clear that she was not one of them. She never would be. And Niall had chosen his brothers over her. So be it.

She would keep her appointment with Bobby after all. The important thing now was to find him and for them both to get as far away as possible before the Riordans began searching again in the morning. She glanced out the window at the black sky. She had no idea of the time, but she estimated that it might be just a couple of hours before dawn. Bobby might already be waiting for her.

She looked around the bedchamber where she and Niall had shared such bright passion over the past few days. In the faint glow of the fire, it looked dark and ominous. Niall had collected an odd assortment of clothes for her until her own could be made, but she left everything in place except for the frock she was wearing and a cloak that she grabbed at the last minute to ward off the night chill.

She made her way silently along the narrow hall and down the grand staircase to the entryway. As she neared the doorway, something shot out from the front parlor and slithered across her feet. She pressed her hand against her mouth to keep from crying out, then relaxed as she saw that the nocturnal creature was a large gray cat with white front paws. It was no doubt Boots, the pet Ultan had so proudly offered to show her, she thought with a twinge.

There had been moments over these past few days when she had had daydreams of having a child just like that—a little boy with a crooked Riordan smile and thick wavy hair. A little boy to love and a husband to raise him with.

But they had just been dreams, she reminded herself. She'd known since that day at the Valley of Mor that she'd never again have such a normal life.

She belonged in the woods with Bobby. The cat had stopped to watch her curiously from the far side of the hall. She gave it a bittersweet smile, then slid the bolt and slipped out the front door.

"If you were going to lie awake the whole night tossing about, you might as well have stayed in the house," Eamon grumbled, giving his brother a shove.

The brothers had camped out around the estate armory with the group of assorted Riordan kin and estate workers Cormac had recruited to help in the search for Bobby Brosnihan. Niall had hoped the rough camaraderie of the male company would help him take his mind off Catriona, but the men had mostly gone to sleep early, leaving Niall turning restlessly on his bedroll. Eamon, who had been beside him all night, had a right to his complaints. "If you and Cormac hadn't made me stay in bed all day yesterday, I might have been able to sleep last night."

Eamon gave him a scornful look. "Oh, aye. 'Twas your brothers' bullying that kept you there, and it had absolutely nothing to do with the fact that your wife decided to join you in bed."

Niall rolled to a sitting position with a groan as the various wounds he had received protested the restless night and the hard ground. "I reckon she had something to do with it."

Eamon sat up beside his brother. Around them the other men were slowly getting to their feet and rolling up their blankets. "Even though she'd just been meeting with her former lover," Eamon said pointedly.

"Brosnihan's not her lover."

"How can you be sure of that?"

Niall sent his brother a glance out of the corner of his eyes. " 'Tis the one thing of which I can be sure, Eamon.

I'm not exactly sure what Brosnihan is to her, but he was never her lover."

Eamon looked puzzled for a moment, then comprehension dawned, and he mumbled an embarrassed, "Ah, well, then."

"Exactly." He gave a deep sigh. "And I probably shouldn't have been so short with her yesterday when she was trying to tell us about her meeting with him. After all, she could have gone away with him yesterday at dawn. She didn't have to come back to tell us about what she had learned. I'm not sure why I reacted so strongly when she told us."

"You were jealous," Eamon said with a smile.

Niall looked at him for a moment, then admitted, "I warrant I was."

"Mayhap you should go tell her that before we have to ride out today."

She would still not be happy with him, Niall reasoned. She didn't want them to look for her old friend. But his brother was right. He had treated her shabbily the previous evening, leaving her so abruptly. He should go try to put things to right. Somehow the prospect of settling their differences made the whole day seem brighter.

He bounced to his feet. "I think I'll do just that, brother," he said.

He snatched his blanket from the ground and, without taking the time to roll it, took off toward the house in a fast lope. He nearly knocked over Cormac as he burst into the front hall. "I'll be out with you in a few minutes," he told his brother without stopping, then ran up the stairs.

He took a minute to catch his breath as he walked down the hall to his room. It wouldn't do to arrive panting. He wanted to have his wits about him so that they could discuss the previous day's events in a sensible fashion.

He reached for the latch and pulled open the door. His bed appeared to be untouched and a quick glance around the room showed him that it was empty. Catriona was gone.

"I knew ye'd come, scamp," Bobby said, breathing hard as the two made their way up yet another hill at a quick pace. Catriona had told him that she wanted to get as far away from Riordan lands as possible to avoid a possible confrontation. "I knew ye'd realize that ye were not cut out to be with the likes of them."

"The Riordans are no different than we are, Bobby," she argued. "All they want is a peaceful land to keep their homes and raise their families."

"Aye, and what about the revenge for what was done to yer father?"

Catriona shook her head. "I'm not sure I believe in revenge as I once did. Mayhap I'm seeing that other things are more important."

"Things like what?"

"Like living the life we have now instead of living for the past. Things like loving and being loved. Having children."

Bobby stopped and turned to her with a scowl. "Ye're not—"

She shook her head. "Nay, er—I don't think so."

"Now, that's a relief," he said, moving again.

"Aye," she agreed. If she'd had Niall's child, she'd want to be able to raise it in a loving home, not on the run with a bunch of rebels.

They came to the top of a rise and stopped, surveying the land beneath them. "Don't ye remember the day we watched like this while they burned yer home in front of yer face, Cat?"

"Of course I remember."

"Then how can ye say it should be forgotten?"

She shook her head slowly. " 'Twill never be forgotten, Bobby," she said. "But neither do I want to spend my whole life reliving that day. I'm ready to put it behind me."

"Ye owe it to yer father—"

She put a hand on his arm to stop him. "My father was a peaceful man, Bobby, as well you know. What do you think he'd rather have as a legacy—more dead, English and Irish alike, or . . . grandchildren?"

Bobby didn't answer. After a moment he started down the hill, and Catriona followed him.

The men were assembled and ready to go back out on the search, but Niall and his brothers had moved into a corner of the stable where their argument wouldn't be heard by others.

"She's gone away with him," Niall said, his voice brittle. "That's an end to it."

"Just because Catriona has joined them doesn't mean that the Clearys won't still come after us, Niall," Cormac pointed out.

"He's right," Eamon agreed. "The easiest thing would be to find the lot of them while they're still here in our part of the country."

"Find them and what?" Niall asked. "Kill them? Kill Catriona as well?"

Eamon and Cormac were silent.

"What they wanted was Catriona," Niall continued. "Now they've got her, and they have no reason to bother us further. I say we forget about the whole thing."

Cormac gave his brother a concerned look. "Are you sure she went of her own free will? Could they have somehow coerced her, kidnapped her or—"

Niall held up his hand. In the hour since he'd discovered his empty bedchamber, Niall had done his best to come up with some kind of explanation like the ones his brother was suggesting, but none of them made sense. "We had guards posted all around the house. If a group of armed men had invaded us last night, they would have seen."

"But none of the guards saw her leave, either," Eamon pointed out.

Niall gave a rueful smile. "I believe my wife had developed something of a skill for stealth in her days in London spying for the rebels."

Eamon persisted. "So you intend to simply let her go, never see her again?"

Niall stiffened. "'Twas her choice, not mine."

There was a long moment of silence. Finally Cormac said, "I'll tell the men to go back to their homes, but to keep alert for signs of anything out of the ordinary."

"She and Brosnihan are probably clear out of the county by now," Niall said.

"Just the same, I want everyone to stay on guard."

Eamon nodded agreement, then the three brothers turned to go tell the assembly of riders that there would be no search that day after all.

Alger Pimsley stood at attention in front of Lord Wolverton. In spite of the fact that the nobleman was in bed, dressed only in a nightshirt, his jaw packed with a poultice of mud to ease the pain of his bad tooth, Pimsley addressed him with all the formality of a military adjutant. "Our scouts tell us that after the attack the Riordans assembled a number of men from around the estate. It's a greater number than I had thought, though many did not look like seasoned soldiers."

"Seasoning doesn't seem to matter with these bloody Irish," Wolverton grumbled, his words distorted by the swelling. "They fight like the very devil."

"Aye, but now it would seem that they've let the men go. This morning most of them rode out toward their own homes—"

Wolverton clutched his face and rocked in agony. "God's blood, Pimsley, can't you see I'm in pain, here? I don't care about the details. I just want the thing done. I want to get out of this cold, wet, godforsaken country and back to England."

Pimsley hesitated. "Shall I send for the serving girl to pack your cheek again?"

"The bloody wench doesn't know a thing. I need a real doctor. An *English* doctor. Or at least—" His expression was pitiful. "Don't they have a medicine woman in this village? I need some herbs. The thing's feverish."

Pimsley shook his head sorrowfully. "I've asked the innkeeper, milord. There's no one. The nearest doctor is a half day's ride."

"Damn, primitive savages."

Pimsley hesitated, then asked, "Do you want me to go ahead with the attack on the Riordan estate, then, milord?"

"I don't care, damn you! Just do it. Finish it! Then get me out of here." Wolverton's eyes were squeezed shut in misery and drool was dripping down his chin.

"Very good, milord," Pimsley said calmly. Then he gave a formal bow and turned to leave.

The innkeeper Finbar intercepted him at the bottom of the stairs. "How's His Lordship doing, Master Pimsley?"

"His tooth nags him, I believe."

"You really should let me send for the village herbalist. A bit of feverfew and one of her balms and His Lordship would be as good as new."

Pimsley shook his head sadly. "Alas, Lord Wolverton has a rather poor opinion of your country's medicine, I'm afraid. He's forbidden me from sending for anyone."

Finbar clucked his tongue in disapproval. " 'Tis foolish not to seek help," he said. "If he changes his mind, let me know. I can have the woman here in a quarter of an hour."

Pimsley nodded gravely. "I certainly will, Finbar, my good man, and I'll pass your advice on to Lord Wolverton. But I fear he's a man who doesn't change his mind easily."

"More's the pity," Finbar said.

•   •   •

Niall had not come down for either the midday or the evening meal. Cormac had advised Claire to give him time to himself, but she had never been one to let her husband's opinion deter her when she thought she knew better.

There was no response to her first knock, so she tried again, more loudly. After a moment the door opened to reveal her brother-in-law clad only in his hose and breeches. His hair was uncombed and his eyes were red-rimmed. He flushed when he saw her. "Ah, Claire. I thought 'twas the maid come to force some supper on me. I reckoned Cormac would be unwilling to let me starve myself to death. But I didn't think he'd send you."

"Cormac didn't send me. I warrant he's ready to let you do yourself whatever harm you choose, but you have me to contend with, and I'll not be losing a brother over love."

Niall gave a brief smile. "Love? 'Twas hardly that. I barely had time to get to know the lass."

"Love is not measured in hours, Niall. I suspect you've discovered that."

He gave a little grunt of acknowledgment, then went over to a clothes rack to put on a tunic. "So you've come to tell me that I need to forget about the wench and move on?"

Claire studied him as she walked into the room and sat on his rumpled bed. "I've not come to tell you anything. I've come to ask. Do you love her?"

Niall winced. "I've already confessed as much to Eamon, who I suspect has shared that revelation with the entire estate by now."

"Eamon has said nothing, as far as I know, but anyone with eyes and a heart can see that you're suffering, Niall. Yet here you sit, doing nothing."

"What would you have me do?"

Claire clapped her hands in exasperation. "Lord, I'd always heard that the Riordans were the bravest, boldest warriors in all of County Meath, yet it would appear that in matters of the heart, you slink off the field like milk-faced boys at their first battle. You'll recall that the first thing your brother did after our marriage was to run away."

Niall had to chuckle at his sister-in-law's taunt, which he knew was meant to jolt him into action, but he shook his head and said, "There's no battle to fight here. Catriona's made her choice, and that's the end of it."

"Ah, Niall, if your brother had given up on me, I wouldn't be here now. Sometimes love takes a few twists and turns before it finds a true path. She loves you, Niall."

He gave a snort of disgust.

"It's true," Claire insisted. "She admitted it to me herself."

At this, Niall's eyes widened. He'd never known his sister-in-law to be untruthful. "Then why did she run away with Brosnihan?"

"That would be for you to find out. I didn't say that love was easy."

Niall looked down at his sister-in-law's determined face. He was tired and his head wound ached, but, he admitted, he *was* hungry. "If I come downstairs for some food, will I have to endure your nagging for the entire meal?" he asked her.

She gave a firm nod. "You certainly will. You'll have to endure it for as long as it takes to get you to do something to right this situation."

Niall shook his head with a rueful smile but reached his hand out to pull her up from the bed. "Come along, then. They do say that women with child are endowed with a special wisdom."

Claire took his hand and bounced to her feet with a self-satisfied expression. "That we are, brother," she said.

Alger Pimsley sipped his mug of mulled ale, a thoughtful look on his face. He didn't notice when the young soldier stepped into the open doorway of his room at the

River's Cross Inn. Finally the man cleared his throat loudly, and Pimsley lifted his head. "What is it?" he asked.

"Er—I have a report for Lord Wolverton, Yer—er—Lordship," the aide stammered.

"Very well, you may report to me," Pimsley said.

"The lieutenant says I was to report to His Lordship."

"Lord Wolverton is indisposed. I am presently acting in his stead." He stood up and motioned impatiently. "What is it you have to say, man? Speak up!"

"The lieutenant did send me to report prisoners, Yer Lordship."

"Prisoners?"

"Aye. 'Tis His Lordship's ward, along with another bloke. Some of our men found them hiding down by the river behind this very inn."

Pimsley raised an eyebrow. "Catriona? The girl is here?"

"Aye, Yer Lordship. And the lieutenant did send to ask what we should do with 'em. He said since 'twas our mission to dispose of the lass, bein' she a traitor and all, that we need to know if we should shoot her straight away. He said Lord Wolverton was to decide."

Pimsley came around from behind his makeshift desk and walked toward the soldier. "I'll see that Lord Wolverton hears of it. In the meantime, go back to your lieutenant and tell him to keep the prisoners under guard."

"Aye, Yer Lordship. Er—we aren't to shoot her then?"

Pimsley looked thoughtful. "Nay. You aren't to shoot her."

"Aye, Yer Lordship," the soldier said, then turned and rushed away.

Alger Pimsley walked back to the table where he'd spread out a number of papers he'd brought along from Wolverton House. Henry Wolverton was an extremely rich man, Pimsley reflected, and an extremely foolish one. It had been greedy and foolhardy for him to go after the O'Malley estates simply because the land stood in the most beautiful part of Ireland. If the queen had discovered his perfidy, he would have lost his life.

Pimsley, himself, did not intend to make any mistakes.

"So you've come to your senses and decided to go after them," Cormac told Niall as they sat around the big dining table. "Why is it you'll listen to my wife, but not to your older and wiser brother?"

"I've decided to go after *her*, not *them*," Niall corrected. "And I listen to Claire because she speaks with reason instead of trying to bully people into going along with her ideas. Besides, she's prettier than you."

"No argument there," Cormac said with a smile, unoffended by his brother's comments. There had always been rivalry among the three Riordans, but the bond among the three was unbreakable.

"It would make no sense to start now in the dark," Eamon said. "We can leave in the morning."

Niall pushed away his empty plate and patted his stomach with a sigh. Once he'd made the decision to fight to work things through with Catriona, he'd found himself with a tremendous appetite. With Claire urging him on, he'd finished three plates of veal and onion pottage. "I'm thinking it might be better for me to ride after her by myself."

"Nay!" Cormac and Eamon both cried at once.

"Don't be a dolt, Niall," Cormac added. "You've no idea how many men she's riding with. Nor what they might do if they see you. Remember, they've already tried to kill you."

"I don't want this to turn into a fight," Niall argued. "I just want to find her and talk with her. Once I've . . . told her a few things, if she decides to ride away with Brosnihan, I'll let her go peacefully."

"Aye, you know that your intentions are peaceful, but will her companions know that?" Eamon asked. "In any event, the first step is to find them, and for that you need help. A single man riding alone could miss them."

"There's only one main road if they're riding toward Killarney, which is where the Clearys reside and near her old family estate."

"Aye, one road with endless places to hide," Eamon persisted.

"I reckon 'twould not hurt to have you along," Niall admitted. "But when we find them, I must be allowed to go speak with them, alone and unarmed."

Cormac and Eamon continued their protests, but Claire stood as she saw a visitor entering the front hall. "Why, 'tis John Black!" she said, pushing back her chair and going out to meet him. In a moment she was back, ushering the doctor into the room.

"John!" Niall cried, jumping to his feet, and his brothers followed suit.

For several moments there was general confusion as greetings were exchanged, and Claire sent for more food so that John could have some supper. When everyone was finally seated again, Cormac looked at the visitor and said, " 'Tis good to see you, John. Have you come to stay with us awhile?"

John smiled his thanks at a maid who put a plate of food in front of him. "I'm waiting for the O'Neill to summon me to resume the peace negotiations in London. But in the meantime"—he looked around the table at his friends— "I've a story to tell you."

Seventeen

"*This is a* sad story, my friends," John began, "though we may yet salvage something of a happy ending for it. You young people may find this hard to believe, but there was a time when I was young and foolish just like you. Foolish enough to fall in love."

Every face around the table was turned toward the doctor with rapt attention. Niall gave a sympathetic nod and said, "You never talked about it, John."

"I know. The lady in question died many years ago giving birth. Though I'd studied all the arts of healing, I could not save her. The grief nearly killed me as well."

"Was it your child?" Cormac asked.

"Nay. She had chosen another, a nobleman with a kind heart and a small but beautiful estate. I was just a poor doctor with little to offer her."

"The kind heart was there," Niall corrected.

"Mayhap, though I was more impetuous in my youth, prone to temper at times. I don't think she ever regretted her decision. Certainly she would not regret it if she could have lived to see the beautiful woman her daughter has become."

"You know the daughter, John?" Niall asked politely.

He was having trouble keeping his mind on John's tale with his thoughts so full of Catriona. Would he be able to find her? Somehow he felt sure that he would, but he was less sure of what she would say when he told her that he wanted to bring her back to Riordan Hall to live truly as husband and wife.

"I've come to know her well, Niall, as have you. 'Tis your wife."

Niall's mind snapped to attention. "Cat? She is the daughter of your lost love?"

"Aye. I knew from the moment they revealed her true name, but I didn't say anything because I had some investigating I wanted to do on my own."

"What kind of investigating?" Niall asked.

The good hostess, Claire interjected gently, "Dr. Black's food is growing cold. Perhaps we should let him eat something before we keeping him talking all night."

He smiled at her and lifted his fork. "I'll talk and eat at the same time, Lady Claire, if you won't take offense."

"What did you mean by investigating?" Niall persisted. Now that he knew John's story was concerning Catriona, he couldn't curb his impatience.

"After Rhea O'Malley's death, I left Killarney. Every lake and every hill there reminded me of her. I went, as you know, to join with the O'Neill rebels."

"You turned from doctor to soldier," Cormac added.

"I was both, really. 'Twas a great irony on the field of battle, one moment taking a life, the next saving one."

"What about Catriona?" Niall pressed.

"Every now and then I'd hear word of the O'Malley estate from friends in the area. I believed that Rhea's daughter was growing up happy and healthy. Lord O'Malley was a good father and a benevolent landlord."

"Until the English raid that killed him and sent Catriona to Lord Wolverton's household," Niall added.

"Aye, and that was what didn't make sense to me. What was a troop of English soldiers doing all the way down in

County Kerry? The fighting with the O'Neill was all in the north, perhaps a little in the Midlands, but never south."

Cormac looked thoughtful. "Unless some English lord was looking for an out-of-the-way estate that he could illegally seize for himself under pretext of war."

John nodded. "That far away from the fighting, the English generals never even heard about the raid on the Valley of Mor."

"And that English lord was—" Eamon began.

"Wolverton," Niall finished.

"I've just come from Killarney. According to my friends who still live in the area, the estate is now run by an English bailiff who sends all the revenues back to Wolverton House. He's raised the rents so that the tenants can barely make a living."

"So while Wolverton was pretending to be so kind to a poor Irish orphan, the bastard was actually the one who murdered her father." Niall could feel the rage rising in his throat.

"And stole her inheritance out from under her," John agreed.

Cormac looked nearly as angry as Niall. "The queen would not have sanctioned such a raid."

"Nay," John said. "Which is why I suspect Wolverton started to panic when he realized that Catriona was going to be sent back to Ireland. If she found out the truth, his game was up. That's why he sent men after you to the Hart's Horn Inn."

"They were Wolverton's men?" Niall asked, incredulous. "'Twas not Brosnihan at all?"

John shook his head.

"Then he may not have had anything to do with the attack two days ago either," Niall said.

"Though we know he was in the neighborhood," Eamon reminded them.

John had taken several bites of food in quick succession. With his mouth full, he asked, "There was another attack?"

"Aye, armed men came up to us just on the other side of Scota's Hill," Niall told him.

"I'd put my money on Wolverton sooner than the outlaw group," John said between chews. "From what I hear, the Clearys have mostly disbanded and have more or less given up their struggle to stop the peace."

"If the attackers are Englishmen, they've broken the truce by coming here," Cormac pointed out.

"That wouldn't stop Wolverton," Niall said grimly.

For a moment there was silence while John continued to eat. Niall's mind was whirring, but as he tried to make sense of it all, one terrible thought kept surfacing. "If Wolverton or his men are out there, what if they find Catriona before we do?"

He looked at each of his brothers, but their concerned faces told him that they had come up with the same answer he had.

John stopped eating and put down his fork. "You mean Catriona isn't here?" he asked, his face suddenly white.

Niall shook his head. "She left this morning or last night. We think she went to meet Brosnihan."

"Bloody hell," John said.

Cormac got up from the table and went to put his hand on Niall's shoulder. "We'll leave at dawn," he said, "with every man we've got. We'll find her, brother, I promise you."

Eamon stood up and went to join his brothers. "Aye, we'll find her, Niall, and if that bastard Wolverton is anywhere near County Meath, we'll find him, too."

"Judas, Bobby, once again I've managed to get you in trouble, and this time it might truly be the end for us," Catriona said gloomily. They were being held in a stall of a stable behind the River's Cross Inn. Bobby had wanted to stop at the little village, hoping to find some of his rebel friends. Instead of friends, they had run smack into a troop of English soldiers.

"What are they even doing here?" Catriona asked. "As far as I know, the truce still holds. There should be no English soldiers in this part of the country."

Bobby gave her a comforting nudge of his shoulder. He couldn't put his arm around her since their captors had tied their hands and ankles.

"We'll find a way out of this coil, scamp," Bobby replied with his usual optimism. "We've seen worse."

Catriona laid her head back against the wooden stall behind her. "I just don't understand it. How did they know who I was?" The men who had caught them had addressed her by name. "And why did they want to arrest us? The queen herself said she wanted to get me out of England so that she could wash her hands of me. Why would her soldiers take me back into custody?"

"Perhaps she changed her mind?"

"Nay. I'm not important enough for Her Majesty to send men all the way here. 'Tis a mystery."

Bobby looked around the dimly lit stable. "Why they captured us matters less than what we're going to do about it."

Catriona straightened up and gave herself a shake. "You're right. How are we going to get out of here?"

Bobby smiled. "You sound as if 'tis a sure thing."

"It is. I know you, Bobby Brosnihan. How many times have you escaped from English custody?"

"Counting the stay at the Tower? Ah, we shouldn't count that one because the guards were letting us out regular-like and 'twas nothing to—"

"How many times?" she asked again.

"Five, I reckon."

"So now it will be six."

Bobby grinned. "Ye still have faith in me, then?"

"If I told ye how much, ye'd get a swelled head. So let's talk about a plan. What has worked for you in the past?"

"To start, this usually helps," he said. Then he whipped his freed hands out from behind his back.

Catriona gasped in amazement. "How did you do that?"

"Practice," he said simply, bending to untie his feet. Then he turned to Catriona and in seconds had freed her of her bonds. Cautiously he stood and reached a hand to help her up. "I imagine there will be guards around the stable," he said.

"Aye, but they're probably guarding the doors."

At the same time they both looked toward the side wall of the stable where a hayloft led to a small shuttered window. "My clever Cat," Bobby said approvingly. "Together we'd make a fair run at any prison in England."

"I'd as soon not have to try," Catriona said dryly.

Bobby nodded agreement, then they scrambled together up onto the loft. He motioned for silence as he slowly opened the wooden window and looked outside, squinting to see into the darkness.

He closed the shutter and looked back at her. "We're in luck," he said. "No moon. It's darker than Hades. And there don't appear to be guards on this side of the building."

Catriona took a deep breath. "Then let's go."

"The hardest part will be jumping down with no noise. I'll go first and ease myself down, then I'll help you down. After that, stay close to the ground and follow me to the woods. If you hear a commotion behind us, keep running, understand?"

"Aye. Once again you're my savior, Bobby Brosnihan," she said fervently, then went up on her knees to kiss his cheek.

Immediately she realized that the gesture had been unwise. He raised his hand to the place her lips had touched and looked at her with bleak eyes. "At least I can be something to ye, Cat."

Then he opened the shutter and dropped over the edge of the window to the ground.

• • •

"What is it, man?" Alger Pimsley asked impatiently as Finbar the innkeeper knocked gently on the open door of his room.

"Yer Lordship, I thought to tell ye about His Lordship. It do appear he's gone out of his head. I beg ye to let me send for the village woman. She has herbs that could—"

"His Lordship simply does not want to be disturbed by some witch's medicine," Pimsley said with a secret smile. "His orders are clear."

"But, beggin' Yer Lordship's pardon, His Lordship's face has gone swelled up like a bloated cow. 'Tis that horrible a sight. Shall ye go to see him?"

"Has he asked to see the medicine woman?"

"I warrant he's beyond asking fer much of anything. Mostly he just lies there and moans."

Pimsley gave a slight nod. "If he should request that someone attend him, of course we would accede to his wishes. But when last we talked, he forbade me to send for anyone."

The innkeeper shifted nervously. " 'Tis just that, beggin' Yer Lordship's pardon, I warrant His Lordship might die of the poisons, if the pain don't kill him first."

"Ah, now, that would be a grave thing, wouldn't it?" Pimsley carefully reached up and removed his curled wig. The innkeeper stared in amazement at the Englishman's completely bald head. "I'll go see His Lordship in the morning," Pimsley said carelessly.

"I'm not sure—" the innkeeper began, but at Pimsley's haughty stare, he stopped. "Very good, Yer . . . er . . . Lordship. 'Tis in the hands of Providence."

"As are we all, Finbar," Pimsley said. He turned the wick on the lamp to plunge the room into darkness, then slipped into his bed and went to sleep.

The three Riordan brothers, now joined by John Black, had once again gathered their assembly of assorted servants, retainers, Riordan kin, and village folk to set out on another search. Niall had been in a fever of impatience, but his brothers had persuaded him to wait until the entire group was gathered before he set out.

"It won't help matters any to have you run into Wolverton's men and get captured or, more likely, get your head shot off," Cormac had told him. His older brother rarely invoked his authority as head of the family, but Niall knew that this was one time that going up against Cormac would merely cause more delay.

So he had waited while the men dribbled in two and three at a time, and though it had seemed endless, it was not even midmorning and the group was ready to ride.

The last men to arrive had been the Kelly family. Before they had even dismounted, the oldest Kelly son, Patrick, rode in the direction of the Riordans and shouted, "Lord Cormac, I must talk with ye!"

The Kelly farm was located just beyond a village called River's Cross. Between the village and their farm was a small inn, and, as Patrick explained, for several days, there had been a group of armed men camped around it.

Niall looked up at the new arrival with excitement. "How many were there?"

"We're not sure they're Wolverton's men," Eamon cautioned.

"Who else would they be? John told us that the Clearys are mostly disbanded."

Cormac nodded. "Aye, I warrant we've found our English invaders. Now the question is, what do we do about them?"

"And this still doesn't help us find Catriona," Niall added.

Patrick Kelly explained, "We talked with some of the villagers, and they said the troops have been camped there for a sennight. They've stripped the town of provisions and have had the innkeeper and his workers terrified."

"Sounds like Wolverton," John said grimly.

"And they did say that the soldiers took a couple of prisoners yesterday," Kelly continued.

"Prisoners!" Niall grasped the bridle of Kelly's horse to steady it. "Who were they?"

"A man and a woman, from what the villagers do say."

Niall's face went pale.

Cormac stepped next to him and said, "If they're prisoners, it means they are alive. If we ride hard, we can be there in an hour."

Not trusting himself to speak, Niall nodded and started for his horse.

Alger Pimsley was just finishing his morning sponge bath when an out-of-breath soldier appeared at his door.

" 'Tis the prisoners, Master Pimsley. They escaped!"

Pimsley's eyes narrowed to hard blue slits. "Escaped?" he repeated softly.

"Er—they *did* escape, sir, but we caught them running along the river, and we've brung 'em back here."

Pimsley's shoulders relaxed. "Well, then, lock them back up again. Why are you bothering me with it?"

" 'Tis just that the woman, the, er, lady do seem to be doing poorly."

"What do you mean? What's wrong with her?"

"I reckon she were drug along the river a bit by them what caught her. She's a tiny sprig and I reckon—"

"Where is she?" Pimsley interrupted.

"In the taproom. We've got her lying on one of the tables because the lieutenant did say that His Lordship is doin' poorly as well and we weren't to go upstairs and wake him."

The soldier continued to chatter as Pimsley made his way past him and, with a final straightening of his high-set lace collar, clattered down the inn stairs.

The taproom was full of soldiers. In the far corner two men sat on either side of a bound Bobby Brosnihan. Catriona lay on a table in the center of the room, her hands clutching her stomach. There was a thin layer of moisture on her pale face. Her eyes were closed.

"Is she awake?" Pimsley asked the lieutenant who stood at her side.

Her eyelids fluttered and she opened her eyes. "Bobby," she moaned.

Bobby stood at the sound of his name, but his two guards pushed him back down to his seat.

"Your confederate is fine, Lady Riordan," Pimsley said, his tone soothing. "Tell us where you hurt. Were you hit somewhere?"

She shook her head weakly, then struggled to try to sit up. "I'm all right," she said. "I just felt a bit faint."

"Lie still for a few moments," Pimsley advised. "If you like we can get someone to look at you. I'm told there's an herbalist in the village."

Catriona shook her head but took Pimsley's suggestion and lay back on the table. She had felt faint after the soldiers' rough handling, but more than anything she felt despair at being captive once again. She was so sure that she and Bobby had escaped without notice. As dawn had lit the eastern sky, she'd dared hope a little about a new life for herself. It would be a life without Niall, but in time, she vowed, she would forget him. She would be back home, back in Killarney where the lakes sparkled like a queen's tiara and the rivers tumbled through the mountains like dancing silver.

"Are you sure, milady?" Pimsley insisted, bending over her. His face was so close that his long nose looked like a giant beak moving toward her face. She shifted uncomfortably on the hard table.

"I'll be fine. I'm just a little lightheaded." She wished he would move away, but he continued speaking to her from an uncomfortably close distance.

"You know that your guardian is here?" he asked.

"They told me, but I'm not sure why he's here. Has he come to help me?"

"Ah, my dear, I fear you'll discover that 'twas never Lord Wolverton's intention to help you. His interest has always been in helping himself."

"I don't understand. After my father was killed—"

"After Wolverton *ordered* your father killed," Pimsley corrected.

Catriona felt as if the annoying Pimsley had dropped something heavy on her chest. "What are you talking about?" she asked. Carefully, so that she wouldn't bump into the hovering man, she pushed herself up to a sitting position. The movement sent a rush of dizziness to her head. "What did Lord Wolverton have to do with my father's death?"

"Everything, I fear."

From the corner Bobby said, "I told ye the man was a bastard, Cat."

"B-but he took me into his own home," she stammered.

"He needed to keep you under his own management so that you would never find out the truth about the massacre at the Valley of Mor," Pimsley explained, finally straightening up to give her some breathing room.

She took a moment to digest the information. Somehow, in spite of the fact that Wolverton had cared for her these past seven years, she did not find Pimsley's accusation difficult to believe. "Why has Her Majesty sent him here now?" she asked finally.

Pimsley gave a humorless laugh. "Her Majesty knows nothing about it. We're breaking the truce by being here."

"Then what—?" Catriona began.

Pimsley reached out and stroked her hair, which hung loose after her cross-country dash. "Lord Wolverton came here to kill you, my dear," he said gently. Then he drew his slender finger across her neck.

"Leave her alone!" Bobby shouted, and one of his guards elbowed him in the side, nearly knocking him from his seat.

"Shall we do it now?" the lieutenant asked, looking

none too happy with the idea. "My boys are grumbling and ready to go home."

A number of the men in the taproom nodded agreement.

"Lord Wolverton gives the orders, Lieutenant, you know that," Pimsley said with a sly smile.

The lieutenant looked agitated. "Well, sir, do I have your permission to go upstairs to ask Lord Wolverton's permission to finish this matter?"

Pimsley dropped his hand from Catriona's head and turned toward the stairs. "I will speak with him. Wait for me here, and don't let these two move."

"We need some kind of plan, Niall," Cormac told his brother. "It makes no sense to just go riding in like a herd of frightened cattle."

"That's well and good, but while we plan, we have no idea what they're doing to Catriona." Niall had been urging greater speed the entire way to River's Cross, and now that they were on the outskirts of the village with the modest inn in sight, he could hardly keep from spurring his horse ahead and riding in to find her.

"My point exactly. If we attack, I'd not give many chances for Catriona to come out of this alive."

"Cormac's right, Niall. We need to check out the situation, set up our defenses as best we can, then see if they'll talk to us."

"There are fewer soldiers than I'd thought," Cormac observed.

Patrick Kelly, who had ridden next to the brothers because of his familiarity with the area, said, "There are more than that. Either they are inside the inn, or they've ridden off somewhere else."

"We need to assume they may be inside," Cormac cautioned. "If possible, I'd like to accomplish this without violence. As Eamon said, we'll try talking first."

Niall paid little attention as his brothers, John Black, and the Kellys continued the discussion. All he could think about was Catriona in the hands of her monster of a guardian. Wolverton had tried to kill her twice. What if she was already dead?

The thought sent a chill through his entire body. "Are we ready to stop talking and move?" he yelled at his brothers.

Cormac nodded, and with surprising precision for a group of untrained and unrehearsed men, the group followed his orders to the letter, spreading out to surround the little inn.

When all their men were in place, the three brothers, John, and three of the Kellys rode in a direct line toward the front of the inn, holding up their hands to show that they were not brandishing weapons. As they approached, the English soldiers who were camped out got to their feet, and several more appeared from inside the stables and behind the other outbuildings. None of them made a move toward them.

"So far, so good," Cormac said under his breath as they reached the front path and dismounted.

"We may be walking into a trap," Eamon pointed out.

"Aye, but 'tis worth the risk." Cormac reached out and opened the inn door.

As they had feared, the room seemed to be full of English soldiers, but none of them made any threatening gestures. All that was important to Niall was that Catriona sat in the middle of the room, perched on a table. She looked pale and tired, but she was alive. He closed his eyes with a swift prayer of thanks. When he opened them, she was looking at him. His first impulse was to rush to her side, but he hesitated. It was impossible to tell from her implacable expression if he would be welcome. He followed her gaze to the corner of the room, then stiffened as he saw the young man he had glimpsed only briefly at Whitehall Palace—Bobby Brosnihan. The man she had run away with.

Cormac looked around the room. "Is Lord Wolverton here?" he asked loudly.

The apparent leader of the men, a lieutenant, answered, "His Lordship is ill. He's in a room upstairs. You may want to speak with his aide, Master Pimsley."

"Pimsley is here?" Niall asked in surprise. Somehow it was hard to picture the officious little clerk on this kind of a campaign. But just as he said the words, Alger Pimsley appeared at the top of the landing. He was a picture of fashion, from his polished shoes to his black-and-yellow striped jerkin.

"Aye, Master Niall, Lord Wolverton kindly offered me the opportunity to visit your country. Of course, I couldn't refuse." He looked at the other new arrivals as he descended the stairs to join them. "These are your brothers, I trust? Aye, the famous Riordans. The resemblance is unmistakable."

He smiled blandly and made a flourish of a bow in the direction of Cormac and Eamon.

"We're not at Whitehall now, Pimsley," Niall said curtly. "We've come to confront Lord Wolverton and demand an explanation for his butchery at the Valley of Mor."

"And for the attacks on my brother and his wife," Cormac added.

"Then 'tis true," Catriona asked. She had begun to tremble as if she were cold. "My guardian was responsible for what happened that day at the Valley of Mor?"

John stepped toward her and took her hand gently. "Aye, dear one, 'twas Wolverton." He turned to the others with a look of concern. "She's not well."

Pimsley gave a kind of cackle. "Nor is her guardian," he said. "In fact, ye'd best go up to see him now if you want this thing settled quickly."

"I'll go," Niall said quickly, but before he could protest, Catriona boosted herself off the table.

"If 'tis true he was responsible for this monstrous thing, I want to speak with him as well," she said firmly.

"We'll stay here to be sure there's no trouble," Cormac announced.

Niall took Catriona's hand as they made their way up the narrow inn stairs, but she didn't seem to even notice. When they reached the second floor, a door was open directly in front of them. "I still can hardly believe it," Catriona said, speaking more to herself than Niall. "He was always kind to me."

"A salve to his conscience, I suppose," Niall said.

She turned to him then. "He didn't have to let me live. Many were killed that day. I would have just been one more." Then more softly she said, "There were times when I wished I had been."

Cautiously they entered the room and looked over toward the bed at the far wall. The unmistakable imposing form of Lord Wolverton lay stretched out the length of the bed, his feet hanging over the edge. Catriona shrank back in horror. Wolverton's skin was the gray-blue color of death. His open eyes were glassy and bulging. And his mouth was open in a silent scream of agony.

Niall pulled her immediately back and put his arm around her to shield her from the view, but it was too late. Her eyes rolled back, and she slumped heavily against him.

Eighteen

Niall lifted Catriona in his arms and carried her downstairs where his brothers and the English soldiers were waiting uneasily.

"Wolverton's dead," he said, placing Catriona on the same table where she'd been before. John went immediately to her side as Niall turned on Pimsley in a fury. "You knew what we would find up there. Why did you send us?"

Pimsley's expression was unmoved. "I thought 'twould be a conclusion of sorts for the poor child. Sometimes it's a good thing to see our enemies laid low."

"She didn't even know Wolverton was her enemy until today," Niall argued. "As far as she knew, he was her benevolent guardian." He gave a disgusted wave of dismissal, then turned back to the unconscious woman. "Do you know what's wrong with her, John?" he asked.

John was holding her wrist and had a hand on her forehead. "Her heart's beating too fast, but she doesn't appear to have any injuries."

Bobby spoke up. "The bastards dragged her through the river from yonder footbridge to here."

Pimsley pursed his lips and tisked through his teeth. "Such overzealous men," he said. "What a good thing it is for everyone that Lord Wolverton is no longer around to urge them on to such evil."

The doctor looked up at him scornfully. "And I suppose you had nothing to do with any of this, Pimsley?"

The courtier shook his head. "I'm a man of peace, gentlemen. Lord Wolverton, may God save him, always was too aggressive for my tastes. Now that he is gone, I warrant these men and I will leave you all and head back to London. Untie the prisoner," he added, motioning to the guards who held Bobby.

"It's over? Just like that?" Cormac asked.

"What about the murder of this girl's father?" Eamon asked. "The estates that Wolverton illegally seized?"

Pimsley gave a reverent bow of his head. "Nothing can return her father, but, of course, the estates will be restored to the heiress. I'm sure Her Majesty will be quite distressed when she learns the truth of the matter."

"Which she will learn from you?" Cormac asked.

"But of course."

"And as the hero who exposes his treachery, she may just be inclined to reward you with a nice piece of the Wolverton estates?"

"Her Majesty is generous to those who serve her," Pimsley replied.

Niall's attention was on Catriona, who still lay without moving, but he looked up for a moment to add, "You were his right-hand man, Pimsley. If Wolverton was guilty, then so were you."

Pimsley gave a brief smile. "I don't believe the queen will see things that way. Now, if you gentlemen have things in hand here, my men and I will take our leave."

"*Your* men?" Cormac asked.

Pimsley acknowledged his lapse with a little nod. "Lord Wolverton's men."

On the table Catriona stirred restlessly. John bent over her. "Lie still, Catriona. You've fainted."

"Lord Wolverton—" she murmured.

"Aye, he's dead, child. Everything is fine. You're free and so is your friend."

She clutched John's arm with both hands and sat up. With a pang, Niall saw her gaze go directly to Bobby. "Are you all right?" she asked him. At his nod, she smiled.

Niall stepped back from the table and let John tend to Catriona. Bobby, freed from his bonds, stood and went over to take her hand. "Everything's going to be just fine now, scamp," the rebel told her.

There were several moments of general confusion as the English soldiers filed out of the taproom and headed toward their camp to prepare for the return trip. Pimsley made arrangements with the innkeeper for Wolverton's burial, then retrieved his own saddlebags from his room.

"You gentlemen are welcome in London anytime," he said as he was ready to depart. "I'd be happy to offer you my hospitality."

Then he turned to Catriona, who was now sitting in a chair by the fireplace. "And you, my dear. I hope you'll be able to forget these terrible events and have a happy life now that you're here in your homeland."

Catriona regarded him suspiciously, but said, "'Tis kind of you."

Then Pimsley made a sweeping bow to the entire assembly. "Farewell, all," he said lightly. "I can't say I regret my departure, for 'tis devilishly difficult to keep a decent fashion under these circumstances." Then he made a slight adjustment to his carefully curled wig and walked out the door.

Eamon watched him go with a bemused expression. "He's as guilty as Satan," he said, shaking his head. "He knew every move Wolverton was making. I'd not doubt that many of Wolverton's atrocities were his idea."

"Aye, but who could prove it?" John asked. "He's such an officious, fussy little man. No one ever suspects the clerk."

Niall shook his head. "Let him go. The important thing is that Catriona is here and safe."

He looked down at her, but she still did not meet his eyes.

"Aye," Cormac agreed. "Forget the little monkey. Our concern now is with Lady Catriona. How are you feeling, my dear?"

"I'm fine," she said. She started to stand, then had to use her arms to push herself up from the chair. Bobby, who had not left her side, took her elbow to help her up. "Ye're not fine, Cat. They did hurt ye, I fear."

She shook her head. "Nay, 'tis nothing but—" She broke off her words and looked down at herself in horror. For a moment none of the men knew what was wrong, then Niall cried out as a bright red pool of blood began seeping from underneath her skirt.

Catriona looked to John in confusion. "What's happening to me?" she asked weakly.

John, his face grim, went to her side and helped Bobby ease her back into the chair. "It would appear that you were with child, lass. Is that possible?"

For the first time Catriona glanced briefly at Niall. "I—I reckon it could be possible," she whispered, turning back to John.

"But I'm afraid you're losing the baby." John looked up at Bobby. "We have to get her upstairs to a bed."

Niall stepped forward, but before he could reach her, Bobby had lifted her in his arms, disregarding the blood now streaming down his clothes as well as hers.

"The rest of you stay here for the time being," John said, then motioned for Bobby to follow him up the stairs. Niall was left to watch as the stocky rebel disappeared with Catriona around the landing.

Niall thought he would go mad with the waiting. He paced an endless circle around the four tables of the taproom, glancing up the stairs anxiously with each turn.

He'd tried more than once to head up the stairs himself, but his brothers had stopped him. "You'll be of no help there now, Niall," Cormac told him gently.

Bobby had come downstairs almost immediately with the news that it did appear that Catriona was suffering a miscarriage. He'd shot a resentful glance in Niall's direction but had made no further comment as he settled himself at a seat by one of the small windows at the front of the taproom. Since then, he'd spent the entire time staring out the window.

The innkeeper, who looked as if he'd had about as much as a man could stand in the past few days, had offered refreshments, then had leaned toward Cormac and asked discreetly, "My lord, shall I wait a while to have the, er, body brought out?"

His words had given Niall a jolt until he realized the man was referring to Wolverton. In his worry over Catriona, he'd practically forgotten the nobleman's ugly death.

Cormac had told the man to go ahead with the removal of the corpse, but had offered neither his help nor his brothers'.

The innkeeper bustled out the front door and was back almost immediately with four men from the village. They brought Wolverton down wrapped in a sheet. Niall stopped his pacing long enough to watch in silence as they carried him hurriedly out the door. The man who had been so big and powerful in life was ending it unceremoniously like a sack of flour.

Minutes passed with agonizing slowness, but none of the brothers voiced the thought that was in all of their minds. Was Catriona to be another victim of the curse of the Riordan brides? Niall had never been much of a believer in the curse. Of course, unlike his brothers, he couldn't remember any of the three women who had each married his father and subsequently died birthing a Riordan son.

Cormac, on the other hand, did have clear memories of

his two stepmothers—Eamon's and Niall's mothers. He had believed so strongly in the curse that it had almost ruined his life until Claire had given birth to a strong son and recovered to complete health.

Finally John descended the stairs, wiping his forehead with a kerchief. " 'Tis done," he said.

Niall felt the blood rush from his head. "Nay!" he cried.

John looked at him and said hastily, "I mean the babe, Niall. She's lost the child. Catriona's alive, but she's weak. She's lost a lot of blood."

"I want to see her," he said, heading toward the stairs.

John looked uncomfortable. "Nothing should upset her just now, Niall. It would be better if you would wait."

"I won't upset her," he said.

He started to move past John, but the physician put an arm out to stop him. "She's groggy, Niall, not thinking too clearly." He cleared his throat. "She's asked to see Bobby."

The rebel jumped up from his seat. He looked briefly at Niall, then rushed across the room and up the stairs.

Niall looked as if he were considering following him, but Cormac walked over to him and took his arm. "John says she can't be upset, Niall. Leave it for now."

"Will she live?" Niall asked John.

The doctor looked tired. "I can't tell you that, Niall. All I know is that if I could, I would sell my soul to save her."

The river behind the inn was swollen with recent rains. Niall sat on the bank and watched it swirl leaves and broken twigs among the rocks of the riverbed. He'd no longer been able to stand the stale air of the taproom. When Eamon had offered to accompany him outside, he'd refused. He wanted to be alone.

John had gone back upstairs to be at Catriona's side. Bobby was evidently there as well, since he had not come downstairs. Once again, she'd chosen her old childhood friend over Niall. Niall picked up a sizable rock and sent it slamming into the water. It was *his* baby she had just lost, not Bobby's. They should be sharing this loss together, comforting each other, yet she had asked for another man to be by her side.

He craned his neck to look back up the bank at the inn, wishing he could see through the walls to find out what was happening inside. He looked around at the area where the English soldiers had camped. Only a few discarded pieces of trash remained from their occupation. They would be halfway to Dublin by now, and Alger Pimsley was no doubt reveling in the idea of gaining control over the vacated Wolverton estate. Niall shook his head. Who would have thought the simpering courtier would end up on top in the end?

"John says she's better, Niall," said a voice from above him. He turned around to see Eamon walking toward him. His brother scrambled down the bank and took a seat beside him.

Niall's face brightened. "Can I—" he began, then changed his mind and asked, "Is she still with Brosnihan?"

Eamon nodded. "John says he refuses to leave her, and she appears content to have him there. I'm sorry, Niall."

"'Twas my child, Eamon."

"I gathered that, since I can't see how she could have been with anyone else since the trip back from London."

"Not since then and not before, either."

"That would be between you two, I reckon. But this man is obviously close to her. Perhaps 'tis like having one of her own family nigh."

"I want to see her, Eamon."

"As soon as John gives the word. You'd not want to do anything that would harm her."

Niall rubbed his eyes with his fists, then said vehemently, "God's life, Eamon, she was carrying our baby."

"Aye, and she may yet die of the effort."

Niall looked away from his brother, his eyes stinging. "Do you believe in the Riordan bride curse, Eamon? I never asked you."

Eamon was silent for a long moment. "If there was some kind of hex on our family for wrongs done centuries ago, I warrant the penance has been paid a hundredfold. A new day is dawning in the world. We no longer dance in the moonlight around pillars of stone."

"But women still die bringing their children into this new world."

"Aye, I reckon they always will, but, nay, I don't believe in any curse. Claire is healthy as a prize heifer, and God willing, your lass will come out fine, too."

"Though it would appear that she's not *my* lass."

Eamon had no answer for this, and for a long time the only sound was the rushing river at their feet.

Though she hadn't known that she carried a child, Catriona felt the loss like a tremendous hollow in her midsection, even while she still marveled over the discovery. She and Niall had made a baby. Somewhere during those warm and passionate and tender moments together, a new life had been created. But now it was gone. The tears that seemed to have been running in an endless stream for the past hour continued.

She wondered how Niall felt. Surely by now they had told him, yet he hadn't come up to see her. She'd called for him, she remembered, but it had been during that hazy time after the doctor had carried her upstairs. She'd thought that she was calling his name over and over, but she couldn't find him through the fog. Then she'd awakened, and Bobby had been by her side. Dear, dear Bobby, who had always been there when she most needed him.

It was dark outside. How many hours had he been sitting beside her? she wondered. At the moment he appeared to be dozing.

She turned as Dr. Black appeared in the doorway. He'd been her savior these past few hours. She couldn't imagine what she would have done without his calm, gentle care. She mustered a smile.

"You look much better, lass," he told her in a low voice, glancing at Bobby. "More rested than your friend here, I warrant."

"He's exhausted," she agreed. "He tells me that he sleeps little when he's on the move."

John nodded, then moved carefully past the sleeping man and sat beside Catriona on the bed. "Some of the color has come back to your face," he said, placing a hand on her forehead.

"Thanks to you," she told him.

He shook his head. "Nay. You're a brave lass, just like your mother."

Catriona's eyes widened. "You knew my mother?"

"Aye."

There was a look of sadness in his kind eyes. Her voice softened even further. "How did you know her?"

"I grew up in Killarney, child, just as you did. Only I was not privileged to live in a grand mansion like O'Malley House. My parents were poor farmers who barely had enough to live on."

"But you knew my mother there?"

"She lived on the neighboring farm. We grew up loving each other, but it turned out that her love was not the same for me as mine for her. Once she met your father, she had no doubts about the path her life had to take."

Catriona looked over at Bobby, who was still sleeping. She understood exactly what the doctor was describing. Over the years she had regretted not being able to give Bobby the kind of love he wanted from her. Now she ached for the doctor's hopeless love and for her mother, who surely must have felt his pain just as she felt Bobby's.

Shifting her gaze back to Dr. Black, she was surprised to see tears glistening in his eyes. She reached for his hand. "There are many kinds of love," she said.

He nodded, then leaned over to kiss the top of her head. Behind him, Bobby stirred, then opened his eyes. He looked at the doctor with alarm and asked, "Is anything wrong? Is she all right?"

The doctor turned around to him with a smile. "Aye, she's doing just fine, son. I'll leave you to ask her yourself."

With a final squeeze of Catriona's hand, he stood and left the room. Bobby took his place beside her on the bed. "How are ye feelin'?" he asked.

She wanted to tell him about Dr. Black's revelation, but the similarities to her own story with Bobby gave her pause. It was a conversation best held when she was feeling stronger, she decided. "I reckon 'twill be a day or two afore I'll be able to best ye in a footrace."

He grinned at her. "Ah, ye do sound better, scamp. It does me heart good."

"I am better. You don't need to sit here."

"I'd not leave ye, Cat. Not until we're sure that ye're well. Besides," he added wryly, "I've already had a sample of the accommodations here, and I think I'd do better in the chair."

"They'd not put you back in the stables, Bobby. I'm sure the innkeeper would see to it that you had a room. Or—" She hesitated and flushed. "The Riordans would see to it. That is, if they . . . are any of them still here?"

Bobby studied her face. "Is Niall still here, do ye mean?"

She had always been honest with Bobby. "Aye, that's what I mean. Is he here?"

"I've not been downstairs, Cat, so I honestly don't know, but I'll tell ye this—if the man has left ye alone while ye're here suffering from the loss of his child, he's not worth a hair on your head."

"You think he's left, then?" she asked forlornly.

Bobby gave a sad smile. "'Twould not be my luck," he said. "My guess is the man is down there wearing through the floorboards of the taproom with his pacing as he did for the hour we waited for the doctor to tend ye before he told me I could come up here."

Catriona let out a sigh of relief as Bobby watched her with knowing eyes. "Why hasn't he come to see me?" she asked.

"Dr. Black said ye did ask for *me*, Cat. Ye haven't yet asked to see Riordan."

"But I thought I—" She tried to remember. She knew she had been calling Niall's name, but everything had been so misty. "He could have come anyway," she said.

Bobby shook his head. "Not when I was the one ye asked for, scamp. Do ye know nothing of a man's pride?"

The word irritated her. "What's more important—pride or—" Then she stopped. She'd been about to say "pride or love." But Niall had never said he loved her. "Do you think he wants to see me?" she ended.

Bobby gave a snort of exasperation. "Are ye now askin' me to advise ye with yer love life, Catriona Mary O'Malley? For that would be goin' a league too far. What was I just sayin' about a man's pride?"

He softened the words with a rueful smile, and she put a hand out to touch his arm. "Would you ask him to come, Bobby? I ken 'tis hardly fair to ask you, but, you see, I have no one else to ask. You're my only friend."

Bobby leaned forward and looked directly into her eyes. "I reckon ye could ask me to jump off a cliff and I'd do it playin' the pipes, if 'twould please ye. So, aye, I'll bring yer husband to ye, though he be not half good enough for ye, nor ever will be."

"Thank you," she whispered.

"God keep ye, scamp," he said, then stood and left the room.

Nineteen

John and Niall sat by the taproom fire. The events of the long day seemed to have left them with no further energy for conversation.

Both men had insisted on staying at the inn with Catriona until she was well enough to be moved, but Eamon and Cormac had returned to Riordan Hall. After several moments of silence, John asked, "Do you suppose that little weasel Pimsley knew all along that Wolverton had cheated Catriona out of her estates?"

"I wouldn't be surprised. He was always the quiet one, working behind the scenes, licking Wolverton's boots if called upon, but now look who ends up on top."

"At least Wolverton himself met a fit end."

"Aye, and without bloodshed," Niall agreed. "In spite of everything he did, I wouldn't have wanted to be the one responsible for killing the man Catriona had regarded as an uncle."

"So now what happens?" John asked softly.

Niall shrugged and turned to warm the palms of his hands at the fire. "She'll go home to the Valley of Mor, I reckon. 'Tis what she's always wanted, and now that she'll have her estates back, there's nothing to prevent her."

"I'd hope there might be something that would make her want to stay here."

"Don't worry, John. We won't let her head south until she's fully recovered."

"I'm not talking about her health. I'm talking about her happiness."

Niall knew exactly what his friend was talking about. By now he had reasoned that John had left him alone with Catriona in Dublin precisely to give the young couple the opportunity to fall in love. His plan had worked—for a while.

"We can't relive the past, John. You think that if Catriona and I could be together, it would be some kind of redemption for your loss of her mother, but life doesn't work like that."

John leaned over to grab Niall's shoulder and turn him around to face him. "You bloody idiot. I wanted to see you two together because I know you to be a bright and good young man, one worthy to be husband to such a marvelous and spirited girl. It had nothing to do with me or what once may have existed between me and her mother."

Niall gave a brief smile. "So you were simply playing matchmaker, eh? Cormac's right, John, you have turned into an old woman."

"I'd sooner be an old woman than a young fool who can't see a treasure when it's waved under his nose," he retorted.

Niall turned back to the fire. "I see her well enough. But you forget, Cat made her choice. If you'll recall, before her plans were interrupted by the English, she was on her way back to Killarney with Brosnihan."

"And you think she's in love with him instead of you?"

Niall shrugged. "It would appear so."

They turned at the sound of a heavy step on the stairs. Bobby rounded the corner and said, "The doctor has the right of it, Riordan, ye be a bloody fool."

Niall stood and for a long moment the two men looked

at each other without speaking. Finally Niall asked, "How is she?"

"She's still weak, but doing better. She'll do better yet when she sees ye."

"She wants to see me?"

"Aye," Bobby said. When Niall hesitated, he continued with some irritation, "Well, what be ye waiting for? If 'twere me she loved, I'd have been by her side hours ago."

Niall waited no longer. He turned and bounded up the stairs. When he reached the doorway, he stopped.

Catriona's eyes were closed. She looked frail and frighteningly pale, lying on the bed with her long hair spread out around her like a funeral veil. The sight gave him a chill. Noiselessly he approached the bed. When he was standing next to it, her eyelids fluttered open.

"I lost our baby," she said.

His throat full, he nodded. "I know, *a stór*."

A tear slid from the corner of her eye. "My guardian—" she began weakly. "He's dead? I did not dream it?"

Niall took her limp hand. "Aye, Cat," he told her. "Wolverton is dead."

"He killed my father."

Niall nodded. "Don't think about it now, sweetheart. The important thing is that you are safe and that you're going to get better."

"Bobby."

He could barely hear the word, but it made him stiffen. Bobby's last words had implied that Niall was the one she loved, but Niall had yet to hear her express a choice. He forced himself to keep his voice steady as he asked, "What about Bobby, Cat? Did you want him to come back up here to be with you?"

She shook her head. "I thought I had to go with him. I thought you didn't want me."

Niall's chest expanded with relief. "Sweetheart, John says you're not to upset yourself. All you have to think about now is getting well."

"Back home," she murmured. He wasn't sure if she was talking about Riordan Hall or about her own home in the south, but he said soothingly, "As soon as John says you can be moved, I'll take you home. You'll get better there. Claire will be with you."

"And you," she said. He thought she was trying to give his hand a squeeze, but she was so weak that the pressure barely registered.

"Of course. I'll be there whenever you want me."

She smiled, then her eyes closed again and she drifted off to sleep.

Catriona was dreaming that she'd borrowed one of the queen's fur robes and was rubbing her face back and forth in its softness. When she opened her eyes, she found that the fur was real. It was attached to a large gray cat.

The cat's owner was kneeling on the edge of her bed in Niall's room back at Riordan Hall. Memory came flooding back. Niall and John had brought her from River's Cross the previous day in a large cart. She had not found the journey difficult, but once they'd arrived, Niall had insisted she go directly to bed. From the look of the bright morning sun shining through the bedroom window, she had slept round the clock.

"You wanted to see Boots, remember?" her young companion asked. "See how his eyes are green like yours?"

Catriona struggled to sit up with the big cat still perched on her chest. "So this is Boots, eh?" she asked the boy. She grasped the cat firmly and moved it down to a more comfortable position on her lap.

"These are his boots." Ultan pointed to the cat's two white forepaws. "Only they aren't really boots, they're just fur," he added with a giggle that made Catriona's heart melt.

"They look like boots to me," she said. "Is Boots your very own cat?"

"Aye. He eats mice sometimes," Ultan informed her gravely.

"I should think so. That's what cats do."

The little boy appeared relieved that she had not been disappointed by his revelation.

"Ultan Raghnall Riordan!" Claire's voice was unusually sharp as she came hurrying into the room. "I told you that you would have to wait until Aunt Cat got better before you brought Boots here." She scooped the cat off the bed and dropped it to the floor with a look of apology to Catriona.

"Nay, Claire, don't scold the lad," Catriona pleaded. "He's a love, and I'm quite delighted to make Boots' acquaintance."

Claire took a step back and looked at her. "Ah, you're looking much better, dearie. You gave me a fright when they brought you in yesterday. You were so pale, it was almost enough to set me to believing Cormac's curse."

Catriona smiled. "How many children will you and I have to produce before the Riordan brothers will put aside this curse nonsense?"

Claire gave a delighted laugh and reached over to take both of Catriona's hands. "So you *are* staying! I'm to have a new sister, after all."

"If Niall will have me."

"He'll have you all right. The Riordans may be unruly, but they are none of them stupid."

"I'm not sure your husband will be as pleased as you are," Catriona observed.

Claire waved her hand as if to dismiss the notion. "All Cormac and Eamon want is what is best for their brother. They'll come around as soon as they see that you're making Niall happy."

"I hope I can do that."

Claire leaned over to give her hand a pat. "I know you can. You already have."

Ultan was rocking back and forth on the edge of the

bed. "Aunt Cat thinks it's proper for cats to eat mice, Mummy," he said, oblivious of the adult conversation.

Claire shook her head and lifted her son in her arms. "You must not jump on Aunt Cat's bed, Ultan, because she's a little bit sick."

The little boy looked at Catriona with a frown. "Will you have to take fish oil?" he asked with a grimace.

"I don't think so," Catriona told him. "I'm almost all well again."

"But she won't get well if we don't let her rest, son," Claire admonished. "You may come back to see her tomorrow."

"With Boots?" he asked, looking at Catriona.

"Of course with Boots," Catriona agreed.

Claire started walking out, carrying Ultan with her. Before she reached the door, she paused and asked, "Have you told Niall yet that you intend to stay?"

Catriona shook her head. "I'd rather have him *ask* me. Up to now, other people and other events have interfered to determine our fate. Now I want to hear from his own lips that this is what he truly wants."

Claire looked a little doubtful. "Sometimes 'tis hard to get a man to talk about the things that mean the most to him. The creatures are better at action than speech."

"That may be, but if he wants me, he'd better be willing to tell me so, at least this once."

"You've a right to that, I expect. Good luck, sister," she ended with a wink.

Claire and Ultan had no sooner disappeared out the door when John entered. "How's the patient?" he asked cheerfully.

"Hungry," she answered.

He looked pleased. "Ah, lass, you'll be fit as a fiddle in no time at all. It gladdens this old heart."

"I feel fine today," she told him, and was surprised to discover that it was true. Only yesterday she'd hardly been able to climb the stairs without Niall's assistance, but today she felt completely normal. "The only thing that still worries me is—" She hesitated.

"Whether you'll be able to have more children?" John supplied. At her nod he smiled. "I see no reason why you should not have a dozen healthy youngsters, if you choose. You're a strong lass. You've a tougher constitution than your mother had," he added with a sad smile.

"I'd like you to tell me more about her."

"I shall. We'll have many a good talk about those long-ago days. I knew your father, as well, of course. He was a fine man," he added with a rueful smile. "That was part of my agony. I knew that Rhea was right to choose him over me."

"My mother was a lucky lady to be loved by two such men," Catriona told him gently.

"She deserved the love." He reached inside his jacket and pulled out the small leather book he'd once given her to read. "I think she'd want you to have this," he said, handing it to her. "I'd given it to her as a gift, but she returned it to me when she made the decision to marry your father."

"Oh, I couldn't take it," Catriona protested.

He laid it on the bed beside her. "I insist. 'Tis my wedding present to you."

"But it's your lucky piece, you said."

He put his hand on her cheek. "If you will honor me by taking it, child, it will be as if the book has come full circle. It's time for me to let it go."

Catriona could see that the gesture was important to him. She picked up the little volume and held it to her chest. "I shall love it always," she told him.

He nodded, and she thought she saw the glisten of tears in his eyes.

"Is everyone in the household to know that my bride is awake before I do?" came an indignant voice from the door. Niall came striding into the room and looked from Catriona to John. Evidently sensing some emotion in their expressions, he stopped and asked with concern, "Is anything wrong? She is better, isn't she, John?"

The doctor nodded. "She's nearly back to normal, though you're not to forget those warnings I gave you."

Niall had turned his gaze to Catriona, his eyes shining.

"You won't forget, will you, you randy young pup?" John asked more sternly.

Niall waved him off. "I won't forget. Catriona and I will do nothing but take tea and discuss politics until you pronounce her completely fit again."

Catriona blushed as she realized the gist of the "warnings" the doctor had given.

"However," Niall continued firmly, "I would appreciate a little time alone with my *wife*."

John smiled. "I warrant you two have a few things to talk about," he acknowledged. "I'll be back to check on you this afternoon, my dear."

She lifted the book he had given her and said again, "Thank you, Doctor. I'll treasure it."

He nodded and left the room. Niall waited until he left, then closed the door behind him. "Are you truly well?" he asked, walking back to take a seat beside her on the bed.

"Aye. I warrant I could go help Molly in the kitchen this afternoon."

"I warrant you could do no such thing. You'll not leave this room for at least another day. I intend to take better care of you this time around."

He seemed to be taking for granted that she would be staying at Riordan Hall, and she found that she was a little piqued by his presumption. After all, he'd still never told her that he loved her.

"I can take care of myself, thank you, Master Riordan," she told him tartly.

He grinned at her, unwilling to take offense. "I've seen that, Lady O'Malley Riordan, but it so happens that I've decided that I enjoy taking care of you."

"You do?" she asked, softening.

He leaned over to kiss her nose. "Aye."

The admission was nice, but it was still not completely what she wanted. "Why?" she asked.

"Why what?"

"Why do you enjoy taking care of me?"

He moved up to the head of the bed and pulled her carefully onto his lap. "Because you're beautiful and warm and because it makes me insane every time I smell that lemony scent of yours. Where the hell does that come from anyway?"

She smiled. "Women's secrets," she told him. "But let me understand you, Master Riordan. You enjoy my company because you find my body attractive?"

Niall gave a little groan. "Why do I have the feeling that no matter what I say here, 'twill not come out right?"

Catriona remembered Claire's words about men not wanting to talk about the things that mean the most to them. "Perhaps you'd be more interested in showing me than telling me?" she suggested, running her hand along the inside of his thigh.

He immediately snatched it away. "Oh, no you don't, witch! I'm not to touch you for a month. Doctor's orders. And I intend to—"

She stopped his words by leaning up to kiss his mouth. For a few moments he kissed her back, their tongues and lips melting together in the instant heat they always seemed to generate. Then he pulled away, lifted her off his lap, and got off the bed. "I'll not be tempted, vixen," he told her. Then his voice softened. "I'll not do anything that would risk hurting you, *a stór*. Not ever again."

"I've hurt you, as well," she said in a low voice.

She moved over to sit on the edge of the bed and offered him her hands. He took them and sat beside her. "We've hurt each other, I reckon," he agreed. "But I'm willing to start again, if you're sure this is what you want."

"I'm sure."

He hesitated a moment, then asked, "What about your friend Brosnihan?"

Catriona sighed. Bobby had disappeared as mysteriously as he had appeared over the years without taking leave of anyone. "Bobby will probably always be part of my life, Niall. In a way, he's the only family I have left."

"Do you think he's gone back to the outlaw rebels?"

"I don't know. He told me that the Clearys are disbanding. But he still has a lot of anger left in him. He may find another group of hotheads who don't want to give up the fight."

Niall smiled. "I seem to remember having a run-in with one of those hotheads back in London. A beautiful chestnut-haired vixen."

"It seems a lifetime ago," she acknowledged with a smile. "I understand Bobby's anger, because I had it myself."

"I don't mean to tease you, Cat. I can't even imagine what you went through when your father was killed. Your desire for revenge was understandable."

"Understandable, perhaps, but, as you say, hotheaded and probably foolish. I see things differently now. Revenge is not what my father would have wished for me."

"What would he have wished for you? Perhaps he would not have been pleased to see his heiress daughter married to a poor third son."

"Hardly poor, Niall. I'm sure my father would have respected the power of the Riordans. But he was always one to judge a man by his character, not his station or his wealth."

"I wish I had been able to know him," he said.

"So do I. But you will know something of him when we go to the Valley of Mor. You'll have to take me there, you know, now that it's to be mine again."

He nodded. "I'll take you wherever you want, my beautiful wife."

"And you can truly forgive me for everything that has happened between us?"

"We'll forgive each other, sweetheart. We're starting fresh from this day forward." He slipped from the bed to kneel before her. "Catriona O'Malley, will you do me the honor of giving me your hand in marriage?"

She looked down at him, her throat full. "I thought I'd already done that."

He shook his head. "Nay, the queen of England gave me your hand. Now I'm asking that *you* give it to me. And your heart as well. For, my love, you already have mine."

The tears welled in her eyes as she looked down at his face and saw the love in his eyes. "I give you my hand and my heart, Niall Riordan," she said. "You've brought me home."

Then she slipped down into his arms and they sealed the bargain with a long, tender kiss.

Irish Eyes

From the fiery passion of the Middle Ages
to the magical charm of Celtic legends
to the timeless allure of modern Ireland
these brand-new romances will surely
"steal your heart away."

The Irish Devil by Donna Fletcher
0-515-12749-3

To Marry an Irish Rogue by Lisa Hendrix
0-515-12786-8

Daughter of Ireland by Sonja Massie
0-515-12835-X

Irish Moonlight by Kate Freiman
0-515-12927-5

Love's Labyrinth by Anne Kelleher
0-515-12973-9

All books $5.99

Prices slightly higher in Canada

Payable by Visa, MC or AMEX only ($10.00 min.), No cash, checks or COD. Shipping & handling:
US/Can. $2.75 for one book, $1.00 for each add'l book; Int'l $5.00 for one book, $1.00 for each
add'l. Call (800) 788-6262 or (201) 933-9292, fax (201) 896-8569 or mail your orders to:

Penguin Putnam Inc. P.O. Box 12289, Dept. B Newark, NJ 07101-5289 Please allow 4-6 weeks for delivery. Foreign and Canadian delivery 6-8 weeks.	Bill my: ☐ Visa ☐ MasterCard ☐ Amex _____ (expires) Card# _____ Signature _____

Bill to:

Name _____

Address _____ City _____

State/ZIP _____ Daytime Phone # _____

Ship to:

Name _____ Book Total $ _____

Address _____ Applicable Sales Tax $ _____

City _____ Postage & Handling $ _____

State/ZIP _____ Total Amount Due $ _____

This offer subject to change without notice.   Ad # 868 (7/00)

SEDUCTION ROMANCE

*Prepare to be seduced…by the sexy
new romance series from Jove!*

**Brand-new, full-length, one-night-stand-alone
novels featuring the most seductive heroes in the
history of love….**

❏ **A HINT OF HEATHER**

by Rebecca Hagan Lee   0-515-12905-4

❏ **A ROGUE'S PLEASURE**

by Hope Tarr   0-515-12951-8

❏ **MY LORD PIRATE**

by Laura Renken   0-515-12984-4

All books $5.99

Prices slightly higher in Canada

Payable by Visa, MC or AMEX only ($10.00 min.), No cash, checks or COD. Shipping & handling:
US/Can. $2.75 for one book, $1.00 for each add'l book; Int'l $5.00 for one book, $1.00 for each
add'l. Call (800) 788-6262 or (201) 933-9292, fax (201) 896-8569 or mail your orders to:

Penguin Putnam Inc.   Bill my: ❏ Visa ❏ MasterCard ❏ Amex _____ (expires)
P.O. Box 12289, Dept. B
Newark, NJ 07101-5289   Card# _____
Please allow 4-6 weeks for delivery.   Signature _____
Foreign and Canadian delivery 6-8 weeks.

Bill to:

Name _____

Address _____City _____

State/ZIP _____Daytime Phone # _____

Ship to:

Name _____Book Total $ _____

Address _____Applicable Sales Tax $ _____

City _____Postage & Handling $ _____

State/ZIP _____Total Amount Due $ _____

This offer subject to change without notice.   Ad # 911 (8/00)